THE ORDER

THE CULT OF SERENDEE

ANGEL LAWSON

FOREWORD

Readers!

Welcome to Serendee. It's a peaceful utopia designed for living the perfect, off-the-grid life. It's also a place where darkness and manipulation fester under the surface. Greed and corruption. There's worse stuff too. That's what we need to talk about.

If you're a fan of the Royal's series...understand this book will not be that dark. Sam brings out my inner demon. But this series explores the fictional world of cults based on too much research and years of obsessive interest. Are there triggers? I think so. Will they send you hiding under the bed like Lords? Probably not, but here they are...

Warnings: this book contains dub-con, an arranged marriage, mental and emotional abuse, self-harm, coercive-control, manipulation and general mind-fuckery.

Angel

PROLOGUE

Before I step off the path, I glance behind me, making sure that no one else is around. The trail marker is nothing but a gash in the wood—nothing noticeable, unless it was pointed out. Which it was for me, by my mother.

Once I'm past the tree line, and starting up the hill, the trail is more noticeable. The terrain rocky, and less overgrown, although with every step I feel the sharp slap of weeds against my bare calves and relish every one.

Starting tomorrow, my legs will be covered when I go outside. Clothing requirements for females over the age of twelve require modest dress. Tomorrow is my birthday and I'll move into the domum with the other girls. But tonight, I'm still eleven—a child—and although physically I don't feel different, the teachings of the community say otherwise. Tonight is my last night of this kind of freedom, and I'm willing to make the risk because of it.

I see the outcropping up ahead and scramble up the swollen granite rock that provides a flat ledge and a view out at the community below. It's dusk, and soft light glows from the windows of the houses that dot the horizon. I can see the Main House and the dot of blue that marks the swimming pool. Beyond that is the fencing that surrounds our lands, and even further the small town just outside.

On the eve of my birthday, I should be at home celebrating with my family, but now it's just me and my father—my mother has been gone for a while. This was our special place—somewhere she told me she found while surveying the property before Anex bought it. It's on the edge of the property, the highest point and unfettered by a boundary line. It's quiet. Peaceful. And mine.

Or that's what she told me the night she left.

I wait for the sun to drop in the distance, offering a blessing for its warmth and light before the moon rises behind it. I'm focused on this, trying not to think about the changes coming tomorrow— the clothing and the lessons. The rules and preparation. Too focused, because by the time I realize I'm not alone.

Someone is already here.

"What the hell are you doing here?" he asks, standing before me, tall and lanky. I blink at the boy. I know him. *Everyone* knows him. Even at fifteen his cheekbones are sharp and defined and his shoulders unusually broad. I glance around, searching for the friends that are notoriously glued to his side, but after a beat I realize he's alone.

That makes it worse.

"I-I'll go," I stutter, knowing I shouldn't even speak to him.

"Why?" he asks bitterly, "so you can tell everyone you saw me up here? Tell my dad." He picks up a rock and tosses it over the ledge. The fading sunlight makes his pale hair shine like a halo. "Don't worry, he won't care."

I don't have to guess why he's here. I can see the dark smudges under his eyes. He looks tired. I know the look. I see it every time I look in the mirror.

"I'm sorry," I offer. What else is there to say to someone's whose mother has just died? His died a week ago. Unlike when mine left, there was a big ceremony for Beatrice, wife of Anex, mother of Rex. A parade through the center of the community. A celebration of her life and service.

"Shut up." He scowls, lip curled up. "I don't want pity. Especially from someone like you."

"Like me?" I clamp my mouth shut. My mouth. It gets me in trouble. I never know when to stop. Even now, alone with a dangerous boy, on top of a hill where neither of us should be. I will be the one in trouble if we're found. I will be the one scorned and shamed.

"I know who you are," his eyes flick over me with dark anger. "Imogene Montgomery. Your mother was the Regressive. A scar on this community."

I don't deny it.

"She's the one that should have died."

The word land like a punch. He's right. My mother betrayed us, Anex most of all, while his mother was devoted and true. I take a step back. I need to get out of here. I've heard the rumors about him and his friends. He senses that I am about to run and lunges at me, grabbing me by the wrist.

"Are you going to hurt me?" I ask, knowing he could destroy me.

His grip tightens, digging into my flesh. "Does it ever get better?" he asks. When I don't answer he adds, "Knowing they won't come back."

Oh. "No," I tell him truthfully. "Not really."

He nods, like it was what he wanted to hear and sits down on the rock. His back is to me and I should take the opportunity to run, but there's something about the slouch in his shoulders that glues my feet to the rock, knowing how much trouble I could get in for being alone with him like this. He's older than me, and I am almost twelve—old enough to know better than to be with a boy like this.

"It was so sudden, you know?" he says, picking up another stone and throwing it in the distance. "One minute she was there. The next gone."

"You father teaches us that when someone dies...The Way has determined that they are fully Integrated. Their work here is done. It's an honor."

His expression darkens. It doesn't make him less attractive. "Yes, I know what my father says. Which is why I'm up here on this rock, talking to the daughter of a Regressive. Everyone down there thinks we should be celebrating." He looks up at me with watery blue eyes and whispers. "I just want her to come back."

"I know."

I stare down at his hand for a long time until an urge overwhelms me. I pick it up and slide my fingers through his, feeling the warmth of his skin next to mine. It's wrong. Deceitful. But I understand what he's going through. How painful it feels and how much he must crave the touch of someone kind.

His fingers lock with mine and we sit on top of that rock until the sun vanishes completely and the moon shines high above. I know that tomorrow I will be a different person—a woman—but tonight it's just the two of us: Imogene and Rex.

Two kids, one powerful, one not, bound together because of what we've lost.

1

IMOGENE

Six Years Later

"It doesn't work, you know."

I've just stepped out of the building, canvas bag gripped in my hand. I cut my eyes to the guy speaking to me, while definitely not making eye contact. He leans against the wall—a friend next to him, scrolling on a device in his hand. They're both in jeans and a T-shirt.

I keep walking.

"Hiding under that frumpy skirt and sweater," he continues from behind me. "It just makes us want to know what's under there even more."

My skin prickles at his insinuation. I also feel shame for being out on the street so late. I'd stayed late to help clean up after the meeting, volunteering to stay long after everyone else had left. That was foolish of me. Walking back and forth from my neighborhood to the strip of shops a few blocks away is normally not an issue, but with the University students back at school, the odds of running into someone that doesn't understand our lifestyle is amplified.

"She's one of those freaks, isn't she?" a second voice says. I guess his friend decided to join in. "Do they make you wear those skirts?"

I push past a line of people waiting to get into a popular restaurant. There are outdoor tables and people milling around. Rock music blares from speakers and the chaos makes it a good place to slip away. A small part of me wants to call out to the patrons for help and ask them to make these guys go away, but I don't. First, we're not supposed to talk to anyone outside of Serendee if we can help it. Second, I can see the judgement in their eyes. They think the same thing as the men following me; that I'm a freak.

I cut through the crowd, ignoring the looks and stares about my long, braided hair and plain clothes. I'm used to it. I grew up this way—with the locals thinking that those of us that live in Serendee are different. We are *different*, that's the whole point, but that doesn't mean we're freaks.

At the end of the building, I cut down the alley toward Serendee. The building is on one side of me and a short, picket fence on the other. My skirt swishes at my ankles and I use one hand to lift it high enough that I don't trip. The iron gate of the community comes into sight and I exhale, the feeling of safety coming back over me.

A shadow steps out from behind the building. No, two.

"Thought you could get away?" It's the man that spoke to me first. I catch the scent of stale cigarettes on his clothes. "We just want to know more about you." He jerks his head in the direction of the community. "Know more about what you people do in there."

"We don't do anything," I say defensively. Then press my teeth down on my tongue. A punishment. "Leave me alone."

"She speaks!" The second guy says, eyes bright with amusement. "I heard you aren't allowed to talk to men—or anyone really —outside your little cult. If you do, they'll kick you out."

"It's not a—" I clamp my mouth shut again.

"I heard they're not allowed to watch TV or have the internet."

"Huh," the second guy says, rubbing his scruffy chin, "then how do they watch porn?"

Despite my will, my cheeks burn at his statement—at the scrutiny of my lifestyle. I take a deep breath and conjure up an image of Anex and his intelligent, kind, face. He warned us over and over about people like this. It's why he stared Serendee in the first place.

"Tell me," the first man says, stepping closer, "do you have big orgies?"

"Nah, they only have sex with their hippie guru in charge." His brown eyes sweep over me. "That's what I heard."

I grip the handle on my bag, and I blink back hot tears at the corners of my eyes. The books inside are at least eight pounds. I could crack a head if I swung it hard enough. *A head. Not two.* But I don't want to do that. I just want to go home.

"Do you all have sex with him? I mean, isn't that what cults are really always about? Sex?" Again, I don't answer, but that just encourages him more. "You think you're better than us, don't you? With your weird outfits and innocent vibe." He continues. I follow his hand as it drops to his belt. "What would happen to you if you weren't so innocent? Would they kick you out?"

"Stop," I whisper.

His hand lowers to his crotch, cupping his manhood. "Maybe a little taste of what it's like out in the real world is exactly what you need."

A true flicker of fear rolls in my belly. I've been harassed before. So many times. But never have I been trapped alone like this. "Please," I finally say. "Please stop."

The first guy grins. "Oh, I like the way that word sounds coming out of your mouth. Say it again." His tongue darts out. "Beg me."

A heartbeat. That's how quickly things escalate. With a twisted smirk on his mouth, he closes the gap between us, and I act on instinct, rearing back, swinging the bag filled with books with all my strength. He blocks it easily, but I don't wait around, darting toward the gate. If I can just get behind it, I know they won't follow. I'm almost there when strong hands grab me by the shoulders. Fear drops into the pit of my stomach.

"Don't hurt me," I whisper.

"I'm not going to hurt you," the voice says harshly. I'm spun around. I look up and it's not one of the men in front of me. It's someone else. A member of my community. I know him. His name is Elon.

Behind him there are others—three more men, dressed more casually than is typically allowed Serendee, but these men aren't typical. Not at all. Two of them stand with clenched fists, easily separating my harassers. They're broad shouldered and intimidating. It's not a show, it's a fact. Silas and Levi. My eyes flick to the last one, and the instant I see his pale hair and blue eyes, I suck in a breath.

Rex.

"You dare speak to one of our women against her will?" Rex says, pushing up his sleeves. I can't see his face in the dark shadows of the alley, but I do see the familiar mark inked on the inside of his forearm. "Threaten her?"

The man with the scuff snorts. "At least I think she has free will. What about you? You think she's a possession, don't you? A belonging."

"Elon, get her out of here," Rex snaps, not looking our way. "Take her home."

Elon reaches around me and unlatches the gate. He doesn't touch me, as that is forbidden, but he doesn't need to. Everything about him is imposing, and I fear him almost as much as the men on the street. As I step through, the sound of flesh against flesh echoes in my ear. I glance back, looking around the man, and watch Rex punch the first guy and the other two quickly jump in.

"That is not for you to see," Elon says, ushering me forward. Soon whatever is happening is behind us and we're back in Serendee. Home.

Once I'm safe, I pause and say, "Thank you."

Dark anger clouds his expression. "If you hadn't been so foolish, you wouldn't need to thank me. If it had been up to me, I would have left you out there with the vultures."

His words hit like a slap. "Wha—"

"You should be home. Preparing for the ceremony tomorrow, not flaunting yourself to the men in town."

"I wasn—" The dark flicker in his eyes cuts me short. I know that look—the accusation behind it.

"Are you like her?" he asks suddenly. "Is that why you were out there alone? Trying to run away, too?"

That I understand. 'Her.' I'm well aware of who he's speaking about. It also means he knows exactly who I am. "I was working late at The Center so that the others could leave early to prepare. *For* the ceremony tomorrow." I lift my chin. "And I am nothing like her. Nothing."

He studies me like he's trying to assess if I'm telling the truth. I don't know what he determines, but he heads down the road toward my domum. We walk in uncomfortable silence. Men, they are allowed in and out of the community with no consequence. And men like Elon have even more freedom. The women, because of our nature—our value—we follow more complicated rules. I didn't exactly break them tonight, but it puts my motivations into question. My family's history doesn't afford much leeway.

I'm thankful when I see the building ahead. At the driveway, Elon pauses in the street, hands in his pockets, obviously waiting for me to make it safely inside. I'm still shaking as I take the path to the front door. A nagging question makes me stop.

"Why did he step in?" I ask. The 'he' is understood. A man like Rex shouldn't even spare a glance in my direction.

His eyes narrow. "You really don't know?"

I shake my head. Rex and his friends are an enigma to me. They're different from the rest of the community. Chosen.

"Don't worry, Imogene," he says, my name rolling bitterly off his tongue, "you'll find out soon enough."

2

If today is a disaster, it's my mother's fault. What she did—how she abandoned us—those consequences have followed me for years. But today, I'll know exactly how much.

It's a big day. I can feel it from the instant I wake to the fluttering in my belly, in the current of energy running through the dormitory.

Today is the day we receive our Order.

"I think I may be sick."

I glance over at Maria. Her dark, wavy hair is a rumpled mess. Everything about her is familiar. Safe. We've been roommates since we both turned twelve and entered the girl's domum together. Now we're eighteen and it's the first day of spring and that's why she feels nauseous. I do, too. By noon, we'll have our Order and everything in our lives will change.

I reach over and squeeze her hand. "It'll be fine. The Orders are a direction of The Way. Anex will make a perfect match."

It's something I have to believe. That despite my mother's betrayal, I have done enough. I'm worthy enough for Anex to bless me like the others. Maria smiles gratefully, and together, along with the other eighteen-year-olds, we dress and get ready for the cere-mony. The dresses that we painstakingly made in sewing class are hung at the ends of our beds. The fabric is made of soft, white, cotton, with a high collar and long sleeves. I slide the dress over my head, and Maria and I help one another with the zipper in the back.

Hers is a little tight, and she sucks in her stomach. "I shouldn't have had that extra bread last night."

"Hold on." I wiggle the zipper, easing it up. Normally, our dresses are loose and covering, but not today. The dresses for the ceremony are special, and we're instructed to make the dresses a size smaller—to our ideal weight. Maria is thin, but she struggles with her food logs. There are always slip-ups, which lead to correc-tions. It's all part of the philosophy. Cravings of any kind are disre-spectful to the body and a sign of a weak mind.

"Got it," I declare, pushing the zipper to the top. "See? It's perfect."

"Thank you, Imogene. You're a lifesaver." She spins and holds up a pair of new black shoes with a strap across the ridge of the foot and a slight heel. "I hope I don't trip and make a fool of myself."

"You won't," I promise. "It's a blessed day. Only good things will happen."

I almost tell her about the night before, about the altercation and the men that came to my rescue, but now isn't the time. Maybe Maria will think the same thing they did or already does. That I went out looking for trouble. That I'd asked for it in some way. Maybe, I consider now, I had.

The warning bell rings downstairs, and Maria and I finish up, heading downstairs to meet the others. There are nine of us that are of age, and we've known one another since we were children. Lived with one another since we were twelve—the year Anex thinks a child becomes an adolescent. Once you cross that thresh-old, he thinks males and females should separate entirely, from housing to education to spiritual services. Boys, I grew up with, played with and went to school and services with, were suddenly off-limits, segregated to a completely different world. At first, I was sad, but I trusted Anex to make the right decisions for the community as a whole. Everything he does is for a well-thought-out reason.

Dressed in white, the nine of us leave our domum at the back of a cul-de-sac surrounded by trees. The house next door is for the girls an age level below us, the one next to that the level below. The homes, or domum's, are nice. For a long time, people lived in their own homes, scattered across the city. People had their jobs; working in banks and schools or even at the University, but Anex had a bigger vision for people. An idea that spread like wildfire. He used some of his wealth to purchase acres of property just outside the city. A place with lots of space and room for gardens and hiking trails, meeting houses, businesses and homes. He and the other leaders created this amazing community. They decided to call it Serendee, after the word serendipity.

Community leaders will tell you that although the idea was great, Anex was the one that made it happen. He's blessed with wealth; financial and spiritual, and he used it to make Serendee come to fruition. In return, the residents give him our loyalty. Our trust. We protect one another from the darkness that festers outside our community. Out there, people don't understand what we're trying to do here—what we want to accomplish. They think it's a cult. We know they're wrong.

The nervous energy building among the girls only increases as we walk down the road toward Anex's home. That's where the ceremony will be held. The "Main House" is a mansion that sits at the top of a hill overlooking all of our community. It's white with a wide staircase to the front door and massive pillars along the front. It's a palace. A home fit for a king. For a man like Anex.

"Do you think we'll get to go inside?" Maria asks, nodding up at the house.

The butterflies swirl in my stomach. "I hope so."

During our education classes, we learned that Anex started this life as a regular man. He had two parents, went to public school, graduated with honors and entered the University. That's where he realized he was different. Smarter. Better than the other students.

His IQ is off the charts. His brain operates on a whole different level than those around him. Anex was blessed with gifts and one of those was creating The Way; a philosophy for life and success. At the beginning, it was just a bunch of college and graduate students sitting around, talking about how to live their best lives, but it emerged into something more. A philosophy that includes the body, mind, and soul.

My parents met at one of those early meetings. They saw the brilliance of Anex early on and admired his discontentment. How he always wanted more, and slowly, guided by energies deeper than I can comprehend, he built this world—our world. The one I was born into.

Clarissa, the woman that runs our house, stops at the iron gates in front of the house. She presses the intercom and announces our arrival. A moment later, the gates swing open, admitting us, and we start the climb up the hill. It's warm outside and sweat trickles down my back.

"Ouch," Maria mutters, slowing her gait.

"What?"

"It's just these shoes. They're rubbing my heel."

"Pain justifies the sacrifice," I remind her. "The reward will be worth it."

Her nose wrinkles, but she nods, holding back any other complaints. Today is not the day for complaints. It's a celebration.

As we walk past the side door, Clarissa approaches me and says, "Imogene, please come with me."

"Now?" I ask, glancing at Maria. Her eyes are wide with concern. I have no real idea about the process of today's events, but being pulled away from the others can't be good.

"Yes," she says, instructing the others to continue to the white tent up ahead. Another House Mother is waiting, waving at the girls to continue walking.

"Am I in trouble?" I ask, mind racing. Did someone hear about the night before? About the boys in town? Did Elon, or god forbid, Rex, say something to his father?

Sweat builds on my neck and I struggle to breathe.

"You're not in trouble," she says, giving me a reassuring smile while leading me into the house. I'm so anxious I can't even take in the fact that I'm in the main house. There's no time to get it together either, because Clarissa quickly leads me into a sparse white room.

The only other person inside is a female—Anex's personal healer, and a medical table.

I gape at the scene, looking to Clarissa for help. "Wha—"

"It's just a physical," she says, facing me head on and bracing my upper arms with her hands. "A formality."

"I didn't do anything. I swear."

"I know, honey. It's a formality. Everything is fine." She gives me a stern look. "This is Healer Bloom."

I've lived with Clarissa since I was twelve years old. The look in her eye does not imply that anything is 'fine.'

"Remove your dress," the healer says curtly. I've only seen her with Anex—she's his personal and private healer. Why is she examining me?

"My dress?" I repeat, slightly more upset because I spent so much time getting ready and now, right before the ceremony, she wants me to disrobe. I glance at Clarissa, and she nods reassuringly. My fingers unbutton the tiny pearl buttons I'd just fastened a short time before and I slowly, trying not to wrinkle the linen, step out of it. Underneath, I'm wearing approved undergarments, a cotton tank and shorts. They are the kind that do not encourage the male eye to gaze upon us.

"Those too," Clarissa says.

"Of course." I jump to oblige.

I curse myself as my cheeks bloom red. Embarrassment is a signal of shame, and I know I haven't done anything shameful. But I feel the healer's assessing eyes on me as I remove the undergarments, handing them over to Clarissa. My nipples harden from the cool air, and goosebumps travel down my skin. I've been to see one of the healers many times, but usually there is a robe or a barrier of some sort. I take a deep breath and remind myself that it's another reminder today is different.

The healer whips out a cloth tape measurer. "Are you following your caloric goals?"

"Yes, ma'am. Less than 800 a day." She nods and jots something down in a book resting on a tray attached to the table.

She then wraps the tape around my waist, hips and each thigh, taking a moment to pinch the skin at the base of my behind. "Every day?" she repeats, the question mark hanging in the air. I turn and look at my backside. There's some pesky flab that just won't go away no matter how little I eat.

"Yes. I log everything in my journals."

She raises the tape and circles it around my chest, at the highest point of my breasts. "32 D," she remarks, noting it in her book. She rests her pen on top and cups me with both hands. "Firm, but soft." Thumbs roll over the peaks before lowering her hands. "Sit on the table."

I do as I'm told; the paper crinkling underneath me as I arrange myself.

"It is important as we go into this day that your truth is known," the healer says, standing over me. "Every potential Ordering must be pure. Do you understand?"

"I do," I tell her, even though I'm not completely sure. I've spent my life honoring The Way. Probably more than the others.

She swings a bright light directly over my face, shocking my vision and causing the rest of the room to vanish in a dark haze. "The body doesn't lie, Imogene," she says, although I can no longer see her face. I just feel the weight of her hands and she begins her examination. "Is there anything you want to confess?"

As I search for the answer—she wouldn't be asking if there wasn't some Regression I've been hiding, I hear the soft snick of a door closing shut. Did Clarissa just leave? I blurt the first thing I think of, "Last night, on the street, a secular man and his friend tried to accost me on the way home from The Center." Her gloved fingers run down my throat, pausing to check my pulse. "They harassed me and made threats. Three men from Serendee were there to protect me, but it was my fault for being out alone at that time. I should have asked for a chaperone."

I jump with a start when she moves down to my breasts, fondling them gently with bare hands.

"Sorry," she says, with a small laugh, "I can exam you more thoroughly without the gloves." Her fingers are surprisingly firm and thick. Warm. "Am I the first to touch you here?"

"Y-yes," I say, stuttering over the feel of her circling my nipple. "I am pure. Devoted to The Way."

Her hands travel down my belly, soft yet methodical. Feeling me inch by inch. "You have let no male or female explore your body?"

I shake my head, embarrassed by my physical reaction. Can she tell that my stomach flutters from her touch? That my lower belly feels strange and full of heat? My insides twist with confusion. No one has touched or explored me like this. I gasp as she pushes my legs so that my knees are up and then taps the inside of each one. When she speaks again, her voice is further away—down near my feet. "Spread for your legs for me, Imogene. I need to check your barrier."

The barrier. Every girl has one. It is sacred and should only be broken when Anex decides. I allow my legs to drop to the side and feel the warm hands running up my inner thighs. I've been checked before—we all have—the last time a few weeks ago as we prepared for this day, but only externally. "You're going to feel a little pressure," she says. Pressure? I have no idea what this means, but it's not the soft brush against a sensitive spot, and I don't anticipate the jolt of electricity that shoots from my pelvis to my nipples.

"Oh," I gasp.

"How did that feel?"

I am unsure how to answer, so I go for the truth. "Exhilarating."

"Good. It should." After a pause, she adds, "You're sure no one has done this to you before?"

"No," I shake my head. "Never."

She touches me there again, but this time doesn't stop with one brief brush. The warm fingers roll around the nerves, coaxing and drawing me into a sense of bliss. I grip the edges of the table, trying to keep my hips still, but it's almost impossible. I stare so hard at the light that when I close my eyes all I see is spots. The sounds of the room float to me, the movement of the healer's hand, the repetitive sound of clothing shifting.

"That's right," the healer encourages, before I feel something lower, sharper. The pressure she'd warned me about.

"Oh," I gasp, jerking up, but hands hold me down. Something firm and intentional pushes between my legs. A piercing pain shoots through me, and I feel myself stretch. At the same time, warmth rushes up and down my limbs. Pleasure and pain, confusion and bliss. They're all wound up together in this moment and I don't know which direction to go. The pressure is removed as quickly as it happened, and my breath catches, a wave rushing over me as tiny pulses of release ripple across my skin. I exhale loudly, chest heaving, and feel myself slowly returning to the room.

"She's intact," the healer says. To herself? Did Clarissa return? Her comment is followed by a low strangled groan, as though someone stuffed a fist in their mouth. The light is still glaring in my eyes, blinding me from the rest of the room.

"Are we done?" I ask, feeling shaky and sweaty, not sure if I can handle much more. Is this what every female experiences before the ceremony? It feels like I've been in here forever.

"Yes." I hear that same soft snick of the door, and when I get to a sitting position, Clarissa has her hand on the knob. She smiles at me softly, eyes tense.

"Did I pass?"

The healer's eyebrows knit together. "That is for Anex to determine."

"Of course." Clarissa rushes to my side, ceremonial clothing in hand. As my eyes adjust, I notice something at the bottom of the table, down near where my feet had just been.

A pile of sticky, white, fluid.

Clarissa helps me off the table, my knees wobbly and a strange, hollow feeling at the crux of my body. I turn to look back at the fluid again, wondering with slight panic if it had come from me, but the sound of crinkling paper fills the room as the healer yanks it off the table and carries it over to the trash bin. It's the next thing that she does that makes my stomach twist uneasily.

Standing over the trash can, she peels off one glove and then the other.

I can't be sure, but a weird feeling in the pit of my stomach tells me that she never took them off.

3

"IT'S TIME," I say, banging on the door. The sound is matched from the opposite side of the door, dueling rhythmic grunts, each a little louder than the one before. "Rex. Man. We're going to be late."

"Give me a minute," he calls out, followed by, "you're so tight, you know that, baby?"

I roll my eyes. Leave it to Rex to get one last fuck in before a sacred event.

"Is he coming?" Silas asks. He's standing in the lobby of The Center. Levi is over on the couch, flipping through one of Anex's books, as though he hasn't memorized it by heart.

"Oh, he's coming alright." I glance back at the closed door of the instructional room and hear a female cry out in ecstasy. "I suspect about right... now."

Silas shakes his head, checking his reflection in the glass front door. We're all dressed in all black ceremonial attire chosen specifically for Anex's inner circle. Our leader is lenient with the four of us, but late to the Ordering? Rex's Ordering? That may push him too far, and I'm not interested in being on his bad side.

I walk back down the hall to the classroom door and don't knock this time. I open the door and see my best friend pounding into a redhead bent over the table. I recognized her from the night before. She'd slipped into the VIP section of the bar and glued herself to Rex pretty fast. Now, her tits bounce with every thrust, and her teeth bear down on her bottom lip as he relentlessly takes her. She's hot—they always are. Rex has a type. His eyes are closed as he chases release, his fingers pressing into the pale flesh of her ass.

"One minute," he grunts, picking up the pace. His nose wrinkles and he sputters to a stop, jerking twice more and groaning loudly. "Jesus Christ."

It's not blasphemy if you don't believe in it, right?

"Get dressed," I say to the both of them and walk back to the lobby. I shouldn't be surprised. Rex is taking every last minute before the ceremony to get his jollies off.

"Finally," Levi mumbles when the door opens and the redhead hops out, sliding a shoe on one foot. Her hair is a mess and her blouse buttoned wrong, but she doesn't look phased by the three of us.

"I assume you had a quality first lesson?" Levi asks, jumping off the couch. He grabs a schedule from the coffee table and thrusts it toward her. "We have classes every day this week."

She jerks her thumb back to the office. "Will he be there?"

Silas grins and leans against the door. "We have a rotation of instructors. It's better for you to get a firm grasp of The Way and how the system works from more than one member."

The woman sweeps her eyes over Silas—his handsome face, and easy demeanor and says, "Yeah, I'll think about it."

"Good," he says, swinging the door open and releasing her into the bright sunlight. "Have a beautiful day."

He shuts the door and Rex walks out, tugging his black linen pants over his hips. "Sorry about that, but you know how it is."

"No," I ask, leveling my oldest friend with a look. "Exactly how is it?"

His lips tug into a smile. "That girl wanted a deep and intensive understanding of The Way. I was just educating her."

"You had her bent over a table, with your dick buried so deep inside I'm pretty sure I heard her teeth clink together."

"So?" He buttons his shirt—his matching shirt to mine and the others. Anex likes uniformity. He says it creates authority. "I wanted to be thorough. Not just show her The Way, but let her feel it."

"Are you sure this doesn't have something to do with that incident last night—with the girl?"

The girl. Woman. *Imogene*. We all know who she is. What she is about to be.

Rex shoots me a glare. "No."

"Wait," Silas says, "are you calling your cock The Way now? Because that's too far for even me."

"You're not going to be able to do this forever," Levi says, his forehead creased. He doesn't like it when we joke about the rules and standards of our lifestyle. He believes in it. I mean, we all do... we just also like to have a little fun. "In fact, as of tonight—"

"Don't," Rex says, holding up his hand, revealing the scrapes from the fight the night before. "Please don't bring that up right now."

Levi exchanges a look with me and Silas. "But—"

"No 'buts.'" Rex walks toward the door. "Just because my father insists on me being part of the Ordering tonight doesn't mean my life has changed. I'll fuck who I want, when I want, how I want." He steps out on the sidewalk, looking deadly dressed in all back, and gives me a wink. "Even if it's on top of the conference room table."

4

The lawn is emerald green, the grass thick under our shoes. There are rows of white chairs, nine on each side. Bunches of flowers are everywhere. At the back, behind a white rope, is open seating for the rest of the community. At the front, on a small stage, is a clear podium. That's where Anex will issue the Orders.

"Hurry along," Clarissa says, quickly ushering us to a tent on the left side of the stage, hiding us from the growing crowd. There's another tent opposite us, one for the men. We're not allowed to see one another until the ceremony begins.

I do manage to look out into the audience and spot my father on the front row. His hair is darker than mine, now flecked with gray. The hollow under his eyes is dark, and he looks tired, but when he sees me, he smiles. We've both suffered from my mother's betrayal. He lost his position on the leadership committee, and I carry around her sins like an albatross around my neck. Today is an opportunity for both of us to regain some credibility. I grin and wave in return before ducking beneath the flaps.

"How's my hair?" Renee asks, tugging a coil of her flame red hair. "I should have straightened it, right?"

"It looks great," Maria says, and I nod. Renee is the smartest in our group and was invited to a private meeting with Anex two weeks ago. Something only the most worthy girls accomplish while still in the domum. She didn't tell us what they spoke about—that is confidential—but when she returned, her eyes were glassy and her cheeks flushed. The most we could get out of her was that Anex is wiser than we could ever imagine, and it was the most eye-opening experience of her life.

"Settle down," Clarissa says, walking past and giving us each a small squeeze on the arm. Outside, the crowd grows quiet, which means Anex has arrived. I peek through the flap in the tent and see him up on the platform. He's dressed in his typical black. Shirt and pants. Round, small glasses perched on his nose. His fair hair glints in the sunlight, and his smile is warm and reassuring. His sleeves are rolled up over his elbows and dark ink is tattooed into the skin of his forearm. It's the same mark that I saw on Rex's arm the night before. Behind him are a group of men and women—all his confidants. One in particular catches my eye. Margaret—one of his Spiritual Mates. She's beautiful with dark, stylish hair and piercing blue eyes. She's special. She has to be, or Anex wouldn't have asked her to stand by his side.

Maria grabs my hand, threading our fingers together, and I draw my eyes away from Margaret. I cling back, overcome with the wild hammering of my heart. This is it. It's actually happening.

"Ready?" she whispers as the first name is called. Rebecca, with her white-blonde hair, exits the tent and crosses the yard. Through the narrow gap, I can see a boy—a man—stride from the other tent. His name is Paul, and I drink him in. Tall, lanky, a crooked nose, but kind eyes. He looks nervous as she does, but smiles when his eyes land on Rebecca. They meet in the middle and face the stage. Then they touch their foreheads and bow. Satisfied, Anex gives his Order.

Maria is still looking at me with expectation, her question still hanging in the air. *Ready?* I am, but I'm not. I have no idea what to expect, no clue who is on the other side of the Order. If Anex will punish me because of my mother's actions or why they needed to see me today. What I do know is that whoever he Orders me to be with, it is The Way, and there's no getting out of it.

I'll be betrothed to a man of Anex's choosing.

~

It didn't start like this, or so we're told. Anex didn't originally pick mates for members of the community. That happened later. It's not that he didn't think people shouldn't have free-will, of course we do. It's the twenty-first century. We live in America. But an unhappy marriage affects the whole community. Divorces are complicated. Messy and filled with toxic energy. And after a while, it seemed like a good idea to just give Anex the ability to arrange couples for the betterment of all of Serendee.

"Maria Castillo."

Her name sounds like honey on Anex's tongue. It's a thrill to get any of his attention, even if it's for only a moment. She gives me one last look and a squeeze of her hand before stepping through the flap into the bright sunlight. My breath catches as she trips over the grass, but she rights herself quickly. I exhale and watch my friend cross the yard. The tent opposite of ours opens, and a man comes out. His name is Elijah. I remember him from when we were kids. He has the same flat forehead and easy grin. Maria's smile falters for a second, but she regains it quickly. Elijah is a few years older than us, but that's expected. The rules are different for men. Women prepare for this day their whole lives. Men have to be trained to be good mates. Sometimes they have to wait until Anex decides they're ready.

One by one, the Order is given. Perfect couples, all hand-picked by Anex himself and betrothed to one another. We'll spend the next ninety days in courtship: learning about one another, preparing to be mates for life. Then we'll prepare for the bonding ceremony.

My adrenaline rises, inching up with each match, aware that my time is coming. Finally, it's just me and Clarissa in the tent alone. She gives me a reassuring look, but I see a crease in her forehead.

I'm still standing there, hands damp, when I hear Anex speak from the podium. He can't be finished, can he?

"I don't think people realize how much work goes into The Ordering. It's not an easy task, but you asked me to do it and I have tried to do my best." He smiles warmly out at his community. "These young men and women are the hope and future for our little Utopia. I am confident in their commitment to one another, to the community, and to Serendee."

I look at Clarissa and whisper, "What's happening? Why didn't he call my name?"

Her lips form a thin line, and she presses her finger against them, indicating I should listen.

"This year is special for me. Personal. After much consideration, my son, Rex, will also receive an Order. He's ready to take on the responsibility of a man—and mate."

The flaps of the tent part and Rex walks out, golden-haired and perfect, just as he was the night before when he came to my aid. My eyes drop to his hand. Sure enough, his knuckles are red and raw. Mirroring his father, he's also all in black, dressed fully in Serendee clothing today. It's hard to take my eyes off of him, but movement in the men's tent draws me away. Never alone, Rex's three best friends emerge. Are they to be Ordered as well? My gaze goes instantly to Elon, who looks just as intimidating and angry in the daylight as he did in the dark. Out here I can see the cool gray in his eyes. There's no kindness there.

Levi follows, with his flaming red hair and ivory skin. His coloring matches his sister, Renee, and I see her smile from her position in front of the stage. His green eyes are clear—his expression serious. He's well known around the center for being a dedicated student of Anex's—one of the youngest—and a devout and a strict follower of The Way.

My eyes are drawn to the final man, Silas. He's known throughout Serendee for being a constant companion to both Rex and Anex. Even in a world where physical appearance isn't celebrated, there is no mistaking Silas' beauty. His features are almost feminine. Soft lips contrast sharp cheekbones. Long lashes and lean limbs. His smile is shy yet makes a funny tickle in my stomach. One look at the other females confirms they feel the same. Possibly some of the males. He is a very handsome, alluring person. People have wondered for years if he was going to ever be Ordered, but it seems his place is by Anex's side.

When all three are on the stage, Rex approaches his father, standing in the center of the stage. His features are more defined than Anex, more chiseled. Everyone—the newly Ordered—the crowd in the back gawks at the men on stage. This moment is very unusual, and my pulse quickens at the realization I'm a part of it.

"It took a great deal of consideration to determine Rex's Order, but in my heart, I already knew. I've been watching this young woman for years, blossoming into the perfect mate for my son..."

I feel the weight of Clarissa's hand on my shoulder, heavy and firm. When I look up at her stern expression, it all clicks.

"Imogene Montgomery," my name is called out, settling over the ceremony. Rex's eyes pin to me the instant Clarissa pushes me out of the tent. It's not just the heat of his eyes that I feel, or that of the crowd in the ceremony. It's from the other men on the platform, Silas, Levi and Elon, watching me with a careful eye. My skin prickles and my cheeks flush, but I walk across the grass anyway, the heels sinking into the dirt. Anex grins, lopsided and charming, gesturing for me to climb the small set of stairs at the front and as I do, Rex steps forward, offering me his hand.

"Here," he says softly. I take his hand, warm and strong, and a moment later I'm standing in front of the whole community.

Anex nods when he sees the two of us together. "Good. This is good." He faces the crowd. "In front of all of Serendee, I witness the Order of each of these couples," he declares, hands up in blessing. "Today is the beginning of your courtship. Take this time to get to know one another, how to support and care for one another. To fulfill one another's needs." I may be mistaken, but I feel Anex's eyes flick toward his son when he says that last one. "The bonding ceremony will be on the first day of fall. You have been Ordered."

The audience stands and claps, cheering on the new couples. On the patio, volunteers have set up a celebration—sweets from the bakery, fresh food from the farm. I try to process everything, but I'm overwhelmed. Confused. Did Anex just Order me to his son? Me, the daughter of a Regressive, to the heir of Serendee?

"Congratulations," he says to the two of us, patting Rex on his shoulder, before striding off the platform, heading toward the festivities.

Out in the grass, the couples are shyly smiling at one another, excited about the prospect of their futures. I look over at Rex, the twist of anticipation warm in my chest.

I glance toward the party and say, "Should we—" That's when I realize he's not looking at me and is already halfway off the platform. "Where—"

He jerks his head at Elon. "Take her to her room," he says, "and get her settled. I'll deal with this later."

A moment later he's gone, and I'm being escorted off the stage, toward the massive home. In ninety days, it'll be my home, too. Mated to the second most powerful man in the community.

5

Imogene

I'm handed off three times before I get to my room. First by Elon, who walks me into the house and into the foyer. He doesn't acknowledge me, but I barely notice, too busy taking in the magnificence of the house. I've been to some of the public areas before, but I've never gone into the private quarters, and I'm struck by the opulence. Before I can get too invested in the inlaid floors and crystal chandeliers, I'm handed off to a member of the main house staff who leads me up two floors of the curved staircase. The hallways shoot off in every direction, wings inside of wings, each decorated with the same wood paneling and fine, but nondescript artwork. We pass multiple staircases, and by the time we reach the final handoff; I feel like I'm twisted in a maze. I'm given to Clarissa last, who waits by a set of thick double doors on the third floor.

"Imogene," she says, her smile genuine and proud, "congratulations on your Order, sweet girl. I always knew you'd do great things."

She opens the doors, revealing not just a room, but an entire suite. At the round table, just inside, are my belongings. A wooden trunk and a small suitcase. I walk over and open the case. Inside are my journals and logs, along with a few photos and my lesson books.

"Your clothes are there as well," she says. "Including the new outfits for the courtship."

I'd spent months sewing and creating a wardrobe to carry me up to the bonding ceremony. Now that I know that I've been arranged to Rex, the idea of wearing them for him sends a flurry of nerves in my stomach. Are they too simple? His clothing is always neatly tailored. I'm embarrassed for him to see my lack of ability.

"Did you know about this?" I ask, slowly closing the trunk. "That I was going to be Ordered to Rex?"

"Anex spoke to me about it, yes. I couldn't tell you."

I nod. It's understood that Anex speaks to the house mothers when he's making his decisions. There are other ways he learns about us; how we do in our studies. Are we attentive in lectures? Do we encompass The Way of Serendee? The extra physical makes a little more sense, in retrospect. The Heir of Serendee must have a pure mate, but that's also what creates my fear.

"Why," I finally say, "would Anex choose me for his son? I'm... the daughter of a Regressive. A runaway. An abandoner. Why would Anex want me to be with Rex, and how disappointed is Rex to have me as his betrothed?"

"It's not our place to question his Order," Clarissa replies, leading me deeper into the suite. "The only way this works is if we have faith. Don't you have faith in The Way?"

"Of course," I say quickly, feeling shame for even allowing the question to be asked.

"Then stop worrying," she says, "and let's take a look at your new home."

There is a living room and a well-appointed kitchen. There are two hallways going in opposite directions, and along the back wall is a wide window that overlooks all of Serendee. "There are bedrooms down each hall, including two masters. One for you and one for Rex." She gestures to the left. "Your room is this way."

She takes me down one of the hallways, passing two additional rooms, and leading me to another set of double doors that open into a large bedroom. The bed sits in the middle; the frame made of twisting iron. There's a quilt folded on top of the sheets. I step forward and see a note.

"The Women's Assembly?" I ask, reading their congratulations. "They made me a quilt?"

"You and Rex, yes. The bonding quilt. It's customary."

Me and Rex. In the same bed. It's something I've pushed out of my mind, as I've been instructed to my entire life. But here it is. Now that I'm Ordered the time has come to think about it; sex.

But not now, I think, feeling the heat in my cheeks. Not today. It's one reason for the courtship. Anex knows people develop intimacy at their own pace. I tuck the card, which includes an invitation to the next meeting, back inside the quilt.

"Imogene," Clarissa says, watching me carefully, "I know this is overwhelming, but you didn't just receive an Order today. You were *Chosen*. A position that many others would sacrifice to have."

True. There are many girls that would love to be in my position. And many girls are unhappy with the one they were given. But no one complained or questioned. That was the curse my mother left me with. Her obstinance and curious disposition. Her inability to just *accept*. It's like a disease running through me. I can't stop it no matter how much I try.

Being Chosen isn't something people know much about. It simply means that Anex has determined that you are worthy of being part of a higher circle in Serendee. Being Ordered to Rex elevates me to this level.

Clarissa clears her throat and sits on the end of the bed, patting the spot next to her. I take my place, feeling the soft give of the mattress underneath me. "You have spent the last seven years preparing for this moment. You know how to cook, clean, sew. You know how to maintain a home—"

"Even one this size?"

She nods. "That will be a challenge, but there will be assistance."

"I'm not worried about maintaining the home. I know I am ready." I tug at a thread on the quilt.

"Then what is on your mind?"

I want to push back my curiosity, the questions, but I can't. "At my job at The Center, I've had the opportunity to see Rex, and I know that he has lived differently than the rest of us. He often wears secular clothing and spends a lot of time around people outside of Serendee."

That's the nice way to put it and doesn't even include the gossip that swirls around Rex and his friends. Seeing him out the night before wasn't unexpected. Even in Serendee gossip flourishes, particularly about this group of men. That they go into town often and frequent the restaurants and bars filled with worldly college girls. Secular girls. That they are *experienced*.

"Imogene," she says, taking my hand, "I've taught you not to listen to petty rumors, haven't I?" I nod. "Rex was raised to be a leader, and leadership requires a different approach. His position at The Center requires him to straddle both our world and the secular world. There's no scandal there. Anex can't protect us from the outside world if he doesn't know what to protect us from, can he?"

"No."

"So yes, Rex and his companions have had access to that world so that they can lead Serendee in the best way possible. They are the ones that must bear the burdens of a fast-changing world—a sinful world." Her nose wrinkles and looks me in the eye. "You have been Ordered to be his mate, not to question his affairs. You are here to fulfill his needs as a partner, not as a confidant. That is not your place as his mate or as a member of Serendee. Do you understand?"

"Yes, ma'am."

"This will not be an easy transition for you, Imogene. You are going to be required to do things that feel foreign and strange. Subversive, even, but that is part of being given this honor. You will be the mate of the next leader of Serendee, and with that will come great sacrifice as well as rewards."

What she says makes sense. The pieces click into place. "I guess I'm just overwhelmed by the honor of the arrangement. I never expected—"

"You deserve it. Anex sees something important in you. Something others have questioned." Her smile turns sympathetic. "From now on those questions will end."

Because no one will dare second guess Anex or Rex's judgement. It's a reprieve from the sins of my past and a second chance. One I will not squander.

~

I'm not the only one in a new home today. All of the Ordered are given a house to live in at the beginning of their courtship. Anex believes that during this time all areas should be explored together, making sure that by the time of the bonding ceremony the couple is ready. Outside of Serendee, a wedding is the start of a new life together, but not here. It all begins with the Order. It's another way that we are more advanced.

What I do have to wonder is if my friends are spending their first day alone like I am. Hours pass, and Rex has not made an appearance. I have no idea when or if he will. Anxious from waiting, I decide to take a shower and change, freshen up for if and when he does arrive.

The bathroom is luxurious with a big tub and a separate shower. There's a dressing table already supplied with toiletries. The idea of taking a shower in my own bathroom is a thrill. I've always had to share with strict time limits and limited hot water usage. Those habits die hard and even though I'm the only one here, I bathe quickly, still thinking about what happened the night before with those men in the alley.

It's well known that people think Serendee is a cult. The word is tossed around so frequently, so lightly, that it's something of a joke within the community. We don't prescribe to any specific religion other than a basic spirituality. The Way isn't about a higher deity. It's about living a responsible, accountable life. How can we be a cult? It's laughable. Anex tells us that people slight others when they're jealous or frightened. They're scared to take the risk that the founders did all those years ago. To have the belief that there's something more out there than how they've been conditioned.

The core concepts started with sustainability. Creating a community that relies on the government, the establishment, and corporate systems as little as possible. It was a bold plan, but Anex was an environmental engineer and his friends were skilled in other sciences and educated at the university and what they didn't know, they learned. One of these people was my mother, who was working on her master's degree in community development. Serendee was executed with a plan. We have gardens and livestock. We compost and reuse as much as possible. We use solar energy and limit our carbon footprint. We nurture the earth, and, in return, the earth nurtures us.

I know it all sounds hippie-dippy, but it's not just that. Anex is a brilliant thinker. He's prepared. He's gifted and our little community has been given awards and has been highlighted for how people should aspire to live. We have everything we need inside the walls of Serendee. Everyone has a role. A purpose. A job. There are farmers and builders, teachers and technicians. There's a bakery and a seamstress. A grocery and market. Each adult is given credits for their work and those credits are how we purchase what we need. Any supplies needed from outside the community are processed through the Main House. It's a perfect system, created by a perfect man.

That's what makes the Order today so intimidating.

Rex's purpose will be to take over for Anex one day.

My purpose will be to support him.

After I bathe, I take the time to brush and dry my long, thick hair. All the young girls and women have long hair—as we've been taught to downplay our physical appearance and focus on our inner value instead. Today is the first day I'll be viewed as more than just a girl. I'm a potential mate and I can't help but study myself in the mirror, wondering what he'll think of me. Is my hair too long? Too immature? I've seen secular women in town. They look... different. More sophisticated, exotic.

I braid my hair and change into one of the new dresses folded neatly in my trunk. The color is a soft blue, similar to Rex's eyes, and has a tighter bodice than I normally wear. Looking for hand lotion, I open one of the vanity drawers. I'm surprised to see a collection of makeup. None of the girls in the house wear makeup. It's considered secular—something done outside of Serendee. Nature gave us our looks. We don't need to accentuate it. Quickly, I shut the drawer and step away. Obviously, whoever stocked this room made a mistake.

When I enter the living room, I jolt to a stop, surprised to find Rex waiting for me in the living room. He's facing the window that overlooks Serendee. His golden hair shines in the afternoon light. My stomach flutters as I take in the tight fit of his black linen shirt across his wide shoulders. He has the body of a man, something I'm not accustomed to being around for more than a few seconds of time.

He's also alone.

The smile that spreads across my face isn't false. This is the moment I've been waiting for.

"Hello," I say when it's clear that he doesn't realize I've entered the room. He turns, and I'm struck with how he's even better looking than I realized. His eyes, they're so blue, like the reflection of the sky. His features, the line of his nose and the curve of his cheekbones, are startlingly strong. His hair shiny and pale. I can't help but look for the bruises on his knuckles. They're the only flaw I can see. Red, raw, and exposed.

"Imogene," he says, his voice curt. Jaw tight. "I wanted to stop by and speak to you."

Stop by... as in visit.

He gestures to the couch and I sit with my knees pressed together, hands folded on my lap. I wonder, as he takes the chair across from me and runs his thumb over his knuckles, if he remembers the last time we were alone together? That night when I was twelve, and he was a hurt, sad boy.

"Thank you for that," I say, staring at his hand. I'm not sure where to hold my gaze. "For defending me last night."

"No one should degrade our women." He chuckles darkly. "Or *my* woman in particular."

The statement causes a little thrill, something deep in my spine. It scares me, but also causes some excitement. I've waited so long for my Order, and now that it's here I feel so overwhelmed. I run my hands over my knees, smoothing my dress, daring a glance up at him and find him watching me.

"Would you like for me to cook dinner? Or would you prefer to show me how you want the house kept? Clarissa taught us to make sure everything was in order, but a home this size isn't what I was prepared for..." I trail off, aware that I'm rambling. "Please, tell me how we should proceed."

"That is what I came to talk to you about." He inhales deeply and then exhales. "We will not be proceeding in a typical fashion."

I frown. "What do you mean?"

"I mean that you and I will not participate in this farce created by my father. This life? Serendee... The Way? I don't believe in it. It's bullshit."

My gasp is audible. Everything he's said from the curse word to his statement throws me.

He shakes his head. "This is what I mean. What shocks you more? My vulgarity? Or my blasphemy?" I swallow the lump in my throat, but no words come out. He smirks. "It's both, right? I can see it on your face."

"I don't understand what you're saying."

He runs his thumb over his tattoo. It's a small circle depicting the sun and the moon. He got it when he was sixteen. There was a ceremony, and we all watched as the tattooist inked it on his forearm. It's the symbol of The Way and worn by the leader of Serendee to remind him to stay grounded. Or, in his case, the next leader.

"I've seen beneath the curtain and what lies on the other side. The good stuff. The real stuff; sex, drugs, alcohol, music, books. I may be forced into this role by my father, but I have no intention of settling down and abstaining."

Each admission is like a wrecking ball trying to knock me off my foundation. Although I understand the words he is saying, I do not understand why. Why would he feel this way? And why, if he did, would he— "If this is how you feel, why did you drag me into it? Why did you get Ordered?"

He laughs and narrows his eyes. "Why do you think?"

"I have no idea. I have no idea why you are saying such terrible, such despicable things."

"Do you think I have a choice? Any more than any of the others here?" He lifts his chin. "Than you? I don't believe, sweetheart, but there is no getting away from my father either. Not without paying for it dearly." He holds my eye. "I thought if anyone would understand it would be you."

"Me? Why me?" I'm dutiful and faithful. I work hard, study, and I follow all of the rules. But the set of his jaw and the lift of his eyebrow answers my question. "Oh. Because of my mother."

"When my father told me that I was to be Ordered this year, he did allow me one concession; the opportunity to choose my future mate. I could have anyone, obviously, but I didn't need the most beautiful girl or the most obedient." His eyes turn cold as the truth spills out. "I needed someone that no one else wanted—someone that was flawed and couldn't make demands. Someone that couldn't make a fuss when she learned the truth about the parameters of our relationship. He wasn't happy about it. He doesn't like the idea of having someone like you so close to our home, but I told him I would handle it, *you*, and ultimately he agreed."

A hot tear streaks down my cheek. There's no holding it back. I suck in a breath and ask, "What does that mean? For me?"

"It means you will live in this house, and we will pretend on the outside to have a perfect bonding. It will be a farce, but if we do not uphold it and convince the members of Serendee then we will both pay the price."

"Wait," I say, hopping out of my seat. All of this is moving so fast. "If we pretend on the outside, why can't we just try to make it work. Even if you don't..." I swallow, "believe in your father's teachings, I am ready to be whatever you need me to be. I can make you happy."

Laughter rumbles from his chest, this time genuine and pure. "No, sweet Imogene, you cannot make me happy."

"Why?"

"Because...I want things that you can't give me." He stands inches away and rakes his eyes down my body. "Things I require to live like a man. Gluttonous, sinful, secular things." He reaches out and grazes those raw knuckles across my cheek, wiping away a tear. "Things a girl like you, no matter how much you're like your mother, could never provide me."

"That's not true. I've prepared my whole life for this. I can do—be, whatever you want."

He laughs, demoralizing and cruel. "Sorry, but no. I don't want home-cooked meals and a tidy house. I want a woman with meat on her bones, who doesn't look like she'll break when I bend her over the nearest surface and bury myself inside of her." His eyes narrow. "Do you even know what that means?"

I want to say yes, but it's a lie. Everything he says is confusing, but I know the tone. It's mean. He's mocking me. "No."

His fingers trail down my neck. "Figure out how to use that body of yours, and how to please me, and maybe we can talk."

My body reacts from the way he looks at me; embarrassment, humiliation, horror... but there's something else. Something deep inside that flickers like a hot, dangerous flame.

"So what do I do now? Everything I've prepared for is worthless."

The look he gives me is sympathetic—or maybe pitying. "You'll continue on as normal, going to your position at The Center, attending meetings, and we'll present as a couple when it's required. We'll go through the ceremonies and get bonded in the fall. Outside of this house, no one will know the difference." He takes a step back, and I think he's going to leave. I *hope*. But he stops and says, "You know this isn't the end of the world for you, Imogene. If it hadn't been for me, my father wouldn't have Ordered you with anyone at all. Not with your reputation." His words are cold and harsh. True. "I've given you a gift. This way, you've entered the most powerful home in Serendee. You're not just Ordered, you've been Chosen, and there are perks to being in this position even if it isn't what you expected."

With that, he walks out of the living room. I hop up and follow him to the front door. "Where are you going?"

"I'm not staying here. I have my own suite. You'll remain here."

"But—" I start, panic starting to rise. He vanishes, closing the door behind him. I'm left alone for the first time since I was twelve, in a strange house with nothing but my disgrace.

6

The look on Imogene's face when I leave the suite is exactly why I don't play with the females in Serendee. They're wound up so tight, caught in the layers upon layers of my father's manipulations, that they don't even know what's real and what's not.

Which is exactly the point.

I stride down the hall, pushing aside the image of those big blue eyes looking as though I had snakes coming out of my eyes. How dare I say I don't believe in The Way, or even worse, the teachings of Anex? *Blasphemy!* I knew she would struggle to even hear it, which is exactly why I told her. Imogene Montgomery is nothing but a sheep, but that doesn't mean she shouldn't know the truth about what's about to transpire between us. We are Ordered, after all. And if she needs to understand one thing up front, it's that I am not giving up my freedom for some innocent little virgin my father thinks will keep me latched to this bullshit society forever.

I enter my personal rooms, along the opposite wing of the house. I should be moving into the suite with Imogene today and beginning our courtship, but that's not happening. I walk into the den and see my best friends lounging on the couch. Silas and Elon are playing video games. Levi has his nose shoved in a book.

"So," Silas asks, "how did she take it?"

"Well enough. I didn't give her much choice." I pick up the controller but after a few movements toss it aside after the throbbing pain in my knuckles makes it too hard to play.

"I feel a little bad for her," Silas says. "She spent the last seven years preparing for this day and you completely crushed her dreams."

"Yeah," I admit. "She seemed ready to fulfill her role. She asked if she could make me dinner."

"I don't know why you have to push back on this," Elon says, striking a match. Sulfur fills the room, and he lights a rolled joint and takes a drag. He hands it off to me. "You're not leaving Serendee. Why does it matter?"

Because I'm not getting attached, I want to say. "Because my father Ordered me this season because he's trying to control me. He's the one that opened the door and showed us that there's a bigger life outside of Serendee. He taught us how to straddle the line. He thinks that if I get Bonded to one of his devoted; a damaged, needy, desperate little girl, then I'll come back to the fold."

"But why not just take her as your mate? She's cute. A little too skinny for my taste, but her tits are nice." Silas asks. "She'll probably make a good lay once she figures it out."

"Yeah," I snort. "They are pretty nice. Perky." I may not want to be Ordered to her, but I'm still a man. I'd felt it the other night in the alley when those men were harassing her. I may not want to Bond with her, but that doesn't mean someone else can have her. Especially some asshole from town.

"So you do like her?" Levi asks, glancing up from his books. I can tell from the spine it's one of my father's. Levi's the only one that doesn't game with us. Or smoke, or drink, or fuck around. Despite having more leniency with the standards in Serendee, he does his best to stay on track, unless it's for work. I think my father approved him as one of my confidants because he'll report back.

What dad doesn't get is that he's more loyal to me than him. "It's understandable to be wary. Her mother was Regressive."

Regressive. It's the term we, no Anex, coined for the people that challenge him. The ones that are no longer welcome inside his sacred little walls.

"I'm not wary. She's just not my type."

Silas snorts. "You mean she's a virgin and not some skank at the bar. Think about it, Rex, I bet she's tighter than Levi's tie."

Levi frowns and touches his neck, shooting Silas a dirty look.

I push his arm, making his hand slip off the controller. "I'm not getting tied up with an emotionally stunted, devotee of my father's. No matter how fuckable her tits look or tight her pussy is."

When I turned eighteen, my father began showing me and the guys the other side of Serendee. The business and money and the methods he uses to keep his perfect little town under control. Learning that truth had been Earth shattering. I'd been like everyone else in the community—a sheep—believing all of Anex's manipulations and lies about the evil that resides outside Serendee's walls. About the roles of men and women—about sex and desire. I believed all of it. That if you followed The Way—followed him—happiness and contentment would follow.

I think, for a brief time, that it was true that Serendee had all of those things. The problem for Anex is that he always wants more, and to have more he had to spread his wings. Silas, Elon, and Levi, and I were the wings. We each have our own positions; mine is primary as a recruiter. Levi's is teaching classes down at the Center. Elon's task is quiet—working in the shadows doing whatever it is my father wants or needs. And Silas? My father capitalizes on his best feature; his ability to seduce people in and outside of Serendee.

My connection to The Center is how I knew about Imogene— the daughter of the betrayer. When Anex told me it was time to get Ordered, I already knew who I wanted. I chose the girl that was pretty enough, completely compliant and totally desperate. Someone I can control.

Because there is no leaving. No getting out. There is just...

finding pleasure in one world and tolerating the other. My father is too dangerous to walk away from. The consequences... well, I'd seen what had happened to those that questioned him publicly. The people who had doubts. And he's made sure that I can't leave. I rely on him for everything: money, housing, support. He's sullied my hands. He has leverage. Even if I risked it, where would I go? Even with a foot in the secular world, I don't know how to exist there. Not the way I do here.

My father created my world, a world that one day will be mine. Even if I think every single word out of my father's mouth is a lie, I have to pretend otherwise. We all do. Now we're just four fucked up, directionless men, straddling two very different worlds.

And that's how it will continue—except in ninety days I'll have a woman by my side that needs to understand the truth. My truth. I will never be the mate she wants or needs, nor will I use her for my pleasure, because I refuse to put her in that kind of danger.

The sooner she understands that, the better.

7

———————

My mother wasn't always an embarrassment. She'd actually been one of the original members of Serendee, one of the innovators. She'd studied urban and community planning. She loved horticulture and advocated for the gardens that feed and nourish the members. For many years, Anex, along with everyone else in Serendee, relied on her intelligence and friendship. It's one reason her betrayal hit so hard.

As a mother, she'd been kind and fun. Strong. She took me with her to work as often as possible, showing me how to tend to the gardens. She told me all about her long-term plans to grow more vegetables, herbs and fruits. There would be a bigger greenhouse and the backfield would eventually be cleared and plowed. She advocated for less housing and more green space. That was something she and Anex disagreed on. It may not be why she ultimately left, but it was part of it. The real reason was her ego and pride, her lack of faith. But mostly, her questions.

Anex's vision is to continue to grow Serendee in land and population. Two years after my mother left, one of his dreams came to fruition. The Center—a three story building on Main Street—a visible spot in the middle of town for people to stop in and learn more about The Way. He could have built it inside the gates of our community, but that's not what he wanted. He wants the world to know about our way of life. We can't do that by hiding.

It's another reason we laugh at the idea of our lifestyle being a cult. Do cults set up shop for any and everyone to enter? We have no secrets, Anex says, just opportunities. And the opportunity to explore The Way is for everyone. That is, if they're willing to do the work.

It flies in the face of our detractors, that and the fact they think women aren't allowed to hold positions, but they're wrong. Anex tells us often, females are the glue that binds the community together. I'm the perfect example. I was given the position of managing the front desk at the center a year ago, when I turned eighteen.

After spending the night alone, where I was caught in restless sleep about Rex and his whereabouts, I came in early to get my mind off the odd turn in my life. There are three floors of offices, all strictly used for Serendee business. Floor one is for seminars and meetings. The second floor is for real estate and the day-to-day management required for a community the size of a small town. The third is the private offices for Serendee Leadership. They aren't used that frequently, and when they are, people tend to come in and out of the back door that leads directly to the staircase. Anex rarely comes in at all. Everyone wants a moment of his time. He's in high demand with people in and outside of the community, but it's widely understood he doesn't like traditional meetings, preferring to have more casual interactions down by the lake or playing a game of basketball at the gym. Which is why, when I hear the chime on the front door and look up from my desk, I'm shocked to see him walk through the door.

I drop the pencil and quickly touch the spot in the center of my forehead while bowing slightly. "Good morning."

He smiles warmly. "Good morning to you as well, Imogene. I hope you slept well after the excitement of yesterday."

"I did, thank you." It's a lie. One I will jot down in my journal later.

"I wanted to speak to you."

"Oh, yes. Of course." I step away from the desk. "Would you like my seat?"

"Thank you, dear." He moves behind the desk and sits in the chair. I don't miss how he assesses everything in my workspace. I move quickly, anxiously. Anex has never given me a reason to be uncomfortable around him. It's the opposite. He's so kind and generous. So wise with his knowledge. To be in his presence is to feel blessed—favored. "It's my understanding that you met with my son yesterday after the ceremony."

"Yes, I did."

He leans back in the seat. "And he told you his feelings about Serendee and The Way."

"He did." I add quickly, "I made it very clear that I did not agree with his views."

"Of course not. You are a loyal member of this community, Imogene. It's why I trust you in this position at The Center. In fact, it's why I agreed to his request for you to be his mate." He smiles. "You know what it is like to be betrayed by a family member."

It always comes back to this. "I do."

"But you also know how important it is to not let them go—to fight to keep them close."

"Yes, I do understand that." My father and I failed Anex when we couldn't make my mother stay.

"Your father fought for her," he says, as though he can read my thoughts, "but she was too far gone. Too poisoned." Hearing this is surreal. No one discusses my mother and if she is ever brought up at all, it is as a warning. "You were too young to do anything when Alia made her decision, but that is not the case today."

I frown. "What do you mean?"

"My son needs you, Imogene. He needs your guidance and your support. To be nurtured like plants in the garden." His eyes are clear and determined. "But most of all, he must stay in Serendee and continue to work toward leadership." He tilts his head. "I need him, Imogene, as much as you do."

The statement comes out softly, but the threat is there. I need him to make me reputable again. This is my shot at redemption in the eyes of the community. Anex and I look at one another for a long time, but all the apprehension drifts from my body. If I felt lost last night talking to Rex, things are much clearer now.

"I am at your service," I tell him, "and will do whatever must happen to keep Serendee on its righteous path. Tell me how to help your son."

~

What he asks of me is startling. Shameful. Uncomfortable.

"I don't blame my son for his... needs. All men have them, but those of use that believe in The Way, do our best to channel them into more productive activities." He sighs. "It's my fault, really. I gave Rex too much access to the secular world. I wanted him to have the same education and opportunities that I did, assuming it would only bolster his abilities for leadership. Instead, he has been swayed by the pleasures of that society and he doesn't want to give it up."

"I know nothing about the outside world," I tell him. "I don't know what I can do to help him."

"You show him that you can be everything he needs to be happy and successful."

Rex told me himself that he wants sex and drugs and fun. "I'm sorry, but I don't know how to provide that."

"I'm sure you don't, but... well," he looks around the office, picking up a few things on my desk, "did you know how to manage an office when you first started working here?"

"No. Not at all." I point to a bookshelf. "I studied books on office management, and I asked for help when I could. But the best

46

method is trial and error—" I clasp my hands together and my skin turns hot. "Oh."

"Like with any new skill, you will need to be taught—trained." Anex stands and walks around the desk. The uneasiness in my stomach grows. "I believe in you, Imogene. You are resilient and determined. Like your mother, you are very smart, but unlike her, you are loyal and will give what is needed to protect this community for the future."

"When," I swallow back my heartbeat, "when does my training begin?"

"Tonight. At your suite in the main house. I have assembled a skilled team to teach you everything you need to know about pleasing a man like my son. And although there will be times where it seems confusing or trying, understand that everything asked of you has been approved by me and is part of The Way." He reaches out and glides a hand down my hair and rests it on my shoulder. My skin prickles from his touch. "I have faith in you, Imogene."

It's an honor to have Anex believe in me like this, but I still fear what comes next. I close my eyes and brace myself, but it's unnecessary. His hand is gone and when I reopen my eyes, so is he.

8

I WALK DOWN the patio steps, toward the small cottage at the back of the main house property. It was built for guests, primarily new recruits, that Anex wants to ease into Serendee. Although I was raised here, and our way of life seems normal, I know enough about the secular world to understand that at first glance, things around here seem... different.

They're right.

Serendee is a haven compared to the outside world. It's quiet and peaceful, with fresh air and locally grown food. Our lives are controlled, days filled with meditation and self-improvement, seeking enlightenment, but what most people in the community don't understand is utopia comes with a price. One I pay as part of my duty to Serendee as part of Anex's inner circle.

I pass the pool, the crystal-clear water refreshing and clean. This area is sacred to residents of the main house and Anex's personal guests. Many are secular, which means they must be kept separate from the main community. My job is to help potential members get comfortable. Anex saw my gift when I was just a teenager and helped me cultivate it.

I enter the guest cottage, which seems small in comparison to the main house, but is a nice size. There's a living room and kitchen, two bedrooms. There's the room I will attend to our guest—a woman named Kayla—heiress to the Montclair publishing company. They specialize in books focused on health and nutrition, as well as sustainable living. Anex has worked very hard to get her attention.

I knock on the door. I'd asked Kayla to be ready for me when I arrived.

"Kayla, it's Silas, are you ready?"

"Yes," I hear, the words slightly muffled. I step inside the room, dimming the lights, as I take in Kayla on the massage table. She's on her stomach with a white sheet draped over her body. Her shoulders are bare and even in the faint light, I can see the emerging gray streaks in her hair.

I take a moment to light candles around the room and turn on some soft music. I stop in front of a mirror and try to see past my reflection to the other side. It's impossible. Approaching the table, I say, "Are you ready to take another step toward enlightenment?"

She cranes her neck slightly and looks at me. I see the surprise in her eyes when she sees my face. I'm not just handsome, but appealing. Calming. I have a kind face. I know this. Women like it and I work it to Serendee's advantage. "If that means you'll work the knot out of my shoulder, then yes, I'm so ready."

Laughing, I squeeze a liberal drop of oil into my hands. I warm them up and start to work on her shoulders. She's right about the tension. I feel the knot almost instantly and begin rubbing that spot gently.

I took my first massage therapy class when I was sixteen. Anex felt this would be a good place for me to focus my gifts. I enjoy making people feel better, helping them with their aches and pains. The best, though, is when I'm working with a woman like Kayla. She's seeking more in her life, or she wouldn't be here. She wants to unblock her mind and release what's holding her back.

I know exactly how to help her.

Carefully, I push the sheet down to her lower back and begin focusing on that area. Next, through the sheet, I work her glutes, then the back of her thighs, her hamstrings and calves. She groans softly and shifts a little on the table. The movement is enough to let the sheet fall. I let it and wait for her response. When there is none, I continue to make passes up and down her body, easing the tension from her muscles.

Incrementally, my fingers knead into her glutes, dipping between her cheeks, and then a slow sweep between her thighs until I 'accidentally' brush against the lips of her pussy. Her body jolts. I wait a beat and her legs widen just a bit, and I know she's ready for me. She's ready to take the step toward enlightenment.

I'm just here to guide her.

My tactics change slightly, moving to long, deliberate strokes. Occasionally, I'll touch her pussy again, dragging my fingers over the opening, but then spend the majority of my focus elsewhere. I feel her tense, straining, wanting me to touch her there again and when I finally do, she exhales and spreads her legs a bit wider, giving me more access.

There's nothing rushed about this process. It's all part of the higher awareness of following The Way. Patience will get you where you want. Faith will guide you to pure joy. Enlightenment is within reach. When I touch her again, she's slick and ready and I massage around her opening. I put in the tip of my finger in applying pressure. When she's ready, I push all the way in. I've developed my own technique—one that I know with release the tightly wound energy pent up inside of this magnificent woman.

Once she comes, there will be no obstacle to her pathway.

I slide in a second finger, then press both against her inner walls. She hums in approval, toes curling on the table.

"Does that feel good?" I ask, moving them in a circular motion.

"Yes, god, yes."

"Good. I want you to breathe deep and enjoy the sensation. Open your mind, heart, and body. Embrace the moment."

It's all a little woo-woo, but I believe in this. Anex believes in it

and as I feel her walls quivering around me and the moan of pleasure crossing her lips, I know she will too. A pink flush spreads
across her skin and her hips writhe as her hands grip the edge of
the table.

When she regains control, she blinks up at me and I pick up the
sheet and place it back over her body. "Thank you for sharing that
moment with me. I'm going to leave you now so that you can
change. Anex will be waiting for you in the next room. He'll
continue your journey there."

"Thank you," she says, getting herself to a sitting position. "That
was quite extraordinary."

"Not when you're part of Serendee," I tell her, reaching for the
door, "Revelations like this happen every day."

I exit the room and shut the door. Anex walks out of the
adjoining room, straightening his shirt, and smiles at me. I bow
slightly, and he claps his hand on my shoulder. "You're truly gifted,
Silas."

"Just using the talents given to me by The Way."

He nods and meets my eye. "You understand what you're to do
next?"

He's made his directives clear, who and what we're supposed to
focus on next. "Yes," I reply. "I understand completely."

9

————————

My heart leaps when I open the door of the suite and hear someone in the living room. Maybe Rex has come to his senses, and he's ready to begin our courtship. Maybe all of this was confusion. Cold feet. He wouldn't be the first Ordered male that struggled with the decision. Jonas Baker was ordered to Catherine Stillwell two years ago. He completely panicked and vanished for three days, returning with a black eye and smelling of alcohol. He was corrected by Anex and he and Catherine were bonded six months later. Now, they have a child.

But it's not Rex in the living room. It's his three best friends and confidants; Silas, Levi, and Elon.

I pause in the doorway, not sure how to proceed. I've never been in the presence of three men my age at the same time, alone, even at work. The simple sight of them; their broad shoulders and sharp features, is unfamiliar, yet intriguing. I consider running, but no, this is my house, and these men are confidants of my betrothed. Still, I don't move, and they pay me no attention until Silas, with his shaggy brown hair and perfect chin, looks up at me and grins. "She's here."

Elon, who has been pacing back and forth in front of the large window, stops and faces me. His dark gray eyes assess me, and that hard expression that is always on his face doesn't fade. "Where have you been?"

"At The Center. My shift doesn't end until after the last session." I'm not sure why I have to answer to him. "Is Rex here?"

"No," Levi replies. He stands from where he was sitting on the couch, a book in his hand. I recognize the cover. It's one of Anex's about how to incorporate The Way into all of your daily activities. We read it in school, and it is suggested we read it several times a year for a reminder. "We were sent by Anex."

The uneasy, uncomfortable feeling I'd carried all afternoon blooms brighter in my chest.

Silas throws an arm over the back of the couch and says, "We've been sent to assist you into acclimating with your Ordering."

Elon clears his throat and pushes his hands in his pockets. "We're responsible for training and preparing you for mating with Rex in the fall."

Nausea rolls over me and I clutch my stomach. "You'll be the ones training me? The three of you?"

I'd expected Clarissa, or maybe one of the other older, bonded women in the community to instruct me. There are other knowledgeable people: healers, high leaders, educators.

I did not expect three handsome, young, intimidating men. I did not expect Rex's closest friends.

"This can't be right," I mutter, anxiety building in my chest. "What Anex wants of me... it would be improper." We are kept apart all through adolescence to maintain purity for our Bonding. This would throw all of that away. Just being in this room together, talking about these matters, is enough to cause a problem.

"What's improper is for you to question the will of our leader," Elon grinds out. "Did he not tell you he approved of this? That he is orchestrating it?"

I lower my eyes. "Yes. I just don't understand. Isn't Rex your friend?"

"Yes," Silas says, "but, despite our friendship, like everyone else in Serendee, our priority is adhering to The Way above everything else."

"You mean, like everyone but Rex." I look to Levi, notably the most devout of the three, for confirmation, but he refuses to meet my eye. My hands tremble as realization washes over me. These men will train me to be a good mate to a man like Rex. A restless, selfish, spoiled man, who does not believe in the world or standards we live in.

After all this time, all these years of waiting, I realize it's happened.

I'm finally, truly, being punished for my mother's betrayal. *This is the punishment.*

And I have no choice but to let it happen.

~

They moved in while I was at work, taking the additional bedrooms, leaving the right-side master for Rex, although it remains empty. They don't have many belongings, just the loose cotton clothing all the men wear in Serendee, although they seem to prefer darker fabrics.

While they settle in, I shift into motion, forcing myself into the role I'd been trained for. The only difference is that my actions aren't for my mate. When I step into the kitchen to prepare dinner, one look in the refrigerator reveals that it's already stocked for this number of inhabitants. Obviously, I was the last to know about the assignment from Anex. Even the house managers were aware. It's an unsettling feeling, but what about the last twenty-four hours haven't been? This is my new life. One I must accept.

To people outside of Serendee, the gender roles of our community seem archaic. It's not that men can't cook. Or that women must take on the household. Anex is a historian and believes there are many reasons these roles have been upheld throughout time. It's not always about what people can do, but what brings them closer to The Way. Men feel stronger when they are using their bodies and minds. They are less likely to lose focus if they are protecting and providing for those they love. Whereas women feel more secure and less prone to anxiety when they are nurturing their families and creating a safe, functional, home. Efforts in the secular world to undermine these positions are one reason why there is so much strife and pain. Serendee is about harmony. Mental and physical. At home and at work. Balance is important. As are sacrifices for the greater good.

It's something I am forced to think about when we are all sitting around the table, a full meal plated before us. The roasted chicken turned out well, but the vegetables are a little mushy. I want to apologize as I set the dishes on the table, but I'm too stubborn. I didn't invite them here, although they certainly have no problem making themselves at home.

Silas comes to the table last, carrying a bottle of wine. He uncorks it and pours it into each of our glasses. I stare at the dark red liquid while the others pick theirs up.

"Lift your glass," Silas instructs.

"Using substances is not part of The Way," I refute, "unless it is part of the ceremonies."

"Well," he says, lips quirking, "consider this a ceremony."

Again, I glance to Levi for help. Even from a distance, it was obvious he was always studying and following Anex's words carefully. He is well regarded at The Center, but he too lifts his glass. I must have been wrong about his dedication.

"I would rather not," I say.

"Pick up your glass, Imogene," Elon growls from two seats away. "Or would you rather me force it down your throat?"

The dark spark in his eye makes me think that even if that's not what I want, he wouldn't mind. With a shaky hand, I pick up my glass and hold it level with the others.

"The next few months are going to be a challenge," Levi says, taking over for Silas, "but I have faith in Anex and The Way. He is guiding us down the righteous path, toward the road to retribution and certainty." He looks at me. "Silas is correct. This is a ceremony, one confirming our devotion to the future of Serendee."

The others murmur their toasts, then clink their glasses together. I follow their moves, not wanting to be reprimanded again. The wine is bitter at first, but after I swallow, I taste the tang of sweetness on my tongue. The men move on to their meals, eating ravenously, and I feel pride that they are pleased with what I prepared, even the vegetables. I'm not a complete fool when it comes to serving the needs of men.

Conversation is light while we eat—they speak of business— something I don't completely follow. Selling and trading; things that take place outside the walls. I know that most of the harvest from our garden stays inside Serendee to feed the community. What isn't used is sold at the local farmer's market. Nothing as complex as what they are talking about. They refer to measurements and weights. Dollar amounts. I pay it little mind, feeling the warmth of the wine spread through me. Midway through dinner, I notice Silas watching me.

"Is something wrong?" I ask.

He nods at my plate. "Why aren't you eating?"

"I'm eating," I say, looking down at the modest amount of food on my plate. I'd actually measured it out before cooking—taking into account how many grams of fat, protein, carbohydrates and overall calories I am consuming. "I just don't eat as much as you do."

"That's barely enough food to survive on," Silas adds. "A tiny piece of meat. Six green beans. No bread."

Typically, I pride myself on my control. Anex's teachings are very specific. It's not about weight—but about health and keeping oneself away from toxins. I glance at the wine and feel a conflicting twinge of guilt.

"She's following the standards," Levi says. "Imogene is faithful to the teachings she learned while living in the girl's domum." He scoops chocolate up on his fork and nods at me. "Do you maintain your logs?"

"Yes. Faithfully." Females are taught from a young age to document every morsel of food that goes into our bodies. These, along with our daily journals, guide us through The Way.

Silas' mouth opens and closes like he wants to argue, but Levi holds him off with a glare. I'm thankful for his defense. At least one person around here seems to understand.

I continue drinking, the warmth now buzzing in my head. When his plate is clean, Elon drapes his arm over the back of a chair and watches me with narrowed eyes.

"What?" I ask, not feeling as self-conscious as I should.

"I think we should begin our lessons."

"Tonight?"

"Why not?" He takes the last swallow of wine. "Come here."

I glance at the dishes and say, "I probably should—"

"Lesson number one: don't make me ask you to do something twice."

His voice is hard. Mean. His eyes filled with wicked intent. I stand, pushing my chair out behind me. I pass Levi, who chews a bite of food, and Silas, who takes a sip of wine, both watching me like an animal in the zoo. I approach Elon. He pushes back his own chair but remains seated, running a hand down his thigh. "Come. Sit on my lap."

"Excuse me?"

His jaw clenches, and he grabs my arm, yanking me down. When he speaks, his breath is hot in my ear. "Lesson number two: Rex can get his needs met by other women at any time. He probably is right now." From across the table, Silas snorts. "Which means that you do not want to give him any reason to turn away. The goal is to keep him interested in his home, in Serendee. Defiance isn't appealing." He pushes the hair off my shoulder, sending a wave of cool air across my neck. "Well, to most men, at least." I tremble as his fingers run down my arm. Goosebumps popping up in a shiver. "I know this is new, but you need to get used to the touch of a man."

I sit silently as he runs his hands along the bare skin of my arms and the column of my neck. His hands are big, and although he uses a gentle touch, I'm frozen in fear. I feel the eyes of Silas and

Levi on me as Elon explores my body, each stroke taking a bit more liberty, moving up and down my sides, flattening over my belly. Despite my efforts, my breath becomes labored and my skin tingles as though it's on fire. I feel heat in places I didn't know could grow so warm. Damp.

"She's pretty," he says while exploring. "Don't you think?"

"Elon," Levi says. His voice is stern, but his eyes follow his friend's movements.

Elon's hands make a pass over my belly and then up to cup my breasts. I gasp, fighting the intrusion, but he holds firm. "She's skinny, but we were right, her tits are nice."

"Stop." I say, squirming against him. His body is like a wall, blocking me from moving. "This is wrong."

He ignores me, pulling at the neckline. His warm hands meet my skin and a rush of heat courses through my veins. "They fit perfectly. Right in my hands." He squeezes, pushing them together. I cry out in protest, but just laughs. "Silas, feel them yourself. You know you want to."

I'm thrust toward Silas who catches me by my breasts. To be fair, he drops his hands quickly with a look of pity on his face.

"Anex made it clear you are to do as you're told. To listen to us. To be trained," Elon says as I try to cover myself. "Why do you disobey the words of our leader? Are you truly like your mother?"

Anger and humiliation rush through me and my reaction is impulsive—my palm flattens across Elon's cheek. The slap echoes through the room and the look on Elon's face morphs from shocked to murderous. He takes a step toward me, but Silas slides between us.

"Go," he commands.

"I'm—" An apology stalls on my tongue. I'm not sorry. I'm raging.

"Imogene," Silas repeats, "go."

I spin on my heel and run down the hall, locking the bedroom door behind me, hating the sobs that heave out of me. I catch sight of myself in the bathroom mirror, and I walk into the room, making an effort to fix the top of my dress. The neck gapes, and there are streaks of red down my chest. I don't miss the hard points that press against the fabric, a clear sign of my arousal. I face my reflection and see my splotchy cheeks and red eyes. I see something else that I haven't noticed before.

My mother. I look very much like her during those last days before she left, when she always looked as though she'd just been crying. Like she was hiding something.

"Are you truly like your mother?"

Am I?

Am I disloyal?

A betrayer?

Am I defiant?

Do I not believe in Anex's guidance and The Way?

I don't want to be any of those things. I want to be good. Pure. Faithful to the end. I want to please Anex and help him with this complicated problem. I want to be a force for Serendee, not a destroyer.

I want redemption.

Is this how I get it?

Tomorrow, I'll figure out how to manage this. Maybe Clarissa knows. Maybe I'll have to speak to Anex again. But tonight, there is nothing to do but hide in my room, hoping none of these men decide to come to my door overnight.

10

Levi

"Was that really necessary?" I ask, leaning against the back of my chair. The last sound was Imogene's door slamming down the hall. Silas and Elon still face one another, caught in a tense standoff.

"Yes," Elon says, shoulders easing. "She needs to be tested."

"By you mauling her?" Silas asks.

"Sorry if I haven't been trained in the art of seduction," Elon snaps, shaking his head at Silas. He's right. We haven't been trained the way that our friend has. "I wanted to know what she would do if I treated her like one of the women outside of the community."

"She rebuffed you," Silas says. "Does that mean she passed?"

"No," I reply. "No, it doesn't. We don't know what she is capable of. What her motives truly are."

"Her motives are to mate, have babies and further The Way," Silas says. Suddenly, he's the most trusting of us all. You'd think with the women he's been with, manipulated, he'd have clearer eyes. "She's not a Regressive."

"How do you know?" I ask.

"I just do," he replies, sitting back at the table and pouring another glass of wine. "She's a normal girl."

"She's a sheep," Elon adds. There's no kindness in the title.

"Or a lamb on the way to slaughter," Silas points out.

"I'm with Elon," I tell him. They both look at me in surprise. Siding with Elon is rare for me. He's a brute and I'm an intellectual, but not in this situation. My gut tells me to be wary. "Imogene Montgomery is dangerous. Her blood is tainted. Her motives unclear. Rex and his father are playing a game that could catch us all on fire."

Elon runs his hand through his dark hair and narrows his eyes at me. He's always suspicious—even when I'm agreeing with him. It's one reason he makes a good bodyguard for Rex. "You're saying you're ready to test her? Really test her?"

I nod, swallowing back the apprehension. On the outside, testing and training Imogene goes against my nature. But according to The Way and the literature, this is what I have been preparing for my entire life. I'm protecting our community, potentially ferreting out a Regressive, and securing Rex's position as heir.

I've been given an honor by Anex, albeit an uncomfortable one. That's what makes it all the more important and prestigious.

Despite the fact that the dark glint in Elon's eye makes me nervous, and Rex's behavior is questionable, I will do as I'm told, and I will not let Serendee down.

11

———————

My sleep is fitful. I dream that Elon breaks through the door and drags me from the bed. His hands are all over me. Silas and Levi sit by and watch. I wake breathing heavy with a strange feeling in the pit of my stomach and a pounding headache. My tongue is dried out and tastes of old, bitter wine. A knock at the door forces me to sit up, and I hold back the swell of bile in the back of my throat.

"Imogene?" It's Silas. "Are you okay?"

My whole body is clammy and hot. "Go away, please."

"Imogene." The doorknob rattles. "Will you open the door?"

With every word, I think of the few moments his hands cupped my breasts. Oh god.

I take a deep breath and walk over to the door. I open it but only a crack. He looks relieved to see me in one piece.

"Can I come in?" he asks.

"I'm not presentable."

"I don't care." His eyes hold mine. "We need to talk about last night—to make sure that doesn't happen again."

Slowly I open the door, while walking to the closet and grabbing a robe to cover myself. Silas stands in the doorway, the strap of a slim bag hung over his shoulder. He runs a hand through his shaggy hair.

"I want to apologize for last night. It was never my intention to touch you like that."

"No?" I ask, crossing my arms over my chest. "I have a hard time believing that. Isn't that all part of my training?"

"Well, yes, but...this is complicated for us as well. You need to understand that."

I laugh darkly. "I doubt that. You have all the power here. All the knowledge."

"True, but that experience is a gift for you. This is a test for all of us, Imogene, one set up by Anex. If we all pass, then we will go on to glorious things in Serendee. But we have to pass. All of us."

"How can I pass a test I don't know the answers to?"

"Are you implying that you don't trust Anex to make the right decisions concerning you or his son?"

"No, I just—"

"Your questions say more about you than anyone else, Imogene. You need to dig deep into why you're fighting back."

He's right, of course. This is my flaw, not his.

"That is where we can help you, but you have to trust us."

I shake my head. "There is no way I can trust Elon. Not after last night."

His hand grips the strap of his bag. "Can I give you an important lesson?"

"Does it involve someone groping me?"

He dares a grin. "No, groping. Promise."

I exhale. "I'm listening."

"Not all men are the same. We don't have the same personalities, the same habits, or the same desires. I have no interest in forcing a woman into things she's uncomfortable doing. It makes *me* uncomfortable. Last night... I felt terrible. It's not how I would have handled this situation. I almost came to apologize a dozen times, but it seemed better to leave you alone."

"Smart."

"I have my moments." He laughs. "Levi? He is devoted to Anex and will do anything and everything he asks. He truly believes in Serendee and The Way."

"Does that mean you don't?"

He shrugs. "It means I've seen enough to understand why Rex struggles, but this is my home. My life. I have no intention of giving it up."

"And Elon?" I ask, swallowing back a lump of fear. "What about him?"

"It's important that you not test Elon. Do as he says, and things will be easier."

"You think I should just let him... do things like that to me?"

"I think that he knows better than anyone what Rex wants in a woman."

That answer turns my already tumultuous stomach. I push my hair out of my face while I try to hold back tears. It's pointless. "I don't understand what I'm supposed to do. All of this is foreign to me. It goes against everything I've been taught."

"Which is what I want to help you with." He reaches out and gently wipes a tear off my face with his thumb. "If you'll let me."

His touch is warm—gentle—nothing like the manhandling the night before. I don't imagine that I have many options and if Silas is throwing me a lifeline, I should take it.

12

"I think I calmed her down," I say, walking into the living room, "and hopefully did a little damage control for last night."

"I'm thinking it's time to stop treating her like a baby bird. She's out of the nest, Silas," Elon says, "it's time to fly."

"Yeah, well, what does that make you? The cat waiting at the base of the tree, ready to eat her?"

He grins. "Something like that."

I glance at Levi, who has said little this morning. "And you? You still think his tactics were the right decision?

"I think that Anex chose us with intention. He knows Elon's ways, just like he knows yours and mine. Together we'll create the perfect mate for Rex."

"So, he'll smash her into pieces, and I'll pick them back up? What will you do?" I ask, honestly wondering. "Report everything back to Anex?"

"Yes. I'm here to make sure that she stays on track and doesn't reveal anything that goes on here to others in the community. I'll monitor her journals and logs. I'll document her comings and goings as well as her progress." His mouth sets in a hard line. "This is a very delicate situation, if anything should go wrong—"

"It won't," Elon says, walking to the kitchen and opening the refrigerator door. He stares inside for a long moment before shutting it again. "Honestly, she's a good choice. Innocent and pure, yet very willing to please Anex. She wants redemption, and that makes her more pliable than most."

"She asks a lot of questions," I point out. Which is something I like about her. There's a spirit in her that seems unbreakable. That is hard to find in some of the women in the community. After being around secular women, the females in Serendee often seem a little robotic. That's not the impression I get from Imogene. She seems genuine. *Beautiful* and genuine.

"She won't for long," Elon says, taking a sip from his glass. "Give me one night and I'll shut that down."

I sigh and run my hand through my hair. That is what I'm most afraid of. To what length with Anex have us manipulate this girl? And how willing will she be to change?

It all feels risky to me—something Anex should know firsthand.

When he told us that we were chosen to help him with this task, I felt a sense of pride. Being singled out by him is a great honor. We're already in his inner circle, with a strong understanding of the inner working of Serendee, from business holdings to his visions for the whole of the community. It's much more complex than what is visible to the residents. Anex has created not just a utopia inside Serendee, but an empire.

Joining Anex's inner circle can be dangerous. It requires sacrifice, and it's a burden of information. At first, it's a bit of a mindfuck. Sometimes, his behavior and what he asks of us seems to go against the spirit of The Way.

But once I truly understood what we were doing—what Anex was doing, I realized that he truly is a genius working on a higher level than the rest of the community. Leadership isn't easy—neither is being a visionary. That's why he's in charge and it's why everyone follows.

What I told Imogene about this being a test for all of us... it's true. We all want to rise to our next level. Doing this together may be our only chance.

67

13

Imogene

The next morning I stand outside the Beatrice House in one of my new dresses, preparing myself to go in. Once a woman is Ordered, things change. One of the changes is an invitation to the weekly women's meeting. It's for bonded and ordered women only. A club every young girl inside Serendee wants to belong to. It's always seemed exclusive and secretive. Now that I'm finally here, under my circumstances, I feel less excited and more nervous. Will they be able to tell my Order is a sham? Do they know that Rex doesn't want a mate, and that I have to degrade myself to keep him in Serendee?

Faking contentment is something I'm used to—I learned how to do it after my mother abandoned us. I had to pretend like I didn't care about her anymore and that I was as disgusted as everyone else. In my heart, I missed her and had so many questions. Questions that I wasn't allowed to be asked.

"Imogene!"

Maria waves from the sidewalk. I lunge forward and pull her into a tight hug. "I've missed you," I tell her.

"I've missed you, too. It's weird not waking up from you talking in your sleep every night."

"I do not," I laugh. But it's an ongoing joke. Apparently, when I'm overwhelmed, I yammer along. I can only imagine what I've been saying the last few nights. It's a blessing no one is around to hear it.

"Can you believe we're finally here?" She looks up at the house and back at me. "Is it weirder because of Rex?"

Beatrice House It's named after Anex's former wife, Rex's mother. She died when he was a child, and the family couldn't bear to live in the house any longer, so they donated it to the women of Serendee—as a place to gather in her honor.

"Everything about this week has been a little weird," I confess. "I guess this is no different."

"True."

"How have you been?" I ask. "How is Elijah?"

She grins, and there's no mistaking the warm glow in her complexion. "Better than I ever thought. He's sweet and kind. Very attentive. I've enjoyed getting to know him."

"That's wonderful."

"And you? What's it like being Ordered to the most important single man in Serendee?"

The truth sits on my tongue, but I swallow it back. "It has been full of surprises. Every day I learn something new about the man that will be my mate."

"I bet," she says. "He's always been an enigma."

I nod. Enigma is putting it lightly. I haven't even seen him since the day of the Ordering and after last night...I am not sure I could ever face him again. That morning, I told the men that I wasn't going to fight them anymore. I was committed to the training Anex had requested. Silas looked relieved, while Levi just scribbled notes in his journal. Elon... well he looked at me as though I'd just issued him a challenge.

"What about his friends?" Maria asks, as though she can read my mind. "Are they around?"

"Yes, they are still thick as thieves. I get the feeling they can't breathe without the other in the same room."

She laughs and opens the gate. "Be careful or you may end up with four mates instead of just the one."

My eyes widen and I glance around, hoping none of the other women walking up to the house heard her. "Maria!"

She tries to stifle her giggles with her hand. "I'm just kidding." She rolls her eyes. "Can you imagine handling four men?"

"No." I smooth the front of my dress. "That sounds like a nightmare."

"I can barely figure out one," she agrees. "I've spent the last few days trying to figure out as much as I can about him; his favorite foods, how he likes his shirts ironed, what color he prefers me to wear. All of those little things."

This conversation only proves how different my situation is from the others. No one else is being asked to do something like this—to be trained to meet a man's subversive needs.

"I kind of feel bad for his friends," she says, as we enter the house. The first thing I see is a large portrait of a family. Anex is young, looking more like Rex now than I could imagine. Beatrice is beautiful, her golden hair shining like a halo. And Rex? He's a small, fair-haired toddler, clinging to his mother's side.

"Why?" I ask, drawing my eyes away from the portrait. "Why do you feel bad for them?"

"Because Anex didn't give them their own Orders. They must want women and families of their own?"

I think of the dark glint in Elon's eye and the way Silas' hands felt on my breasts. They're wise to Rex's needs and seem to have experienced them themselves. "It's none of my concern what they want," I reply. "The only person out of the four that matters to me is Rex."

"Come," she says, directing us toward one of the round tables set up for tea, "I'm hopeful that some of these more experienced women will help us understand better how to serve our men's needs. I realize now that Clarissa was holding back on us on some of the finer details."

I grab her arm and lean in. "Have you done something with Elijah? Intimately?"

Her cheeks redden, and she glances around. Quietly she says, "He kissed me. Using his tongue."

My eyebrows raise. "With his tongue?"

"It sounds weird, but it felt good."

Silas' hands on my breasts felt nice, too.

"Has Rex not tried to kiss you?"

I shake my head. "No, not yet." He'd have to be around to try something like that.

"I'm sure he will soon, but it's also okay to take things slow. That's what the courtship is all about, getting to know one another." The door opens and shuts behind us and Maria looks over my shoulder. "Oh, Renee! We were just talking about your brother."

Hearing that Levi's sister is behind me brings about another wave of discomfort. I know they aren't close. No male and females remain close after age twelve, even siblings, so I shouldn't worry that she knows what has transpired in our house but it still makes me uneasy. Renee's eyebrows rise in question.

I quickly reply, "Only because he's one of Rex's closest confidants."

"Ah, of course. They have always been thick as thieves—the four of them."

"Still seems that way," I reply.

"Imogene," a soft voice calls from behind me. I turn and see Margaret, Anex's Spiritual wife. Instinctively, me, Maria and Renee drop to a slight bow. "I was hoping to get a chance to meet you today. I'm Margaret."

"Yes," I reply. "I know." I blush at how stupid I sound, but Maria giggles next to me, which seems worse. "This is Maria."

She greets Maria and Renee but quickly shifts her attention back to me. "Can I speak to you for a moment?"

"Of course." I turn to my friend. "Talk soon?"

Maria still looks a little in awe as she and Renee walk toward the tea tables. I'm sure my expression is the same. Getting an audience with Margaret is almost like being in Anex's presence.

"I'm excited that you are joining our family," she says, once we're alone. "I'm sure you are feeling overwhelmed by the events of the past few days."

"Overwhelmed is an accurate description." I wonder how much she knows. Is she aware of what Rex told me? Or the training suggested by Anex? My skin prickles at the thought, but I don't give that away. "I'm definitely ready to serve the needs of the community."

She reaches for my hand, and squeezes it with hers. "I know you are. Anex wouldn't have chosen you if he didn't think you and Rex weren't perfect for one another."

"Thank you for the vote of confidence."

She leans in a little. "You're not alone, Imogene." Her voice is soft. "I host a small, exclusive, group of women in similar arrangements, and I would love for you to join us."

There are others like me? "That would be wonderful."

Her expression turns serious. "It's a place where we explore our personal growth and how to become better women and mates. Sometimes it takes a deeper introspection to find our truth, The Way, and the first step is to stop focusing on our own selfish desires."

"Yes," I say, both mesmerized by her words and the sound of her voice. "I would love to belong to that group."

"Ladies!" a voice calls from the front of the room. "Please find a seat!"

Margaret releases my hand and with one last small we're ushered to different tables. We're served tea and small cakes made down at the bakery. I'm introduced to the other women at the table, all bonded and mated. They talk about laundry and recipes and juggling home and their work to Serendee. None mention sex or a mate that's uninterested. None mention training. But none of these women are me. They don't have a scarred family past or a tarnished reputation that follows them. They aren't betrothed to the next leader of Serendee. None are Chosen.

In a room filled with women, and even my best friend, it has never been clearer exactly how alone I am. Except, just when I feel even more lost, I lock eyes with Margaret across the room, reminding me that maybe I'm not as isolated as I think I am.

〜

I'm thankful that when I arrive back at the main house that no one is home. The men do have jobs—whatever they'd discussed the night before. Something that requires them to come and go from Serendee on Anex's orders.

Their absence gives me time to build up my courage. I have questions, and I want answers.

I'm thinking about what to cook for dinner when Silas comes through the front door. I pause when I see him. His clothing isn't exactly secular, but lines of his jacket reveal the broadness of his shoulders and the linen of his shirt is a purplish blue, that looks nice against his olive skin. Men here mostly wear black, white or tan and the burst of color is surprisingly appealing. I look away when I catch sight of his hands.

All I can think about is how they felt on my body the night before.

"Good evening, Silas," I say. "Do you know if the others will be home soon?"

"Actually, no," he says, shrugging out of his jacket. "They won't be home for dinner. I came back to change and then I'm going to meet them."

"Oh," I say, not sure how to feel. They make me so uneasy that the thought of a night alone isn't unappealing. On the other hand, I should be deep in my courtship during this time, or at least receivethe lessons. I suck up my disappointment. "Thank you for telling me."

He nods and walks down the hallway toward his room. As he reaches the door, I blurt out something that has been on my mind all day. "Do you think what Elon said last night is true? That Rex is getting his needs met by someone else?"

He walks back toward me, his expression careful. "Yes. Most likely."

My stomach drops and a wave of sickness rolls over me. But I don't stop. "What does he do with them? Does he kiss them with his tongue?"

His lips quirk and I wonder briefly if they are as soft as they appear. "I would assume so, among other things."

"What other things?"

"Things you'll learn in your training."

The flicker of apprehension fills my chest. "But that's what I want to know. What will my training involve? Until last night, I'd never been touched by a man in such a...intimate way. Until today, at the women's meeting, I didn't know a man kissed with his tongue." I clasp my hands together. "I need to know what to expect from these lessons. What you want from me."

He studies me closely for a moment and abruptly walks to his bedroom door. He opens it and looks over at me. "Come with me."

He enters his room, and I follow, stopping at the door. His room is large, although not as big as my own. There's a king-sized bed and a small sitting area with a couch and two chairs. A desk sits against the wall. He lays the bag from his shoulder on the surface and pulls out a thin, silver device.

My pulse quickens. "What is that doing here?"

"It's mine. For work."

"Devices like that are not allowed in homes. You know that." Computers, phones, televisions... they're all forbidden outside of a regulated work environment. Anex doesn't want our daily lives swayed by the outside world.

"There are exceptions for everything, Imogene. You must know that."

"I didn't. Not until the last few days. I'd been raised to think that there was no leeway, and if you bent the rules, there will be consequences. How do I know I won't get in trouble from having this kind of contraband in my home?"

"It's my contraband," he says, laughing at me. "I assure you,

Anex is well aware that I have this device. He's the one that gave it to me."

He did? I swallow. "Then I shouldn't be here. If it's part of your work, then I should leave you alone."

"No." He sits on the couch and rests the laptop on the coffee table. "Didn't you just ask me to explain more about what you should expect?"

"I did."

"Then let me do that—by using the resources provided to me by *Anex*."

When he puts it that way, it's hard to argue. I just can't imagine what he wants to show me on the computer that is relevant to my questions.

Silas pats the cushion next to him. "Sit next to me."

I do as I'm told, circling the table and sitting on the firm cushion. It's strange being so close to him. He smells good, manly, although I get the slightest hint of something flowery—feminine. I watch his face, the slope of his nose and the length of his eyelashes as he works. He pays me no attention, focused on the computer. It's not the first time I've seen one. In fact, we have an entire class dedicated to the evils of technology. How they seem like useful, yet benign devices. Things that make life easier—but an easy life can be deceiving. It makes a person lazy and compliant.

Like everything else, Anex thinks it's important that segments of the community maintain knowledge of dangerous things and certain people in the community are given that burden. Silas, and I assume the other men in our shared home, have been chosen to lift that weight off the rest of us.

A renewed sense of respect swells inside of me. Anex must truly find him to be an outstanding member of the community. Even so, as he presses buttons and the screen comes to life, I twist my hands in the fabric of my dress, trying to soothe my nerves. His fingers move quickly, confidently, and I'm in awe of his knowledge as much as the machine itself.

"You use this for work?" I ask, feeling the need to fill the air.

"Yes—all the time, actually."

"What kind of work do you and the others do?"

"Well, I work closely with the new recruits, making sure they are comfortable and ready for their decision to join the community. And, as you know, Levi works at The Center. Rex and Elon are involved with another side of Serendee. They distribute some of the local products to the secular world—things that don't have much use in the community but are valuable out there."

"What kind of product?" The community is prolific. Besides the garden there is the bakery, tailors, and other artisans. There are also skilled workers in farming, carpentry and welding. Everything that makes our little world run smoothly without outside intervention.

Silas draws his eyes from the screen and gives me a small smile. "Nothing for you to worry about. It's not very interesting."

I nod. "And this... product distribution... Rex works with you?"

"He does. We've always made a good team."

Obviously, or why else would they be trusted with training me? "I'm glad to hear you all are so close and have jobs Anex deems important."

"Very important," he agrees, taking a final swipe at the computer keyboard. He tilts the screen in my direction and it's frozen on a picture of a group of people. They're all young and strange looking. Pretty by secular standards. I've seen men and women like this in town near the University. Shiny hair and heavily made-up eyes and red lips. The men have clean-shaven faces and hair that swoops artfully away from their faces.

I can't take my eyes off of it.

"What is that?"

"It's a TV show. Have you ever seen one before?"

"No, but I've heard Anex speak of them in his lectures. Not positively," I add.

He shifts on the couch, turning to face me, and our thighs touch, sending a current of energy up my leg. "It's basically a story told in pictures. Moving pictures, obviously. And there are a million different kinds of stories, but one of the most popular types is a romance or love story. I think it may help answer some of your questions about what to expect."

"This is the kind of show that Rex watches?"

He laughs. "No. Not exactly, but the men and women, how they interact with one another, that is what a man expects from a secular woman."

Although the method makes me uncomfortable, it is better than being manhandled by Elon again. "Thank you. I will watch this and see if things make a little more sense."

"You can use the computer whenever you want."

I eye the machine. We were taught that computers have the ability to track and collect data. "Can I keep it in here? I don't feel comfortable taking it into my room."

"Sure," he says, his lips twisted in amusement. "I know this is moving fast for you. Believe it or not, I felt the same way at one point, but it's important that you try to make progress. There are obligations coming up, including the summer solstice, where you will need to be ready."

His hand rests on top of mine, and he squeezes it gently. It's the kind of touch that Maria and I would have shared, but the feeling behind it is very different. Sparks shoot through my body, igniting a million different emotions. I glance over at him, wondering if he feels it too, or is it just me and my naivety. His dark eyes hold mine and then dart down to my mouth. I yank my hand back and turn away.

I stay that way as he goes into the bathroom and changes. It's only after he leaves that I move, leaning toward the computer and pressing play.

14

———

The house is big and ornate, sitting on the edge of the lake. Just outside of town is a quiet, but expensive, vacation area that draws in wealthy families. The house buzzes with life—a full-blown party is going on just past the large front porch. It's the kind of event nearly everyone in Serendee would feel uncomfortable attending, but not us.

I'm the one that gets us in the door. I inherited my father's easy smile and ability to lure people in. It's a gift. Of course, that's not all. It's the expensive car and clothes, the gold watch, but it's more than that. There's something mysterious about the three of us— members of this exclusive community. Good looking and rich. Entitlement oozes off us and people want that. They want what we have, even if they don't know exactly what that is. And they, unknowingly, have what we want.

They just don't know it yet.

"You came!" I hear, turning toward a pretty blonde. Her name is Jasmine West, heir of the Cobra tequila company. We'd met at the country club gym a few days before, and she'd extended the invitation. She approaches me and gives me a kiss on both cheeks, leaving a wake of her perfume in the air. "I didn't think you would."

"Why?" I ask, sliding my arm around her waist. "You think they lock us in after dark?"

Joking about the community is the first way to lower outsider's guards. She laughs and shakes her head. "I figured you'd be too busy. I told all my friends about the fascinating man I met from Serendee. They didn't believe me."

"I'm here for proof." I tilt my head toward the guys. "I hope it's okay that I brought a few friends."

Her eyes flit over each of them, lingering on Elon. She laughs. "You didn't need to bring me a gift—much less three."

"I never attend a party without bringing something for the hostess."

She drops her hand on my ass and gives it a playful squeeze. "Just make sure you save one for me, okay?"

"You got it." I reach into my pocket and pull out a small box. It's custom made in the Serendee workshop. "Oh, here's a little something else for you, too."

She opens it and takes a deep sniff. "I'm inviting you guys to all of my parties."

She walks off, tucking the box into her pocket and turning back to give Elon one last flirty grin.

Elon's eyes are zeroed in on her. "I call dibs."

Silas claps his hand on Elon's back and gazes into the room of beautiful women. "She's all yours, brother. I think there's plenty of fun for us all to have here."

He vanishes into the group, the mask already slipped into place. Between the four of us, by the end of the night, at least one of us will get laid, we'll have a list of names to pass on to my father, and I have no doubt we'll have secured new business for Serendee.

Tonight isn't about fun, it's about community; it's about building a future.

One that gets me as far away from here as possible.

15

———

ELON

WHILE THE GUYS attend to business, I follow Jasmine through the crowded living room. My only job is to keep Rex safe, and at a party like this, he needs a little space. We have a lot of product to sell—acres of it—and a high end party like this is the perfect place to make new connections. The sway of Jasmine's hips leads me into the state-of-the-art kitchen. It's less crowded in here. Most people are out on the deck or down by the lake.

I'm not going to deny that I want one thing from this woman. I've been horny as fuck for days. It's not that I'm not always horny, but a flip switched in me when I was messing with Imogene that first night. Dragging her light little body on my lap and feeling her tits. It wasn't just her body that got me hard—it was the way she fought back. The stinging slap on my cheek. I almost followed her into her room, pushed her down on the bed and showed her what happened to women that rebelled against me or Anex's rule.

But she's not mine to have. So I lay in bed at night, thinking of the Little Lamb a few rooms away, pretending to be all innocent and naïve, while I rub myself raw.

"You're following me," Jasmine says, cutting into my thoughts. She leans against the marble countertop, a little smile on her lips. My eyes are drawn to her blonde hair. Soft like a lamb.

"Just looking for some water."

"Follow me." She walks over to a door, and I follow her into a large pantry. It's immaculate and well stocked. She bends, opening a small refrigerator under the cabinet and pulls out a glass bottle. Looking back at me, she slowly screws off the top. Her nails are manicured into sharp points, and they drag against my hand as she gives me the bottle. This woman is everything that the women in Serendee aren't. Sleek, poised, confident. She eyes me with curiosity.

"What's it like in there?"

I take a sip of the bubbly water. "Can you be more specific?"

"In your compound or whatever. That place. Serendee."

"It's beautiful," I tell her truthfully. "Clean, self-sustaining, all organic and natural food. I'm lucky to call it home."

"What about the culty-stuff?"

Heat warms the back of my neck. I try not to get defensive about Serendee. Anex has taught us how to deal with people like this. We speak with honesty. Truth. A woman like Jasmine has the kind of wealth that Anex likes to get his hands on, but it's not always a good fit.

"If you think maximizing and understanding personal growth is culty, then I guess we're guilty as charged."

She steps forward, leaning over to give me a view of her cleavage. "I heard there are some kinky sex things going on in there."

I laugh. "Kinky?"

"Yeah, like, big orgies out in some field. People say they can hear the drumbeats from miles away during them."

"Hmm." I finish off the bottle and screw back on the cap. "Do you think I'd be at a party here if there were orgies going on in there? It's much less exciting than you think. It's just a bunch of people seeking enlightenment."

Her fingers tuck over the waist of my pants, her nails pressing against my stomach. "I know a really good path to enlightenment."

I tilt my head. Now that we're this close, I can't help but notice how much makeup she's wearing. How much perfume. I wrinkle my nose and suddenly my desire wanes. There's no thrill here. No chase. When did I stop wanting it so easy?

I place my hand over hers to remove it, but her thumb loosens the button. A moment later, my cock is in her hand and she's on her knees. Any other night, and I'd be down for some easy head, but again... there's that word. Easy. Is this what I want?

I look down to nudge her away, but I get a glimpse of the top of her head—the shiny blonde that's more yellow than white but still... close enough. Exhaling, I shove my fingers in her hair and pull, eliciting a gasp from the woman on her knees. She tries to look up at me, but I force her eyes down, and twist my fingers in her hair, "Don't," I tell her, allowing my own lids to fall, "don't look up and take me deep."

It may not be what I want, who I want, or the way I want it, but when do I get any of those things?

I'm at the mercy of a dictator, living in a paradox of gluttony and deprivation. As Jasmine's mouth closes around my cock, warm and wet, I think of a different blonde and remember that this is The Way. It's what Anex wants for me. My sacrifice for the greater whole.

16

IMOGENE

Hours pass. *Hours.* And I understand more than ever why Anex discourages technology. It's addictive. Consuming. Distracting.

I can't stop.

These people and their lives; I had no idea. It's flashy and bright and moves so fast that sometimes I have to press the button again to make it slow down, to repeat over again, so I can try to understand their words. It's so much talking and laughing and drinking coffee and wine. There are men and women, but it's the women I can't stop watching. With their shirts that show their flat, smooth stomachs, and strain across their breasts. Their pants are tight, and the skirts are short, revealing long, exposed legs. But it's not just their looks I'm obsessed with. It's the way they speak first, and take control, and have their own lives.

Then there's the kissing. With tongues. And all the hands. And the sex. So much sex. In jokes, in reality, it's in everything. It's not hidden or forbidden. It makes them laugh. Cry. Moan. My cheeks burn red.

It's terrifying.

I don't look away until the door opens, and I glance over and blink. Silas has returned. I fumble forward, jabbing the button with my finger. "You're back," I say, feeling like I got caught with my hand in the cookie jar. "What time is it?"

"Late," he says, easing off his coat. "After midnight. Have you been watching this the whole time?"

"Yes," I admit. "I couldn't stop."

He laughs. "I bet. It's called binge watching for a reason."

I frown. "Binge watching?"

"Yeah, when you start a show and can't stop. That's what they call it. A binge." He then kicks off his shoes, revealing dark socks. "How did you like it?"

"It was...overwhelming."

"I'm sure. I found all of this overwhelming at first too."

He'd said that before. "You did?"

He shrugs. "Sure. I was raised like you. It wasn't until Anex came to me and I started my own training that I understood the power of intimacy and that I had a gift to share with the community."

"How old were you?"

"Sixteen."

"But you still believe in Anex and The Way."

"I do. It took a while, but I understand my place in both worlds."

"But Rex doesn't. He wants to be in that world." I point to the laptop. "All the time."

He grimaces. "He's struggling. I believe with our help—your help—he can find his way back."

It's weird that for Rex to find his way back, I have to lose a little bit of myself, but I've already accepted this is my fate. "So, the women he is attracted to, they are like the ones on the show?"

"Sort of. Not specifically, but it's a good example." He sits next to me. "Did you learn anything useful?"

"Useful may not be the right word. I'm not sure any of them do anything useful other than talk too much."

He laughs. "You're funny, Imogene."

"I am?"

"Different." He takes my hand again and this time I force myself not to panic.

"Being different has always caused me problems."

He tucks a piece of hair behind my ear. The soft pads of his fingertips elicit a shiver as they trail down my cheek to my chin. "Are you ready to show me some of what you learned?"

My heart pounds wildly, banging against my ribcage. I want to escape, but his hand is on mine and I know there's no more running. I can learn this lesson from Silas or from Elon. Silas seems the better option. I don't want to fail Anex and his son and I realize that is what this whole night has been about.

"I don't know what to do."

"I doubt that, Imogene." He bends, brushing his lips across mine. They're warm and soft. A tingling sensation buzzes on my mouth. Silas grins. "See?"

He's not finished coming in for another kiss. This time it's harder, his mouth applying more pressure, his lips blistering and hungry. Panic builds in my chest—this is wrong, he is not my mate —but his hand moves to my back, keeping me in place. I open my mouth to suck in air and his tongue sweeps in, licking against mine. It feels like an explosion in my mouth and I lean into him, wanting more, taking more, until we're both breathing heavy.

"I'm sorry," I say, pulling back. "That was—"

"Perfect," he says, moving his hand behind my neck. "Are you sure you haven't done that before?"

"Of course not!" If possible, my cheeks burn hotter. I struggle to my feet and see his grin. "Don't make fun of me."

"I'm not," he says sincerely. "That was a very nice kiss. With tongue even."

Now I know he's mocking me. "Stop."

He grabs me and yanks me close, nose grazing mine. "I'm not making fun of you. That was a very good kiss. One, with a little practice, Rex will definitely approve of."

"You really think so?"

He nods. "I know so."

I exhale. "Good. And thank you for the lesson. The expectations, although way out of my wheelhouse, seem a little clearer now."

"I have no doubt you can do what you need to do to win Rex over." He smooths my hair and once again his lips brush against mine, and although it's not as shocking as the first one, when he releases me, it still leaves me feeling lightheaded. "You should go to bed. Get some sleep."

I nod and exit his room, feeling wobbly on my feet. Later, I lie on the bed, running my fingers over my lips. If this is what all of my lessons are like, then I may have something to look forward to.

SINCE I WAS TWELVE, my daily logs and journals have been filled with repetitive, neat documentation. What I consumed that day. How much I exercised. The hours I volunteered. The minutes spent studying, meditating, and giving to Serendee. There were occasional notes about celebrations or something unique; on March third, I saw a rainbow. On September ninth, we harvested the garden. On December twenty-first, we brought the gifts that we'd created to Anex, honoring him for his sacrifice and leadership. But mostly it was the mundane—something, after my mother disrupted my world, that I cherished. Watching those calories and grams add up to nice, appropriate numbers. Seeing my thoughts smooth into acceptable conformity, while internally chanting, *"I'm not my mother. I'm not my mother..."*

The peace I received from documenting the details of my life has slowly faded since moving into the main house. Sure, my food goals are still on target. Actually, I may be ahead of target, having skipped dinner last night. But that food was replaced by binge watching a TV show, which I dutifully record. That was followed by me kissing a man that is not my future mate. I know all of it was for the better good, but still...

I'm more aware than most that these logs... they aren't exactly private. Members of Anex's leadership council have the right to review them. After my mother betrayed Serendee, I was required to turn them into Clarissa so that they could assess my state of mind, my loyalty.

It's with that knowledge that I speak the truth about what happened. Lying...it never ends well. Anex has a way of knowing. Plus, this was his idea. The lessons are what he wanted. Despite my concerns, I have faith in my actions.

I place the journal in the wooden box on my desk and take one last look in the mirror. I'm in one of the dresses I made for my courtship. It's long, grazing my ankles as is required. My arms and collarbones are covered. It's fitted at the breast and waist—an offering to my betrothed. The fabric is pale gray. Nothing flashy. Nature provides the color and vibrancy to Serendee.

It took a while to get used to the clothing changes that began when we entered the domum. Before age twelve, females are allowed a more casual dress, shorts or pants. Boys could wear jeans or sweats. Whatever was made for play.

But Anex noticed that as members of Serendee reach adolescence, the boys and girls are driven to distraction by one another. He blames hormones—the desire to show off to one another for attention. Outlandish colors, skin revealing outfits. It's just another weakness that falls in the same category as food, and Anex was convinced that it is something that can be controlled if a person is dedicated. That's when the mandates for clothing came down. Girls over twelve must wear loose fitting, ankle-length dresses. Boys, cotton pants with a button-down shirt. Neutral colors only.

What I'm about to do will be in exact defiance of Anex's mandate.

As I secure my hair in a low ponytail, there's a knock on the door. Silas stands in the hallway, and his eyes dart immediately to my lips. They tingled all night, and it starts again when I see him.

"Am I late?" I ask.

"No. I just wanted to see you before you left for the day. To make sure you're okay about last night."

It's impossible for me not to watch his mouth as he speaks. My heart thrums, wanting to taste him again. "I'm fine."

I glance down, afraid that he can tell him I tossed and turned, thinking about him. His fingers press against the underside of my chin, lifting my face. His head is tilted and before I can think, his hand is on my lower back and his lips cover mine.

He tastes spicy, like mint, and there's less fumbling this time. I know to follow his pace, to try to anticipate his moves. My body explodes like someone has set fireworks off under my skin and I clutch the fabric of his shirt. The move forces his hips to brush against mine and that sends another, different tremor through me. I'm still clinging to him when he pulls away, hair flopped in his eyes and smiling down at me.

"Better than last time."

"Do you think?" I ask, knowing it's true. I feel unsteady on my feet.

"Absolutely." He tucks my hair back. "You're close to being proficient."

"That seems like a stretch." A cough from the living room draws both of our attention. "Is he waiting?"

"Yes."

Elon. That is who I am to spend the day with. I take a deep breath and start toward the living room. Silas's hand circles my wrist before I get there, drawing me back.

"Any lesson you've learned for Rex, you can apply to Elon," he says, grazing his fingers down my cheek. "Understand?"

I nod, but I don't. Elon is mean and angry. He clearly doesn't like me or the assignment he's been given. Which is probably why he's agreed to take me somewhere that will push me completely outside my boundaries.

"Good luck," Silas says.

"Thanks," I reply, knowing how much I'm going to need it.

It's not the first time I've been in a car, but it's the first time I've been in one this nice. I'd gaped when I saw it in the garage beneath the main house—a garage, along with the extensive fleet of vehicles I had no idea existed. Elon walks past each one, shiny and clean, to a black one at the end. Everything about this man is dark. His hair, his eyes, his complexion. He's the opposite of Rex, who is pale and fair. I'm reminded of the symbol of The Way, the sun and moon. These two encompass it, at least in looks. He presses a button that makes the lights blink. I don't know the type, but it looks too small for his large frame. Too extravagant for someone at Serendee.

"We're driving?" I ask.

"Obviously."

"But shouldn't we just walk? There's no reason to waste the resources a vehicle like this must expend and Anex…"

He sighs loud enough to cut me off and rubs his forehead. "How many times do I have to explain to you that all of this is approved by Anex?"

I swallow but don't respond and he starts to the driver's side door. He glances back, noticing I'm still in the middle of the garage. His exhale is deeper this time, but he circles around and opens the opposite door. "Get in, Imogene."

I glance at his face, and the directive is unmistakable.

Don't make me ask twice.

I hurry past him, getting a strong whiff of his spicy scent. The seats are low, and I gather the hem of my dress to get in properly. Once I'm settled, Elon slams the door and walks around to the other side. His big body fills the seat, but he doesn't look out of place. He looks comfortable—commanding. The stylish clothing and his dark looks make my heart stutter. His hand grips the knob between the seats, and he seems very much at ease.

"We can't walk," he explains, starting the engine. It sounds like a big cat purring. "Because we're not shopping in town."

"Oh," I reply. Of course. I can't be seen in town with Elon. If someone from Serendee saw us there would be too many questions. "Right."

He reaches up and presses another button, which opens a door in front of us. The car glides smoothly through the door and down the back driveway of the main house. I've seen this driveway from a distance, but never wondered too much about where it led. Elon approaches a tall gate and to my surprise, two men emerge to open it. Although they're dressed in black, it's not the standard male outfit. It's a more utilitarian fit. I notice their thick-soled boots and clunky jackets. They give Elon a curt nod, one he returns, and he exits the driveway. A moment later, Serendee is behind us.

"Do those men always stand there?" I ask, glancing behind me.

"Them or a few others." Elon cuts his eyes in my direction. "Anex has guards placed around the property. Just to keep everyone safe."

I look out the window, seeing the countryside flash by. "I had no idea."

"I suspect," he says, shifting the knob again, "that there are many things about Serendee that you have no idea about."

He says it with bite, like I should feel guilty or stupid about this, but how would I know? I've followed all the rules and directives, not asking questions. I'm doing my part.

He takes a sharp turn and I grab hold of the door to keep from sliding over. Truthfully, I don't want to be any closer to him than I have to. Whatever dislike he has for me, I have as much for him. I ignore him, fascinated by the interior of the car, the knobs and buttons, the little computer in the console. Every day in this new world of mine, I learn that what I thought was off limits, maybe really isn't.

Soon we enter the city, with more cars and taller buildings. I've been before—once or twice with my parents to take care of some business or to visit a doctor, but ever since my mother betrayed us, visits outside Serendee are few and far between other than the small town adjacent to the community.

Elon seems completely unbothered by the traffic and crowds. He pulls the car over to the curb in front of a store with big windows and mannequins posed in bright clothes. Even though they aren't real people, the amount of skin they're showing seems improper. I'm gawking at them, at the people on the street, at every-thing when Elon opens the car door and holds out his hand.

I stare at it and remember what Silas told me. To remember my lessons. I don't know much yet, but from the TV show, I know that casual touches are common in the secular world. I extend my hand. He takes it, pulling me out of the car. I trip over the hem of my dress and fall into him.

"Sorry," I say, feeling awkward and out of place. "I'm so sorry."

"Don't apologize," he replies, his voice tight. "Just hurry up. People are watching."

I look around. He's right. People are watching me, staring at my dress and my lack of makeup and plain hair. Maybe I should have used some of the makeup in my bathroom drawer. Elon probably feels as out of place by my appearance as I do—his black clothing fits in with everyone else. He yanks me forward, off of the street and into the shop. Inside I'm accosted by an explosion of color and thumping music.

"It looks like a flower garden in here," I exclaim, reaching for the fabrics. Everything is pink and red and orange. Some glitter with sequins or shiny thread.

"Pick a few things out." He looks me up and down. "Attractive things."

I haven't the faintest idea of where to begin. Everything is too much. Too bright. Too revealing. Elon must sense my problem because he approaches a shop girl and flashes her a lopsided, brilliant grin.

God. I had no idea he was even capable of that.

"Excuse me," he says, as though he speaks to women like this every day.

Maybe he does.

"How can I—" Her entire demeanor changes when she faces him. Her shoulders square and her breasts lift perkily. Her chin tilts while she looks under her long, black lashes. I think I'm more enthralled than he is. "Help you?"

"My cousin," he says, nodding over at me, "is in dire need of some new clothes."

She glances over and her eyes widen. I'm used to feeling self-conscious in town, but the people there are used to us. I've never experienced anything like this. "Oh, you poor thing." She keeps her attention on Elon. "I assume you want something a little more... fashionable?"

"Yes," he says, looking the shop girl up and down. There's a glint in his eye that makes my stomach twist anxiously. "Something like you're wearing would be good."

It's my turn to stare. The shop girl is wearing a skirt that barely covers her thighs along with a top with no sleeves, just straps that crisscross over the shoulders. The neckline plunges, revealing the swell of her breasts. I can't stop staring at the smooth, soft looking skin. I force my eyes upward to the large gold hoop earrings dangle from her lobes, then down to the spikes coming out of the heels of her shoes. I can't imagine going to these lengths for beauty.

"Head back to the changing room," she says, placing her hand on Elon's forearm. "I'll gather a few things and bring it back."

"Perfect," he says, giving her another grin. "Oh, and make sure you add in a few bra and panty sets. If my suspicions are correct, hers definitely need an upgrade."

My cheeks, no, my entire body, burns with humiliation. Our undergarments are made for functionality, nothing else. The seamstress creates them specifically for the women in Serendee and the accusation that they aren't acceptable for some reason bothers me. I fume as I follow Elon to the back of the store and into a back room. There are several stalls with curtains and a sitting area outside. There's an expanse of floor to ceiling mirrors along the wall, and I see multiples of myself. Compared to the shop girl, the contrast is alarming. I look like a frumpy child in my long dress and plain hair and face.

Elon sits in the comfy chair and says, "Undress. Let's see what we're really working with here."

"Undress?"

"It's time to shed the innocent image, Imogene. Rex wants to mate with a woman, not a little lamb."

"But why do you need to see me?" My arms wrap around my middle. "Anex makes this clear. No one should see a woman undressed unless they are Ordered."

"Undress, Imogene, or I'll do it for you."

The intent in his eyes is clear. I have no doubt if I don't follow his directions, he'll do as he says, and then some. My hands tremble as I reach behind my back, struggling to unbutton the top button. He watches my every move with an aloof, cold stare, and frays my nerves. Finally, he sighs and stands.

"I'm doing it," I promise him. "I just...my zipper..."

"Turn around."

I turn and expose my back. I wouldn't think his big hands could move so swiftly, but they do, pushing aside my hair and loosening the button with a gentle touch. I inhale a breath of air as he pulls the zipper down to my lower back. Cool air hits my skin, sending goosebumps along every inch.

He stands behind me for a moment and then runs a warm finger down my spine. "You're too thin."

I glance back and see that same look of annoyance. "Sorry my appearance doesn't please you."

He moves back to the seat and I reluctantly undress, still futilely trying to cover myself. "You're not unappealing," he says, "but you could use a little meat on your bones. Something to hold on to."

I frown and glance at the mirror. My undergarments are a standard two piece, supplied by the seamstress. A white, full coverage tank and loose shorts. "Why on earth would you need to hold on to me?"

A slow grin reveals his teeth. "Sometimes I think you play coy on purpose, Little Lamb, but then I remember how you've been raised."

"The same way as you."

"To an extent, but when I reached manhood, we were assigned to be Rex's confidants, and the veil dropped. It's dropping for you as well. Serendee is more than what you've always known. It's bigger and more complex, and part of that is embracing that knowledge."

"And that means I need to go against the rules Anex imposed to make us all better?" I ask. "Like my nutrition and food intake? Like my clothing and undergarments?"

"It means that you are now one of the Chosen. The few that get to see Serendee for what it really is." He doesn't say this with pride or awe, but as though it's a burden.

"And what is it?"

"For you? It's whatever Rex wants it to be."

"He made it very clear he does not want me."

"He doesn't want the you that grew up in Serendee, but the one we are making—creating—that is one he will not only accept but desire. Then he and Anex will be happy. If they are both happy, then all of Serendee will benefit."

The shop girl enters the room, and I tighten my arms over my chest. She holds out a stack of clothing; dresses, skirts, blouses, and yes, several pairs of thin, lacy undergarments. I blush just seeing them.

"Now, I brought you a few sizes, although you're obviously a small or extra small. The good thing is that means that—"

"Thank you," Elon says, cutting her off. He reaches into his pocket and removes a thick roll of money—twenty-dollar bills. I have never seen so much currency. Where would he even get that? He peels several off and hands them to her. "I think we're good, but make sure no one interrupts us."

She gives me a strange look, but grips the money in her hand and shrugs. "You got it."

A moment later, she's gone, and she's pulled another curtain across the main doorway. It's just me and Elon and a stack of clothing for me to try on. He flips through the outfits, quickly assessing each one. He stops and pulls out a bright blue dress. "Try this one," he says, thrusting it out. He's focused on the lingerie, fingering the straps, before handing it over, too. It's a set, black and lacy. "With this."

My heart pounds just looking at them. Even after all the justifications, the explanations, the confirming that this is what Anex wants me to do, it feels wrong. Like, a test I'm about to fail. I've worked so hard to reestablish my reputation. I can sense it slipping through my fingers.

But...

If Elon's right, and I am one of the chosen to help usher Rex into his position of leadership, then I must do everything to make that happen. Even if that means going against my own beliefs.

"Do you want me to change here or behind the curtain?" I ask, clutching the soft fabric to my body.

Elon's eyes flick over me, his mouth twists in approval. "Since you asked, you may go behind the curtain."

I nod and carry the clothing into the stall and begin the process of removing my undergarments. I've never exposed myself like this in a public space. Not even in front of the girls in the domum. To his credit, Elon says nothing on the other side of the curtain, although I feel his presence. I do my best to ignore him, focusing on the straps and clasps and adjusting the lace. I face myself in the mirror to check to see if I have it on correctly. The bra cups make my breasts look larger than normal. The low cut of the panties extends the length of my stomach. The lace does little to hide the dark-colored flesh of my nipples or the thatch of hair at the crux of my body. My skin is both hot and cold, prickling with sensation. The curtain opens with a jerk behind me, and my eyes meet Elon's in the mirror.

Forcing my arms to remain at my side, I lift my chin, pretending to be brave.

His gaze rakes over me, and he swallows thickly, his Adam's apple bobbing in this throat. The look in his eye is familiar—hungry like the night before. I take a step back, hitting the cool surface of the mirror.

"Hold still."

I don't dare disobey, but my heart pounds and my stomach twists with nerves. He steps forward until we're inches apart. His fingers run down the side of my breast, then graze over my nipple.

His eyebrow arches. "No man has ever touched you before, correct?"

I suck in a breath. "Correct."

He dips beneath the fabric and circles my nipple, forcing it to pebble and harden. "How does this make you feel?"

Dirty. Disloyal. Confused. Warm heat builds in my lower belly. I stare at the curly chest hair peeking out from under the collar of his shirt. "I don't know."

"Are you wet between your legs? Have you soiled those new panties before you even got them out of the store?"

My eyes flick to his. *How did he know?* "Stop. This is inappropriate."

He leans to whisper in my ear. "This is your world now, Imogene." He tugs at my nipple, pinching hard, and pain shoots through me. "It's better if you accept that. It'll go easier." His breath hot. "Do you understand?"

My fingers coil into a fist and that instinct, the one I try to drive out of my system, starts to rear its head but this time, before I can move, Elon's hand cinches around my wrist. "Hit me again and you'll regret it. I'm serious."

I nod.

"Say it, Imogene. Tell me you understand."

"I understand." My words are shaky but clear. I meet his eyes when I say it, holding them longer than necessary. "I will not raise my hand to you again."

Finally, he steps back, tweaking my nipple one last time and says, "I'll go settle with the girl up front. Put on the blue dress and the heels, then meet me at the car."

"You don't want me to try on the other clothes?"

"It's unnecessary. Rex will approve." His aloofness is back, cold and distant. The dark anger from moments before, gone. I can't keep track of this man's emotions. He repeats, "Get dressed and meet me at the car, we have somewhere to be."

"Where are we going?" I ask, reaching for the blue dress.

"To meet Anex."

17

Elon

After paying, I ask the clerk to point me in the direction of the bathroom. The minute I get inside and lock the door, I lean against the sink and unzip my pants. Two seconds later I've got my hand wrapped around the base of my cock. I'd been rock hard all morning, but that little reveal of Imogene in a black lace bra and panties almost made me come in my shorts.

The Little Lamb... she has no fucking idea.

I made it worse by touching her. That hadn't been my plan, but seeing her barely covered in lace... I lost control.

Despite being too skinny, her tits are incredible, and her lips look puffy and soft. I think about how they felt, how aroused she became. I stroke up and down my cock, tugging and working myself to the brink. Underneath all that innocence is a woman that needs to be broken in. Fucked. I'd do it myself if it wouldn't violate Anex's orders. I close my eyes and think of her naked and splayed on my bed, eyes wide as she takes in my manhood for the first time. As sweet as she seems, underneath there's a fighter. I can smell it. The thought of battling her, dominating her as I claim her, ignites a rumble in my chest. It doesn't take me long to reach my peak, and I shudder through my orgasm, teeth clenched, and unload in the sink.

"Christ," I mutter, pushing and pulling until there's nothing left. I hold on to the counter and catch my breath. Getting hard over Imogene wasn't a surprise, but the ferocity of my orgasm was unexpected.

Jerking off is something boys learn to do efficiently at Serendee. Taking care of our needs quickly and without delay is encouraged. Anex understands there is nothing more inefficient and distracted than a pent-up male. These lessons start at age twelve, when we're separated from the girls. We're taught that males have less control over their physical desires, and that can lead to aggression, anger, and violence. Females have powerful attributes and are born with more self-control. It's their duty to maintain decorum with their appearances and behavior because males can't be held accountable for the flaws nature gave to us—the urge to fuck and procreate. The need to spread our seed. Anex demands that we do the best we can, treating women with honor and respect is important. One way to do that is to rid ourselves of the all-consuming tension to keep us from doing something stupid.

For most, what just happened with Imogene would fall into the realm of stupid, but I'm not like other people in Serendee. I'm one of the Chosen. I have a duty and breaking down Imogene's sexual resistance is part of it. If anything, I held back.

When my breathing is even and my cheeks return to normal color, I clean up myself and the sink, then exit the bathroom to pick up my packages at the counter.

"Everything okay?" the clerk asks. "Your cousin is still in the back." She leans over the counter, giving me an eyeful of her cleavage. "Sure, there's nothing else I can assist you with?"

She's been eye fucking me since I walked in. Any other day, I may have taken her into the back room, but things have changed over the last week. I've been given a mission.

"No thank you. Just tell her that I'll be in the car."

"Of course. Come back—any time."

I smile and push out the door, stepping onto the street. The

BMW is parked right out front. I know seeing it had been a shock for Imogene. Hell, the first time I walked into the garage at the main house, I was shocked too. Fancy cars? High tech? My world turned upside down, but Anex was there to right me, to help me understand.

I load up the trunk with the packages and get in the front seat of the car, hoping she doesn't take long. Forcing Imogene to undress like that hadn't been for my own pleasure. Everything I do is with specific intent—that's one reason Anex chose me for this job. She needs to get comfortable with her body and learn how to use it. I know that Silas wants to ease her into it, but Anex isn't known for his patience. He'll want to see results. He's worried about Rex straying too far from Serendee. Understandably so. Every day he gets closer and closer to leaving and if that happens... well, the questions will start and Anex loathes questions.

That is another reason I've been so harsh with Imogene. She's inquisitive. Nosey. It's in her best interest to do as she's told. It's in *all* our best interests. The right girl had to be chosen to fill the role of Rex's mate, but the right girl also comes with risks.

It's my job, along with Silas and Levi, to make sure those risks are minimized.

Anex spent a lifetime breaking Imogene down.

It's our turn to build her into something new.

18

IMOGENE

After parking the car, Elon leads me back into the house, up a different staircase and down a narrow hall. I try to pretend like he hadn't just seen me—touched me. I feel violated and raw—shamed. Every nerve is frayed wire that I'm terrified he'll expose or ignite. It's a valid concern considering the blue dress I'm wearing.

As we walk the endless maze of hallways, I run my hands down my arms, seeking the comfort of sleeves, but instead feeling smooth, bare skin. The sensation is weird and jarring. I'm cold, even though the apprehension in my chest makes me sticky with heat. I keep my eyes on Elon's jet black hair and broad shoulders as we walk toward our destination—toward Anex—thinking they look less tense than before, wondering what changed since he left the dressing room.

"Can you tell me where we're going?" I ask. The hallway is strange, cutoff with no windows or doors.

"To Anex's private chambers. It's an area not accessible to members of Serendee. Only his inner-circle is invited here. No one from the community will see you dressed like that, if that's what you're worried about."

I am worried about it, but I hear the mocking in his voice. "An outfit like this is a symbol of regressive behavior—a punishable offense. After all my hard work, my sacrifices and dedication, if Anex disapproves..." I swallow and heat blooms in my cheeks. "What if he knows what you did to me?"

His gaze flicks to my breasts, making my nipples instantly hard. His smirk is cruel and indicates that he notices. "He won't disapprove, and he won't care that I touched you. It's my job, Little Lamb. How many times do I need to tell you that?"

A million, I think, because I can't process the sudden change in my life. This is not who I am, who *we* are as a community. Elon continues down the hall and I have no choice but to chase after him, clumsy in the unfamiliar heels. When he stops at a wooden door and he looks down at me with those cold, assessing eyes. They settle on my hair. I draw back as he reaches for me, but his hand moves to the back of my neck and yanks out the band holding my hair in a ponytail. Long waves tumble over my shoulders and down my back. "It's not great but it'll do."

Wow, he knows how to make a girl feel special.

He lifts his hand to knock on the door.

"Wait," I grab his arm, "What will be expected of me in there? What does Anex want?"

"He wants to see that we have made progress turning you into the kind of woman Rex will accept." His jaw tightens. "Otherwise behave as normal."

Normal.

Whatever that is.

He knocks and a moment later ,another man dressed in all black appears. Same pants with pockets down the legs, same black boots. More security. How have I never noticed these men before? Elon strides into the room and I follow, knowing now isn't the time to ask questions. Elon definitely knows more about this situation than I do. I've only truly been in Anex's presence independently a handful of times.

Whatever my worries are, they are pushed aside as we walk into the private quarters. It's a large additional wing of the house, with its own foyer and living areas. The room we're in is decorated in expensive looking art and warm rugs on the floor. The walls are painted in rich, bright colors.

I'm mesmerized by all of this—outside of nature, Serendee is a world of neutrals and earth tones, but here, everything is different. When I stop gazing at the rainbow of colors, I realize that we're not alone. A handful of people congregate around the room, settled on plush pillows arranged on the floor. Men *and* women dressed more like the people in town than at home. I want to touch the beads on one woman's dress, or the red paint on another's lips.

Elon stops so abruptly I almost run into him.

Anex sits in the middle of the room on a soft looking plush chair. Women, including Margaret, cluster around him on large pillows. It's not a completely unusual scene—Anex is typically surrounded by his confidants—but the colors, the clothes, the room. It's not the same at all. Even Margaret is wearing a soft pink dress with thin straps instead of sleeves.

There's a young woman standing in front of him, back straight, with her hands flat against her sides. I can tell immediately that she didn't grow up here. I recognize almost everyone, but there's also just a vibe from recruited members. It's radiating off of her.

"Charlotte," Anex says, his tone easy, yet tinged with something sharp, "it's come to my attention you went into town. Alone. Is that true?"

She hesitates, like she's considering her answer, but ultimately says, "Yes. I did."

"And if that wasn't violation enough, you went to a place of business and asked to use their phone?"

"Yes." Her chin drops and her hands twist together. "I was trying to call my sister."

Anex lounges back in his seat, elbow propped on the arm of the chair. "The sister who does not believe in the values of our community and has encouraged you to leave Serendee?"

"Yes."

The tension in the room is palpable. Deadly silent. My heart goes out to this girl, knowing what it's like to be on the wrong side of Anex's judgement. But even as a recruit, she should know better. Outsiders will always try to tear down what they don't understand, and it is clear her sister does not understand Serendee.

I look up at Elon to see what he thinks about this scene, but he stares straight ahead, seemingly unbothered.

"Is there a reason you called her?" Anex asks.

"She asked me to call once a month, to make sure I'm okay." She looks up at Anex. "She's just worried. It's her nature."

"Because she doesn't have faith," he replies. "She doesn't have the care and concern of a tight community like ours. One that builds one another up, instead of tearing each other down."

"Yes. She has none of that," she says, nodding. I can see a fat tear running down her cheek. "It was a mistake. One I won't make again."

He holds out his hand, palm facing Charlotte. "I can sense the internal struggle you have with this. Your genetic family versus your chosen one. It's a dark space."

"Please, help me get back. I want to be at peace with The Way."

"You chose this life, Charlotte, and I want to be here to help you be better. This isn't about me. It's about you." He nods, eyes flicking to one of the guards near the door. The man walks over and stands behind the girl. "You need to spend some time alone, considering what you've done. What you want to happen in the future."

"Yes, Anex."

"And I will be using your collateral."

Her eyes snap up and her body shudders. "No. Please don't."

"You've given me no choice," he says, voice tinged with sympathy. "It seems to be the only way to get you back on the right path."

He nods at the guard who leads the woman out of the room. Our eyes meet as she passes, and an uncomfortable feeling rises up my spine. I don't want to be associated with her, yet I pity her. I know what it's like to want to talk to someone outside the community.

When she and the guard have left, Elon steps forward. I follow, and we both go through the process of touching our forehead and bowing. Anex turns his attention to me and I wait until he speaks, until he finishes assessing me. I've never felt as *seen* as I have in the past few days. These men, they're always looking, watching, studying. Today is different ,though. I'm more exposed than I ever have been before. Physically and emotionally.

"Elon," he says, shifting his gaze, "tell me, how is Imogene progressing?"

I'm slightly taken aback that he's addressing Elon instead of me.

"She's doing well," Elon says. "She's eager to fulfill your Order and to please her mate and it shows in her willingness to make necessary changes."

"Good, good," Anex says, tenting his fingers and refocusing on me. "I wasn't sure if you could manage what was being asked of you, but as usual, you surprise me."

I'm both mesmerized by his blue eyes and trying to figure out if this is a compliment or not when Elon jabs me in the side. "T-thank you, Anex. It's an honor to please you."

He waves this off and picks up a bundle of books. The leather covers are familiar, and although it shouldn't, my stomach drops when I realize it is my logs and journals.

"As you can see, I have access to your books. Levi brought them to me." He nods across the room and for the first time I see that Levi is here, standing against the wall. He went through my things? Read my journals? I swallow back the strange feeling of knowing he knows my deepest thoughts and face Anex, who casually flips through the pages, stopping occasionally to study something I've thoughtfully written. "I'm happy to see that you've provided thorough documentation."

"I try to be diligent in my writings—as you suggest."

He smiles and then glances down again at the book. "I see you experienced your first kiss with Silas."

The kiss? That's what he wants to talk about? Not my food logs? Not my sewing? Not the work in The Center?

"Yes." I search for the right response. "He's a very thoughtful instructor."

He leans back in the chair. "Show me."

My eyebrows raise. "Show you?"

"If you're going to mate with my son, I need to be sure that the training I've directed is adequate." He holds up the journal. "Not that I don't believe you, Imogene, but I've always needed my own confirmation on important matters." He nods at Elon. "Kiss *him*."

I turn and face Elon, a man that has made it undeniably clear that he doesn't like me in the least. A man who violated me earlier in the day and the night before. He towers over me and I don't miss that despite the impassive expression on his face. His jaw clenches tight with disgust. He has no choice here—no more than I do.

My pulse quickens in warning, telling me this is not the man I am supposed to be intimate with, but my mind steels itself against emotion. We've both been Chosen, and this is an opportunity to prove our worth in Anex's eyes.

Elon reaches for me, his large hand sliding beneath my hair to cup the back of my neck. Silas had done something similar, and I sink into him the way I knew was pleasing. The pressure on the back of my neck lifts my chin and I stare at Elon's mouth and the way his tongue wets his lips. I mimic his motions and close my eyes. A moment later, his mouth is slanted over mine, lips parted. His breath enters my mouth, and his tongue flicks, slow and seductive. I gasp in surprise, and his other hand presses against my lower back, dragging me close, not letting me get away. The kiss is warm, deep, and penetrative. Elon's jaw is hard and hungry and over the pounding heartbeat in my ears, I hear a rumble in his chest. An inferno builds in my belly and I'm vaguely aware of his hand sliding lower down my backside, cupping my—

"Enough!"

Elon's hands drop, splitting us apart. He steps aside, looking forward, and other than the red mouth, you'd never know what we'd just done. He's calm and collected. Me? Well, I'm using every ounce of strength that I possess to hold myself upright. My heart slams against my ribcage, my lips tingle like they've been electrocuted, my limbs wobble like gelatin. I face Anex as though everything is normal, like my skin isn't on fire. Like I haven't just violated the sanctity of my courtship.

Anex stares between us, eyes roaming over my face. An apology sits on my tongue, but still tastes like Elon and I can't force it out.

"Acceptable," he says. "Obviously, there is a lot of progress that still needs to be made." he snaps the journal shut. "You're halfway there, which isn't enough to convince my son of your worth." His assessment turns clinical, and he nods to Margaret. "Schedule time to visit with Imogene. Do something with her hair and face."

My face? I lift my hand to touch my cheek, but drop it quickly. "Thank you, Anex," I say, remembering my place. "I want to do everything I can to make your Order go through smoothly."

He lifts his hand, and motions for me to come forward. I do as he commands, approaching his chair. He leans forward and takes my hand. "I appreciate your dedication to The Way and my family. Although we try to maintain other appearances, this has been a trying time for us. Everything about the future of our community hinges on this mating." His fingers wrap around my hand, tightening his grip. "You're a beautiful woman, Imogene. Don't be afraid to use the natural gifts you've been given." His eyes slide down my face, lingering on my neck and collarbone before settling on my breasts. "The Way has always encouraged us to use those gifts to make Serendee a better place."

"That's all I want," I tell him truthfully. "I feel it in my heart and soul. Serendee is my home, and The Way is my compass. Together they will keep me on track."

"Good girl," he says, lifting his hand to cup my cheek. "I knew you wouldn't disappoint me."

He dismisses us, and Elon leads me back the way we came. Levi falls in line, his expression impassive and difficult to read. Despite the emotional rollercoaster, I'm buoyed by the elation I feel from being in Anex's presence. I'd passed the test, all of us had, and that is the most important thing of all.

19

LEVI

THE ROOM IS LOCATED in the basement of The Center with a door to the outside for coming and going. It's windowless and the walls are painted a dark blue and the floors a cream tile. A single desk with one chair sits in the middle of the room. It's utilitarian—as is the business done in here.

I've been in here before—many times—but never as a Guide. Usually, I am the one on the other side of the table, but this is my new role, one given to me by Anex, to ensure that Imogene is who she says she is.

"Oh," Imogene says, pausing in the doorway. She's surprised to see me but recovers quickly. I don't rise. Here I am, the authority. She will stand while I sit. The heavy door shuts behind her, locking from the outside. She can leave at any time, but it would be improper for someone to walk in on us during a session. What transpires in these walls is private. Sacred. The only one that will have access to the recordings is Anex himself.

She stands before me in a pale blue dress that buttons from mid-waist to her throat. The buttons are tiny, mother-of-pearl, and look like they would take small fingers to fasten. The hem of her dress skirts against her ankles. I know she went shopping with Elon the day before and purchased secular clothing. Her eyes go to the leather-bound journal sitting on the desk. I took it from her room earlier and read the latest entries.

That is why we are here today. For me to Guide her through her Lapses.

"I didn't expect you," she says, approaching the desk.

"No, I would think not. Usually, at this phase of your Ordering, you would have a female to lead you through the early stages of your betrothal, but Anex thought it would be best to have someone in the inner circle as you Guide. Someone that understands the intricacies of what you're being asked to do."

"I understand," she says. I notice a flicker of worry in her eyes. Fear? Guilt? Both probably. Her journals have gone from the mundane of Domum life, calorie counting and roommate annoyances, to a flurry of emotions she's never experienced before. "Before we start, can I ask you a question?"

"You can ask. I won't agree to answer."

"What is collateral? Like Anex spoke of yesterday?"

"Ah." This I can answer. "Recruits must offer collateral when they join the community. It's a way to firm up their commitment to Serendee since they do not have ties inside. People offer up something important to them that they do not want the rest of the world to know—something embarrassing or shameful, just for Anex to hold on to. It helps them stay on the path."

Her eyes flick to the book on the desk. "Sort of like our journals."

"Yes, but Anex requires more from recruits. It's risky that he allows them in at all." She seems satisfied with this answer, and I jerk my chin upward. "Are you ready?"

She exhales. "Yes."

I open the journal and my eyes skim the page from the day before, settling on the details of her trip to the store with Elon. She wrote a thorough description of the entire trip; riding in the extravagant car, the brightly lit shop, the clothes she tried on and purchased. She goes into exact detail about the lacy undergarments and Elon's behavior. I'm only focused on one thing.

"You wanted to strike him." It's not a question. She'd written down that when Elon pushed her boundaries, she'd wanted to lash out at him physically again.

She swallows, regret and shame written on her face. "I did."

"And you only stopped because he forced you."

"Correct." She shifts on her feet. "I know my defiance is wrong. I just... I get angry. It surges through me and although I try to control it, I don't always succeed."

She's honest to a fault. It makes it easier to do what I'm here for. The look in her eye. She's almost begging for it.

I close the journal. It's enough. More than enough. Imogene stares at her hands and quietly says, "I'm sorry."

"You do not need to apologize to me," I say, turning to face her. "These doubts imply a weakness. A lack of faith."

"I know, I just... I don't know how to rid myself of it."

"When we are confused, it's best to go back to the teachings. What does the literature say about doubt and fear?"

She lifts her chin slightly, but not enough for me to see her eyes. "It says that it's where evil has taken root and allowed to spread throughout a person. To rid ourselves, we must eradicate it, like a gardener with an invasive weed."

Every person in Serendee struggles with these concerns and must determine their own Correction. Some people meditate. Others throw themselves into working in the community. Others fast. But Imogene, her shame and guilt run deep. I've seen the red stains in her journal. She chooses a more physical form of Correction.

She swallows thickly and reaches for the journal, running her hand over the cover. She pushes her nail into the spine, and slides out something silver. It's a long, sharp piece of metal.

"I have spent years fighting against my mother's Regressiveness. Proving that I am not the same, but I fail. Often."

I nod. "These things push you to Correction?"

She nods.

"Show me."

Her fingers tremble as she reaches for the top button of her dress, high against her throat. Slowly, she pushes each one through until I see the pale expanse of her chest and the shadows that lead between her breasts. The edge of lace surprises me and it's my turn to be startled when she reveals a white lacy bra and not the standard undergarments.

"I was trying to get used to them," she says. "I was going to mark it in my journal."

"Of course," I say, forcing the words out past the lump in my throat. An unexpected rush of heat travels below my belt. I say a blessing to The Way, willing my body to behave. I arrange my face as though seeing this much female flesh is something I'm familiar with. I'm not.

She continues down until she's pushed the bodice of her dress down to her narrow hips. Her thumb rubs just above her hipbone. That's when I see the dark lines. They aren't open wounds, more like deep scratches. Her eyes glance at the tool on the table and I understand that is how she made them. She inhales and says, "One mark is for my mother's Lapse. Another is to quell my strong-will. Any others are for current Lapses, like defying Elon." She runs her fingers over them. "So five today."

I sigh and approach her, tentatively reaching out to touch the wounds. There are thick scars under the fresh scrapes, and I feel the pulse of heat against my thumb. "Rex will disapprove of the cuts—he will view them as another weakness, a sign of his father's control. Personally, I understand the need to find a release for the pain, but we'll have to find another way."

"You want me to stop cutting." The expression on her face tells me this isn't something she's ready or wants to do. Correction can become addictive. Pleasurable even. "I'm not sure I can."

"You must face your fears. Challenge and expose them to the light."

Her hands cover her face, and she whispers, "It's too much. It's wrong."

I stand and circle the table, wrestling her hands away from her face and cinching my fingers around her wrists. "Exploring this is the only way to move past it, Imogene. Shame lives in dark spaces. You must bring it to the light. Embrace these emotions and own them."

She finally looks up. "Will you help me?"

"Of course. That's why I'm here." I position us to face one another and force her to look at me. Her eyes are so blue in the light—so clear. "I will be taking over your correction."

She blinks. "Isn't that highly unusual?"

"It is, but you are no longer a typical woman in Serendee. You are Chosen. Part of the inner circle, and neither Anex nor Rex can have the slightest concern about your motivations."

"I want them to trust me."

"Good. Then you can start by trusting me." I nod in front of her. "Place your hands on the table."

Her jaw drops and I can see the defiance coming—the question —the argument. I raise an eyebrow, daring her to add fuel to the fire. She's already in enough trouble. After a moment of hesitation, she bites down on her bottom lip and swallows it back.

"Good girl," I tell her, moving behind her. I reach for the hem of her skirts and lift them up. I expect the white, chaste panties the women of Serendee notoriously wear. Instead, I get a glimpse of more lace and a scant amount of fabric covering the round curves of her ass. My cock twitches in response. I knew this was going to be hard, but I didn't expect this.

Her knees wobble, making her thighs shake, but her hands remain flat against the table, holding her upright. I don't give her notice before my palm comes down hard against the smooth flesh, her body lurching forward when I make contact, slapping hard.

"One," I tell her coldly, flexing my hand, "for your mother's lapse."

I spank her a second time, hearing a small cry come from her mouth. A coil of desire twists below my gut, something I've never felt before. I slap the flesh again, landing my palm on top of the red skin. "Two for striking Elon."

I continue on, giving her a spanking for each Lapse. The

thought of slapping Elon in the dressing room. The urge to talk back. The constant questions. She falls forward on the third, down to her elbows, and a tear drops on the tabletop. Her knees shake furiously, and I tell her, "Don't you dare fall."

There are five in total, and I breathe heavily with the final one. My cock is rock hard, and something primal takes over. I stare at her for a long time, at the lace and red, blistering flesh. The desire to punish her further—mark her—surges through my veins.

"Straighten your legs," I tell her, annoyed at her slouching. I ignore the muffled grunt as she pushes herself back up. She moves too slowly, and I grab her hips, jerking her upright, while yanking her panties down at the same time. I haul back and spank her again, before dropping the lace on the table and saying, "This is for wearing those slut panties." I add one more. The sound of my palm meeting her ass, echoing through the bare room. There's no reason other than the fact I can't stop.

She falls over the table, her shiny ass red and exposed. Her breathing is fast-paced and shallow, while mine slows, struggling for control. I can see the dark folds of her pussy between her cheeks. I narrow my eyes and discover something else.

She's wet.

I'm not incredibly experienced with women's bodies, but I know the signs of arousal when I see them. I glance toward the famed image of the sun and moon on the wall, and back at the woman on the table.

"That's all," I tell her. "Get yourself together and we're done."

She pushes herself up and brushes the blonde hair off her forehead. Her cheeks are red and sweat dots her forehead. Her breasts are still exposed, and she quickly fastens them, pushing the buttons through the holes with shaky fingers. I walk over and grab the panties, balling them in my fist.

"Leave these. I will speak to Elon about the parameters of when and where you may wear this type of clothing."

"Yes," she says, her tone distant. "Thank you."

My eyebrow lifts. "For what?"

"Correcting me." She licks her lips and glances at me, making eye contact. "For showing me the path to enlightenment."

Something stirs inside of me, deep in my core. This woman. She is strong. Devoted. She takes on the challenge of four men, each determined to break her in one way or the other, to mold her into the perfect mate for our next leader, and she not only accepts every challenge, she thrives on them. The flash of her bare ass flickers in my mind again and the urge to bend her over the table and pound into her is compulsive and strong.

My response is quiet, but forceful. "Go."

She scrambles with the last buttons and leaves, going the way she came. The inner door opens moments after the door closes behind her, latching in place.

"That was excellent work," Anex says, leaning against the wall. "I wasn't sure you had it in you."

"You know I will do anything for Serendee," I say, remembering how she felt in my hands. "For you and Rex."

"The extra corrections were inspired." I feel his eyes on me. I know he was watching. Did he see her arousal as well? "You were right about the cuts. Rex won't like it." He steps back out of the room. "The marks you made on her will fade. Keep working with her. Break down those walls—rid her of all regressive traits. That is something we can't risk."

I nod, and once he's gone, I exhale, feeling like I've just gone through a battle. Like Anex, I didn't know if I had it in me to be so brutal. I also didn't expect to already want to do it again.

20

———

I wake with my face smushed in the pillow, having slept on my stomach because of the lingering pain on my backside. Levi hadn't held back during my correction, but other than the sting from the spankings, I feel strangely refreshed. I'd known for a long time that my own Corrections weren't helping me progress, but having a Guide keep me accountable—one willing to push me to my limits? That changes things.

When he told me to bend over that table, a jolt of emotion ran through me. Fear, of course. I'd experienced being whipped with a leather strap as a child, but also the telltale defiance that brought me there in the first place. I loathe the hot streak that runs through me. It's not that I wanted Levi to Correct me, but I knew I deserved it.

The first slaps were sharp and jarring, more powerful than I imagined Levi could be. But his devotion to The Way runs deep. I accepted each strike, asking for strength and forgiveness. The pain stung, a physical reminder of what my Lapses do to the entire community. One member can weaken the whole. The first five were harsh and punishing. The final two? I've heard of the concept of Enlightenment my whole life. It wasn't until he jerked up my hips and yanked the panties down my legs that I felt it. Suddenly, it wasn't about pain and punishment—my body transcended that. Warm heat builds in my lower belly and every nerve sparked with life. My breath caught in my lungs and my skin ignited with fire.

I knew in that moment that I could truly experience enlightenment. I didn't quite reach it but it was there. So close. And Levi was the Guide that could take me there.

I'm still riding this high when I receive a message from Margaret announcing a visit after breakfast. Although I'm eager to have her assistance, when she arrives its surreal having her in my room. She's beautiful and poised—different from the girls I grew up with. But Margaret didn't grow up in Serendee. She was recruited from the outside—a late joiner, who was quickly embraced into Anex's inner spiritual circle, and joined him as a spiritual wife.

I'd carefully hung up the clothing from my shopping trip the day before and Margaret picks through them. Elon added a few things while I was in the changing room: jeans, tank tops, shoes, and a pile of silky lingerie.

"These are nice," she says, fingering the lace on a complicated-looking undergarment. "You have good taste."

"Oh, I didn't pick any of those out. Elon went with me. It's what he thinks Rex wants."

"He's probably very right." She gives me a little smirk. "Men have little patience and are focused on the flesh. Outfits like this force them to slow down a little."

I nod, pretending like I understand what she's talking about. Everything in my life has gone full speed the last few days. I can't imagine lace and sheer lingerie slowing anyone down. It made Levi angry. It makes Elon mean. For a man like Rex, who is used to getting exactly what he wants, when he wants it, I can't imagine what difference it will make.

"You have some makeup here, don't you?" she asks, folding the clothing neatly.

"In the bathroom," I reply. "How did you know?"

"I purchased it and had it sent up here when you moved in." We enter the bathroom and she opens the drawer. She bypasses the makeup and opens a small, rectangular compact. "I also had Healer Bloom prescribe these for you."

I take the rectangle and open it. Inside are rows of pills. "What is this?"

"Birth control. Take it every day at the same time. If there's an issue, talk to the healer, okay?"

Embarrassment heats my cheeks. Do I tell her that Rex has no interest in me? But she's already moved on and is pulling out the vanity chair. I take a seat, and she runs her fingers through my hair. "God, your hair is gorgeous."

"It's not as pretty as yours," I say. She wears it shorter than the girls I grew up with. Still long, but cut just above the shoulders. Anex feels that long hair is the most practical, requiring less upkeep and, ultimately, less vanity. He's right about it being easier. Pulling it back into a ponytail or just leaving it down takes very little time. I look at Margaret in the mirror's reflection. "Can I ask you a question?"

"Sure." She twists my hair into two ropes. She clamps one section to the top of my head.

"Is it weird having not grown up here? Not living like the rest of Serendee or getting Ordered?"

She laughs, showing her pretty, white teeth. "It took a while to adjust to the ways of the community, but not every female gets Ordered. Some are called for a higher purpose."

"What does that mean?"

"Do you know how Anex and I met?"

I shake my head and watch as she reaches for a pair of scissors in the drawer. "At a coffee shop in town. I overheard him talking about philosophy and his unique way of seeing life. I was working on a paper for school. His words drifted over to me, and it was exactly what I needed to hear. I pretended to work on that paper for an hour, while I absorbed everything he said. He must have noticed because when he parted from his friend, he approached me, and we started talking. I took my first lesson at The Center that week-end. Two weeks later, I had moved into Serendee. Anex told me that I wouldn't be living in the domums or any of the independent houses. I'd been called to The Way, to support Anex, as he guides the community." Her eyes flick to mine in the mirror. "Just like you've been called to support Rex."

My heart thrums from the beauty of her story and the declaration she'd made at the end. I was so enthralled by her words I didn't even notice the inches she cut off my hair until the tips grazed my collarbone. I looked so different.

"I'm going to show you how to use this makeup," she says, spinning me around. "The key is to use it to enhance your features, not overpower them."

I nod, and my skin tingles under her gentle touch as she applies makeup to my eyes and cheeks. She hands me a tube of lipstick and gestures for me to put it on. It's a pale pink and when I run it over my lips, I can only think about the burning heat I felt when kissing Elon earlier.

I look in the mirror again. It's like a different person stares back at me. Strangely, she looks older, more mature. "You're gorgeous," Margaret says, adjusting my hair. "No wonder Rex chose you."

"Rex doesn't want me," I admit. "He made it very clear that doesn't want to have anything to do with me."

"That's just his stubbornness talking. He and his father—they're two lions trying to figure out who runs the den. With your help, things should settle down soon." She puts away the makeup, arranging it neatly in the drawer. "Just keep up with your training. We're not like other females, Imogene. We're different. Chosen. We don't have the luxury of remaining passive. Men like Anex and Rex, they feed off the energy that we supply them. Their mood, their health, their abilities... it's tied back to us. We must always give them the fuel that they need to be the best leader possible."

"I've never considered it that way," I say. "I've been caught up in the strangeness of it all—how to straddle the values that I grew up with, with what I need to do now—but this? It helps."

"Good," Margaret says, giving me a tight hug. "Although it may seem like a sacrifice now, really, this is just another step toward the enlightenment of being a powerful woman."

Her words fill me with a surge of motivation—a purpose—and I vow to do everything that is asked of me to support the leadership of Serendee and fulfill my duty as one of the Chosen.

* * *

"Fuck," Silas mutters as I walk into the living room. He closes the laptop and sets it on the coffee table. "Sorry."

"Is something wrong?" I look down at my clothing, then back at his face. He's studying me closely. I thought I was home alone, but Silas may not like to see me in this clothing any more than Levi. "Is it too much? Should I change?"

"God no. You look…"

"Silly, I know." I changed from the dress I wore to Anex's chambers into a pair of tight-fitting jeans. They stick to me like a sheath. "I've never worn jeans before. They're kind of restrictive." I run my hands over my hips. I'm not used to the feeling of fabric so close to my skin. "I should put on something appropriate."

"No," he blurts. "Don't. It's exactly the kind of thing Rex would approve of. You should get used to it."

"You think?" I tuck my hair behind my ear.

"I know."

I smile. "Good. Elon picked it out, and Margaret did my hair and makeup. I just… it doesn't seem like it's enough."

"Well, you're right, that clothing is just one part of this," Silas says. "When Rex sees you in that he'll be interested and want more."

More. I'm not naïve enough to know this isn't about sex. It's all about sex, but Margaret taught me it's also about something else: a purpose.

"Then show me."

His eyes widen. "Show you?"

"Show me what he'll want. I'm ready." His lips form a line— clearly doubtful that I'm truly ready, but I'm determined. "If our goal, my goal, is to bring Rex back into Serendee I will do whatever it takes. Anex has faith in me, and I have faith that The Way will get me through this."

He nods and picks up the laptop. "Come sit by me. I have an idea."

"More TV?" I'd binged the rest of the show he'd shown me, which is one reason I know this outfit is pleasing to men. I sit next to him and wait as he queues up a show.

"Something different," he says, scooting closer, leaving a small space between us. He places the computer on the table right in front of us. "A new lesson."

Flickers of energy spark through me at his closeness. He smells good. Soapy and warm. He presses play. I'm still enthralled at the way the screen comes to life, showing so many colors and pictures and—I gasp. "Oh."

A woman appears on screen wearing very little clothes. She's in a lacy red bra with matching panties. Her breasts are enormous and her hips curve with so much flesh I didn't even know a woman could possess. "What—what is she doing?" I ask, unable to keep my eyes off of her.

"Watch and see," Silas says, his voice a little rough. His hand moves to the gap between our legs, resting on the couch.

I do as I'm told, studying how this woman walks across the room, distracted by a tightening in my belly, something low and deep. She reaches a bed, and that's when I realize she isn't alone. A man waits for her. He's also wearing very few clothes, just a small pair of black shorts. His body is rippled with muscles, and the sensation in my stomach builds. It only increases when I feel Silas' pinky making sweeping strokes against the side of my leg.

I've seen people have sex on the other show he has me watch. They kissed and touched and then vanished under the covers or are shown the next day looking happy and refreshed. I know they had sex because the characters told me. What I'm witnessing on the screen is more than that. The couple meets at the edge of the bed and their hands are all over one another; grabbing, pulling, pushing. Their breathing is heavy, hypnotic. Their lips bite and their tongues lick. The man tears the bra off the woman, revealing her perfect breasts and round, brown nipples, and she pushes at the waist of his shorts, revealing paler skin and deep cut of muscles and a dark swirl of hair. I'd noticed the front of his shorts seemed lumpy, but when she removes them entirely, I'm struck dumb.

"What is that?" I ask quietly.

"It's his penis," Silas tells me. "His dick, cock, whatever."

I drag my eyes away from the bobbing, swollen appendage and look over at Silas' pants. "Are they always that big?"

He laughs and shrugs.

"And looks like that?" I point at the screen. The woman has his cock in her hands and makes a big show of running her fingers all over it. His jaw clenches and grabs her breasts with his hands, kneading them.

"Not exactly the same. They're all different, like how your tits look different from hers. But the function is the same."

"And what is that function?" I ask, no longer just feeling the warmth in my belly, but between my legs as well. "What does it do?"

"A couple of things," Silas says, placing his hand on my thigh. My nipples tighten, pushing against the thin fabric of my shirt. He leans close to my ear. "But the best one, the one that's in our lesson, is to fuck."

Fuck.

I've heard the word—Silas said it when he saw me. It's a curse, but obviously more. His hand runs down my leg. "Right now, he's going to fuck her mouth."

I watch as he does just that. The girl gets down on her knees, then takes the aggressive cock in her hands like a woman dying of hunger. She dotes on it, stroking, licking and lathing it with her tongue. She swallows it greedily, and the man, he thrusts his hips upward like he's keeping pace with a beating drum. My pulse maintains the same rhythm and Silas' hand continues to glide up and down my leg, fanning the flames of the fire burning inside of me.

"He's going to come," Silas says, licking his lips. "See how his body is all tense? He's about to come in her mouth."

I don't know what that means, but I see the man's body shift from erratic jerking motions to a stiff rigidity, his hips losing their pace. His hand moves to the back of her head and he shoves it down over his cock. A moment later, he jerks twice, and she breaks free of his grip, tilting her head back. Something white and slippery drips over her lips. She licks it and moans before grinning coyly at him.

Silas turns off the video and looks at me while continuing to touch me. My mind is still trying to process it all, but my body seems to understand. It's hot and flustered. Pulse beating in every part of my body, including between my legs. What those two did was natural. Animalistic. It was based on want and desire. It was raw and rough.

I can see why people, why Rex, would want that in his life.

"How did that make you feel?" Silas asks.

"Weird. Like it was wrong to watch such a private moment between two people, but…"

"But what?" he encourages.

"Like I wanted to do it too."

"It made you horny."

"What's that?"

"What you're feeling." He bends and plants a kiss on my neck, warm and lingering. My nipples grow even harder and all I want is for him to touch me like that man touched that woman. Like Levi touched me during our session. "It feels good, doesn't it?"

"Yes, but it also kind of hurts." I think about how bad the first slaps of Levi's palm felt against my skin, how bad they hurt, but then, how they started to feel different—good.

He looks up at me with those pretty green eyes. "I can take that hurt away if you want."

"You can?"

He nods, inching his hand up my side. He brushes the edge of my breast and then cups it with his palm. The feeling is overwhelming, so good, but so intense. These men, Silas, Elon, Levi, they've all been teasing me, taunting me and I feel like I'm going to explode.

His head tilts, and he kisses me, lips firm and hot, tongue

licking against mine. My body feels like it's throbbing, all of it, every inch, and every bit of self-consciousness is gone when Silas' hand flattens over my belly and dips beneath my jeans. "Oh," I cry, when he reaches the crux of my legs. His thumb brushes hotly against a bundle of nerves, sending shivers up my spine. "Oh god."

"Does that feel good?" he asks, kissing along my neck.

"Y—yes."

He does it again, this time pressing down and rotating the pad of his thumb in a small circle.

"Silas," I breathe, burying my head into his chest.

"Almost there," he says, holding me to him. I'm so wound up—beyond wound up—I'm tight like a wire coil, and when he touches me one more time, it springs spreading through my body in pulsing, delicious waves.

I ride out the aftershocks tucked against his body. His hand strokes my hair. "How was that?"

"Unbelievable."

I draw away from him and accidentally brush against the front of his pants. He grimaces and shifts in his seat. I stare down at the bulge—at his cock—that I now understand a little better.

"Oh," I say, feeling foolish. "You're horny too."

He laughs. "A little."

"I'm not sure I can do what that woman did on the show. Not yet."

"I'm not asking you to."

"But I could do to you what you just did to me." I reach for the button on his pants. He doesn't stop me.

"Imogene—"

I don't listen to whatever argument he has. Silas has taught me something today—a true lesson about men and women, one that Anex has discussed before. Our bodies have needs. They have wants. And it hurts if we don't take care of it. I pull his cock out from under the fabric. At first glance, he doesn't seem as big as the man in the film, but he's still thick and warm. Harder along the shaft than I could imagine, but softer at the tip than seems possible.

I run my thumb over the top and a small amount of fluid comes out.

"What is that?" I ask, rolling it between my fingers.

"Semen," he says, resting his head on the back of the seat. His chest rises and falls. "Like what was in the woman's mouth."

"Oh." I frown and dart my tongue out, swiping it over the rounded top. Silas grunts and I say, "It's salty."

"Mmhmm." His arm extends and his fingers thread through my hair. "Show me what you learned."

I make some fumbles, I can tell, because Silas grimaces and gives me little directions, like telling me to lick my palm first or to go slower or than faster, or to cup his balls in my hand. I lick and suck. I stroke and fondle. When he swells big and hard, I suddenly understand the urge to take him in my mouth, but I don't. He fucks my hand, hips rising, and jerking against my palm. I like the way he feels, soft but strong. I like the way Silas sounds right before he comes. His breathing is shallow, and his nose scrunches up and his fingers wind tight in my hair. He comes with a low groan, white, hot, fluid dripping down my hand.

"Oh," I say, realizing how much tidier this was in the movie. No mess. Silas pulls his shirt over the back of his head with one hand and uses it to wipe up my sticky hand.

"Did I do that right?" I ask.

He grins, contentment spread across his flushed face. "Perfect."

I smile back, feeling a strange sense of pride. "Thank you for showing me." I understand that this is my road to enlightenment, to a higher place, where I'll be ready to stand at Rex's side.

"It's my pleasure, Imogene," he says, "and my job."

"You're very good at your job."

"I know." He laughs and drops a kiss on my mouth, and I say a silent blessing to The Way for putting such a man in charge of my training.

21

Levi

I enter The Center at five 'til two. It's almost time for Imogene's break. Calling it lunch would be under the assumption she eats a mid-day meal. She doesn't. I checked her logs.

She's at the front desk when I walk in. Her new haircut is a drastic departure from the style of most women her age, but it's startlingly attractive. It's soft around her face and curls a little without so much weight. Her face lights up when she sees me.

"Hi. I didn't know you were coming in today." She checks the paper calendar on her desk. "Do you have an appointment? I don't see you on the list."

"No," I reply, leaning on the counter. "You go on a break in a few minutes, right?"

Her eyebrows furrow. "Is it time for another session?"

The session. It's all I've thought of for days. Obsessively. But since I can't lock her in a room and inflict Corrections on her each and every day, I've made it my job to know everything about Imogene. I've read through her journals—including the old ones—studied her food logs. I know she's completely devoted to Anex and The Way. She also feels immense guilt about her mother's Regression. I know that this is why both Anex and Rex chose her. That guilt and shame makes her compliant. What they don't see is that she is strong. Very strong. The journals are meticulous. She documents every calorie she consumes, every thought that comes into her mind, every action she performs. Her Corrections are consistent, all part of her faith. That strength is also what fuels the defiant streak. The one I have been asked to eradicate.

"No session. Not yet. I just thought maybe we could talk."

"Oh, right." She seems surprised. "Well, yes. I do have a break coming up."

"Come outside with me," I suggest. "We can go for a walk."

I wait for Imogene outside and a few minutes later she walks out the front door of The Center. She's anxious, fussing with the waist of her gray dress. This is understandable. Until a few days ago, she'd never been alone with a male. Now she's Ordered, and I'm not her future mate. The difference, though, is that I'm one of Rex's confidants. That gives me leeway that most wouldn't have.

"How about we head over to Ash Park?"

She nods and I lead her to a quiet greenspace on the edge of the University. I notice the looks from the students passing by and I'm certain she does too, although she doesn't show it. Her lack of insecurity is another signal of her dedication. I know our hair and clothing seem odd, foreign to outsiders, but we're used to it. Anex has taught us not to fear this difference but to embrace it. It's all just another step toward The Way.

I point to a bench under a large tree, and we sit side by side. I reach into my backpack and pull out a container, and remove the lid. There is meat, cheese, and bread inside.

"Eat," I direct, handing it to her.

She shakes her head. "I can't eat that."

"You can and will."

"This is double my allotment for lunch." She glances around anxiously. "What if someone sees me? It's bad enough that I'm sitting with a man that I am not Ordered to, but this? They'll think I've gone full Regressive."

"No, they won't. I brought you here because no one is watching."

That's probably not true. Anex has eyes everywhere. But in this case, it doesn't matter. He knows I'm here and who I'm with.

"It's way over my calories. Too much fat. And bread? God." Her expression is one of horror. "You've seen my logs. I never cheat."

"I know you don't, and you shouldn't consider this cheating, at least not any more than that new haircut." I resist the urge to tug the ends of her hair. "The goal here is to win over Rex who is resistant to the methods of The Way. Controlling your calories is a way to reach enlightenment and breaking that is one sacrifice you will have to make to successfully draw him back in."

Imogene picks up the cheese and looks at it like its poison. "I can't."

No wonder Anex is obsessed with her. She's the poster child for The Way. I think about it for a moment and say, "What if we come up with some kind of balance. Eat the food that I supply you and in return you can do something that weighs out the actions."

"I like that idea."

"Good. What is something you think would be an appropriate trade off?"

She thinks it over. "How about for every meal I have, we add something to our sessions. Something to help me win over Rex."

"I think that's acceptable. Just make sure you continue to document and log everything—don't neglect that habit."

Imogene pops the piece of cheese in her mouth and slowly chews it as if she's savoring every bite. Fast or slow doesn't matter to me. If this is going to truly work, I need her to put some weight on her thin frame before she sees Rex again.

"This is because he likes women with bigger breasts, isn't it?" she asks suddenly.

"What?" I sputter, feeling the heat rise to my cheeks.

Her own skin is pink, but she continues anyway. "Silas showed me some film. The women in it were much more voluptuous than I am. Breasts, hips, behind and thighs." She nibbles on bread. "Even Elon told me I was too skinny. I didn't understand it, since I've always followed Anex's policies, but now that I've seen some examples, it makes more sense."

I'm not privy to the film Silas showed her, but I can only imagine. I slowly form my response. "There are different features valued in the secular world. As with everything else, Rex finds them alluring."

She glances down at her chest and sighs. "I suspect that no matter how much bread I eat, it will never increase my bust size."

She looks so forlorn at this idea that I feel compelled to comfort her. "No, your... bust size is adequate. Pleasing even." Her cheeks redden even further, and I quickly add, "Rex will surely find you suitable once he actually pays attention."

"I'll do whatever it takes," she says dutifully. "And I trust you to Guide me."

"I will make it my priority," I tell her. "Rex's happiness is important to me, just as your journey to enlightenment. I think with some hard work, we can accomplish both."

The wind blows just as she takes another bite of her lunch, sending a strand of her hair into her eyes. Impulsively, I reach out and catch it with my finger, pushing it off her forehead and tucking it behind her ear. It's a gentle gesture that brings warmth in my chest and is at conflict with the role I played during our session. If I am going to fulfill my duties to Anex, I will need to make sure that my head and body are focused.

Now is not the time to get distracted.

* * *

Once Imogene's lunch break is over, we walk back to The Center. The longer we're out in the secular world, I can feel eyes following us. Men mostly. I think back to the night before the Order, when Imogene was harassed in the alley. We'd stumbled on her by accident. Thank The Way. Who knows what would have happened to her if we hadn't been there.

I'd heard what that man said to her, that the efforts of hiding her body didn't work. That it only appealed to men more—wondering what secrets lie beneath such modest clothing.

Never have I heard such truth.

"Thank you for bringing me lunch," Imogene says, when we're back at the office. "It was delicious."

"You're welcome." I glance at the schedule board over her head. "I think I'm going to take a meeting."

She smiles and says, "I'll mark you down."

Meetings are held constantly at The Center. I'm a member of the Men's Group; VRS. The letters stand for Viri Regum Sunt. Men Are Kings. There are daily meetings here and inside Serendee. Sometimes I even lead them, as it's a skill that has come easily to me as I grow and learn The Way. Anex says that my devotion and loyalty is my gift, but after the last week I'm feeling unsteady in my path. What we're doing to and with Imogene feels different. Altering this female—physically and mentally—seems to go against the teachings I've studied so thoroughly. Women are supposed to seek enlightenment and lose the need for vanity and for outside approval. The opposite of what I've spent the week doing.

But Anex asked me to do this. And I trust him. She trusts him.

I feel weak when I walk into the small room, and I hope that none of the men notice. I know them all. The only access to VRS is to be a long-term member of Serendee and pass through several stages of Anex's approval.

"Levi," Aaron greets me as I walk in. He's about ten years older and has been a mentor since I started coming to the meetings. "How are you today?"

"Feeling the need for a little reinforcement."

"You're working on a task for Anex, aren't you?"

"Yes, a challenging one."

"You need Refortification." His smile conveys sympathy, only confirming my weakness.

"Yes. I do."

Fortification is a process of The Way. Strengthening our mental and spiritual walls against attacks from the outside. It's how we are able to withstand assaults of gluttony, sex, greed, and the pleasures of secular men. Except, I don't always withstand those. Not in this job. I intentionally fed Imogene more food to make her body appear more pleasing to the male eye. Elon purchased her clothing to accentuate her figure. Silas taught her how to please a man using modern technology. Margaret showed her how to use tricks and paint to change her face.

All of these efforts have worked. Too well. I find myself... thinking of Imogene differently. I find my brain and body reacting differently as well. I can't stop thinking of her panties tucked in the back of a drawer in my room.

Hence the need for Refortification.

The room fills, and Aaron stands at the front. A big screen is behind him.

"All of you are here because you want to become stronger, more capable men. You want to be protectors. I know that each of you has that ability inside of you, but to get there, you have to dig past the influences that infiltrate us from the secular world. Past the innate emotions that cling to us biologically. The doubt. The worry. The fear. We must embrace our inner male. The true meaning of who we are."

Remotely, he lowers the lights and turns on the TV. It's a video of people on the street, in a bar. It's all smiles and radiance. Loud music. The women are all dressed provocatively. The camera lingers on one woman as man after man approaches. She rejects each one with a grin. Finally, a man of her pleasing draws her attention. He's handsome. Obviously strong. A winner's smile. She touches his hand, leans close, whispers in his ear.

Aaron stops the film. "This woman is a skilled predator—not because she wants to be, but because she has to be. Society has taught her to seek her own mate, because she doesn't trust these men to protect her. She must dress in revealing clothing, paint her face. She is forced into this position by society. The result is insecurity. Indulgency. A reduction in moral standards. It is why we allow Anex to pick our mates—and to determine when we, as men, are ready." Aaron looks around the room. "The women are already there. It's innate. They are born with a need to be protected. And sure, men are raised to protect—in a greedy, self-absorbed way. It's nature, borne from the hormones that run through our systems—an overwhelming desire to fuck and spread our seed."

The men around me nod. This point has been repeated over and over. Our urge to not just have sex, but to fuck, to claim a woman or women, relentlessly, has been reinforced in every VRS meeting I've attended. It's not the women's fault. It's ours. And VRS is the reminder that we must be better. We shouldn't want a woman that shows her flesh easily or focuses on the outside. We should help them understand that their power comes from the inside. Anex took away that conflict between men and women by Ordering us with a mate of his choosing. If and when we're ready.

When the meeting is over, Aaron walks up and asks, "Do you feel better?"

"I'm more centered," I reply. "Prepared for the challenges ahead."

"Good," he says, resting his hand on my shoulder. "Anex chose you for a reason. Your walls are strong. Your foundation even more so. And when your task is complete, you will be rewarded by The Way."

His words reassure me even more and I walk out of the room, passing Imogene at her desk. She gives me a small wave and carries on with her work. She doesn't know it, but she needs me, and I will do my very best to keep her on the path to righteousness.

22

Imogene

I've been on my new meal plan for several days when Elon enters my room. It's still weird to say that, my room. It's surreal. All of it. The room. The extra food. The clothes, oh and yeah, the handsome man who is not my mate, standing over my bed. That's surreal.

"Get dressed," he says, his voice curt. "And wear something from the new wardrobe. Jeans, a skirt, something secular. Sexy."

I flip the cover of my journal and place it on the bedside table. "Where are we going?"

"Out."

Beyond that, he doesn't clarify, leaving the room as abruptly as he entered. I pick through my closet for what I hope is an appropriate outfit. Sexy. I only have vague notions what that means. I assume it means all the parts of our body that we were told to hide from males because of their weakness for skin and flesh. After watching the video with Silas and feeling his hands on me, I understand that urge a little better.

Now that Silas has shown me what is between a man's legs, how it works and feels, I can't help but wonder about Elon and Levi.

About Rex. Even though I know I shouldn't, I have the desire to see them the same way; caught in the throes of euphoria. Warm and sticky on my hand. The sensation from that day—the burn—it hasn't left my belly. It's a low smolder all the time—ready to be stoked into flame.

I settle on a pair of tight black pants and a pale yellow top that clings against my body. There's a sweater to wear over it and a pair of boots with a slight heel. I take a minute to attend to my hair and face—attempting to replicate Margaret's designs. I'm not very good at it.

Elon waits in the living room, eyes glued to his phone. His gray shirt matches his eyes and is tucked into dark jeans. He doesn't see me at first and I study him; the muscle at the back of his jaw, like always, is clenched tight. He always seems angry and annoyed, like nothing I do is right, like I'm a complete nuisance. Maybe I am. Who wants to babysit a grown woman who has been rejected by her mate?

"I'm ready," I announce. "Is this outfit okay?"

He briefly glances up, then back down at his phone, then back again. Those gray eyes assess me with such intensity that I feel like I can't breathe.

"Take off the sweater," he demands. I slide my arms out of each sleeve. His gaze sweeps over my skin. "You can wear that outside, but indoors, take it off. You need to acclimate to people seeing your skin."

"Okay," I say. "Anything else?"

"Remove the bra. Show off those tits."

I blink. The shirt is so sheer I could see the pattern of lace beneath the fabric. Without it... "Are you sure?"

"Are you asking me to repeat myself, Little Lamb?"

I grimace at the nickname. I know he's mocking me—calling me a sheep. I reach under the back of my shirt and unhook the bra. Then drop the straps down my arms, removing it while keeping on the shirt. My nipples are already hard from the shifting around, and the tank has a slight rib in the fabric, creating friction that only makes it worse. Elon's eyes glide over me and he nods—granting me silent approval.

"Are the others coming?" I ask, balling up the bra and tucking it under a pillow on the couch.

"No. They had to work."

"At night?"

"Serendee's business doesn't end at sunset."

"Can you tell me where we're going?"

"To dinner." He opens the door that leads out of the suite. "At a restaurant downtown. You need to get used to being around more people."

I walk quickly to keep up, but as usual, he seems annoyed to be in my presence. It doesn't get any better when we get in the car. His hands wrapped around the steering wheel in a death grip. The longer we drive, the more uncomfortable I become. Spending time with this man is unbearable. He's rude and authoritative. He may have been sent by Anex to train me, but he has no right to treat me like dirt.

My irritation grows as he turns into a busy parking lot. He gets out and slams the door, walking around to open mine. His movements are jerky and curt. I've finally had enough of his attitude and when I stand, I ask, "What's your problem?"

"What?" He glares down at me and heaves the door shut.

"I said, what is your problem—with me?"

"I don't have a problem with you."

I blink and shake my head. "Okay, sure, just lie to me." I spot the door of what I assume is the restaurant we're going to and head that way.

"I don't have a problem," he says again, closing the gap in two long strides. "I don't give a shit about you." His words should hurt, but instead it's just a relief to hear the truth. "Anex gave me a job, a second job, because I already have one, but I'm doing it."

"I'm glad to know you're dedicated to The Way, Elon, but that doesn't mean you need to act petulant and rude. If you're teaching me how to behave in public settings, with my future mate, I should think you would cut the bad attitude and act civilized."

His eyes narrow, and I wait for a retort, but there isn't one. He simply pushes past me and walks into the restaurant. I follow, prepared to continue to push him, but two steps inside and I stop, unable to do anything but gape at the room in front of me. Music fills the entrance, along with the low murmur of conversation. There are people everywhere, clustered near the door and at all the tables. The phone rings at the pedestal just inside the door. My senses are on overload, visual, auditory, and god, it smells so good. My mouth waters and I try to take in everything at once.

Through it all, I sense Elon's imposing presence, and when my feet seem stuck to the floor, his arm loops through mine and he drags me forward to follow the woman from the pedestal.

"Are all restaurants like this?" I ask, leaning into his side. I'm aware of people watching us. It's a different sort of scrutiny than what I'm used to. Typically, people stare at my long dress and pinned up hair, but the man across from me won't stop staring at my chest. Two women around my age, who split their attention between smiling at Elon and glaring at my nipples. I tug the sweater tighter, but it's futile. "This loud and busy?"

"No," he says, "but you need to immerse yourself. It seems like a good choice. Plus, they have amazing steaks."

"Hope this suits your needs," the woman says when we reach a booth. She gives Elon a small smile. Why are these women always smiling at him? Can't they tell he's a terrible person?

I move to sit across from Elon, but he grabs me by the waist and pulls me down next to him.

"It does. Thank you," he says, ignoring her and glancing down at my sweater. Oh, right.

I remove it, tucking it next to me. If he approves of the gesture, he doesn't show it, instead calling over a waiter and ordering drinks. I'm overwhelmed by the menu—the list of foods I've never seen. Despite my work with Levi, I can't help but try to count the calories and feel a sense of guilt over the gluttony. When the waiter asks what I want and I'm unable to respond, Elon takes the menu from me and orders for the two of us. As annoyed as I am with him, I can't help but be fascinated by his actions. He moves with such ease and determination, like this world is just another layer of clothing.

"Now that we've clarified that I'm just a job to you, then let's get down to business," I say, breaking the silence. "How did you learn to do this? Leaving Serendee to do secular things like going to fancy restaurants and knowing what to wear and what to order?"

"Anex asked me to, and I did it."

I frown. "But what happened? What made you do this? Because it's not usual for the men in Serendee, any more than what I am being asked to do is normal for the women."

He takes a swallow of his drink and sighs. "When I turned eighteen, Anex asked me, Levi, and Silas to join him and Rex in his private quarters. He said that now that we were of age, he needed people he could trust to work for the businesses that fund Serendee."

"There's a business that funds the community? What about Anex's family money? And the classes at The Center? Or the profits from the farmer's market?"

The look he gives me is filled with superiority. It's been taught that the classes alone bring in enough income to support any needs we have on a cash basis. Obviously, that, along with so many other things I was raised to believe, is not entirely true.

"There are several businesses—all of which bring in substantial funds."

"Oh. And you just accepted your new role?"

"It was hard at first," he admits. "I was a little like you, wide-eyed and overwhelmed, but it also wasn't my first time in the secular world. Being friends with Rex allowed certain perks."

"Like what?"

He shrugs. "Vacations. Food. Access to technology."

"You've had that all along?"

"Not entirely. As we got older, Anex allowed more exposure and it felt normal. I'd known that Rex was special—he's Anex's son—but he realized that we were special too. He'd been teaching us individually long before we were of age. He knew that we had a calling and that exposing us to these small indulgences was a test of loyalty."

"You obviously passed."

The corners of his eyes tighten. "Enough that he trusted us with learning about the business, and now, to try to handle this situation with Rex."

"Do you feel bad about that? Going behind your friend's back and manipulating him?"

"Rex is like a brother—family—and sometimes you have to make hard decisions when it comes to family." Our food arrives, and he orders another drink. I stare at the pooling butter under my asparagus.

"Eat," he says, noticing my hesitation. He digs right in, cutting into his steak. "Anex taught us that the feeling you get when you're trying to decide if something is right or wrong—that's The Way nudging you in the right direction."

"I had to make a hard decision about my mother," I say. "When she was still here and was...acting Regressive, she tried to get me to leave with her."

With a knife and fork in each hand, he looks up at me in surprise. "She did?"

"Yes. She begged me to go with her when she ran. I didn't want to leave her, but I couldn't."

"Why not?"

"Serendee is all I've ever known. I was old enough to realize that if we left, we could never come back." He nods while popping a piece of meat in his mouth. I add, "But that wasn't all. Deep down, I have always believed in The Way and if I stayed, Anex would have an important position for me. At first, I thought it was working at The Center, but obviously it was much more than that."

"Way more," he agrees. "You think you're truly ready to do what it takes to bring Rex home?"

I don't need to think. I feel the little nudge that he was talking about, The Way, helping me make the right decision. Without hesitation, I reply, "Yes."

                                      * * *

Of course, I didn't realize he meant immediately.

Elon paid for our dinner with his thick roll of cash and led us down the street to a club. More money exchanges hands between him and the guy at the door, then the bartender, and it's just another difference between here and Serendee that I don't fully understand.

"How did you learn to use money like that?" I ask, watching the roll disappear in his pocket. I know about money—and how secular society is ruled by their ever-loving desire to have more. I've never had any of my own. Just the credits we're given to spend in the community.

"We use cash only for the business, but you get used to it." He hands me a glass with a wide rim and red liquid inside the color of a ruby. He nods to a set of stairs. "Come on."

I follow close, not wanting to lose him. Not that it would be easy. His height and broad shoulders sets him apart. The further we get into the club, the more I notice people—men—watching me as I pass through the crowd. Can they tell it's my first time in a place like this?

"Stay close," he says, pulling me against his side. I can't help but inhale his warm, spicy scent. "I should have made you keep on the sweater."

"What? Why?"

"Because," he shoots a dark-haired guy at the bar a look of death, "because your tits are impossible to ignore and I'm not going to be able to leave your side all night."

"Stop," I say, my cheeks heating up. "They see some naïve little girl that shouldn't be here."

"Yeah, that they'd love to defile six different ways."

Now my entire body turns red. I'm sure of it. "I doubt it. You said it yourself, I'm too skinny for secular men."

"I also said you have nice tits." His eyes sweep over me. "You've put on a little weight. It looks good."

That may be the first and only nice thing he's said about me.

Well, other than the tits one, and I'm not exactly sure that's a compliment.

"It doesn't matter," he says, resting his hand on my lower back, protectively. Warm tingles spread up my spine. "We won't be down here with the riff-raff."

"Where are we going?" Someone bumps into me and my drink sloshes.

He looks up the stairs. "Up there. To a private area."

I follow him up, high above the swarming crowd. There's another large man guarding the top, but he unlatches the rope the second he sees Elon, giving us access to the upper floor. The area is lofted with a second bar and raised platforms establishing distinct sections divided by wispy curtains and strung lights.

Elon steps up to one of the platforms and pushes aside the curtain. The first thing I notice is beautiful women sprawled about comfortable looking couches. The second? Rex.

My future mate is so handsome it hurts to look at him. Golden-haired and bright eyed. He sits on a leather chair with one of the women on his lap. She's got her nose nuzzled against his neck, under his ear, and her hand on his upper thigh. I stare at the two of them, stomach burning, as his finger strokes the outside of her breast.

No new outfits, no makeover, none of the upgrades I've been given in the last week will give me what I need to compete with that.

"I think I'm going to puke," I say, spinning around.

Elon grabs me with both hands. "No, you aren't. You're going to go in there and claim your mate."

"He doesn't want me. He wants... that."

"Then give it to him."

I peek over my shoulder at the sexy, gorgeous woman perched on top of Rex. She's smooth and sleek, dressed in a leather skirt and a top that shows more skin than it covers. She oozes confidence and experience. I can tell by the way she touches him, by how she reacts to his touch. She's a woman that can fulfill his every desire. I have no clue what to do.

"I'm not ready," I tell Elon, knowing that I'll never be ready.

He places two fingers under my chin and lifts my gaze upward. I can tell he wants to say something, but he struggles to find the words. Finally, he grinds out, "You're a beautiful woman, Imogene. You're smart and have intense perseverance. Anex believes in you. I believe in you. Don't be afraid to get what rightfully belongs to you."

Now that is a compliment. A strange compulsion runs through me and I skim my fingers along Elon's strong jaw and say, "Thank you."

I don't falter this time, following Elon onto the platform. Rex's eyes light up when he sees his friend, but then narrow when he spots me. It's not anger, I don't think, it's confusion.

"Babe, move," he tells the woman, pushing her off his lap. She appears disgruntled, but shifts over. He stands and shakes hands with his friend. Then rakes his eyes over my body, lingering on my chest, and a small smile plays on his lips. "Well, aren't you a pretty little thing."

"Thank you." A little thrill runs through me.

"Elon brought you up here for me?"

"He did."

"I'm Rex." He thrusts his hand out. "What's your name?"

I stare at his hand, but years of programming kick in. I touch my forehead and bow slightly. "Imogene—your Ordered."

His eyes flick to Elon and then back to me, before he laughs loud and boisterous. "This is a joke, right?" Again, he looks at Elon. "Are you fucking with me? You dressed her up, took off her bra, and slapped some paint on her face. That doesn't change what she is inside." He glances at me again and barks out, "baaa, little sheep."

"This isn't a joke," Elon says, eyes narrowing in irritation. "And it's time for you to stop running from your responsibilities."

"Unlikely, but thanks for the laugh." He reaches out to slap Elon on the back, but his friend blocks his hand.

"Imogene is willing to do what it takes to get your approval."

"I sincerely doubt that," Rex says. "Nice try, though. Tell my father it'll take more than a slutty dress and a haircut to play his game."

He brushes past us, arm jostling my shoulder. I fall into Elon, who keeps me from totally wiping out. As he rights me, he says, "Let me go talk to him."

"No." I take a deep breath. "He's my Ordered. I'll talk to him."

Elon grimaces, but relents. "Don't remind him that you're his Ordered and don't use any terms associated with The Way. He wants secular, not a reminder of Serendee."

I nod and I walk across the loft to the bar. The bartender pushes a shot across to Rex and he drinks it quickly. Then orders another, paying for both with his own thick roll of cash.

When he spots me walking over, he laughs cruelly. "Don't you ever give up?"

"No. Not on you. I believe we're supposed to be together."

Rex knocks back the shot. "It's not going to happen, Imogene." He says my name with a sneer. "You're not my type." His hand shoots out and circles my arm. "Too skinny." He spins me around. "Flat ass. And you head is way too far up my father's prostate."

He walks away, but not back toward the platform, down a hallway. My eyes burn from his insults, but I know if he'll just give me a chance, I can win him over. Anex has faith in me and I have faith in The Way.

I follow him down the dark hallway, away from the music and crowd. He ducks through a door and when I step through, we're on an iron balcony that overlooks the alley below. Sulfur tickles my nostrils and Rex leans against the railing, smoking a rolled joint. The scent that wafts over is herbal, warm, the kind that wafts over the fields during Anex's birthday weekend, and when he looks up at me, he shakes his head.

"I know you're not this fucking stupid."

"I'm not stupid. Just determined."

"You don't want me, Imogene. I'm not who you think I am. I'm not some fucking savior." He takes a long drag and then blows out a cloud of smoke. "Sure, I'll play the role, convincing Serendee that I can continue my father's vision, but that person? You really won't like him." His words are hard—harsh—and I'm self-aware enough to hear the threat underneath, but Anex sent me here. I have no choice. "Leave while you have a chance, Imogene."

"I can't."

"Because my father said so?"

"Yes. He ordered it," I say, immediately regretting using the word.

"I assume he ordered those clothes and that haircut—the plumpness in your face." His fingers run down my cheek. He noticed that I've gained weight? Rex may have been paying more attention than I realized. "Does that devotion transfer to me? Will you do anything I ask?"

"Yes."

His hand is still on my face, his thumb stroking up and down my cheek. His blue eyes are so distant, so cold, that I feel a chill run down my spine. He rubs the pad of this thumb over my bottom lip, and says, "Fine. Get on your knees."

His tone is so abrupt and his request so strange I blink and ask, "What?"

"Get on your knees, Imogene." His tongue darts out and his hand lands on my shoulder, pushing me down. My knees hit the metal balcony floor. "That's an order."

His hand cups his crotch and images from the video I watched with Silas pops in my head. I know what this is. What he wants. My eyes are level with his cock, and he doesn't hesitate to unzip his pants and reach inside, exposing his length. Oh god. I flinch at the size and look up. "Rex..."

"Shut up." His voice takes an even harder edge. "You're the one that wanted this. You pursued me. I told you to leave me the fuck alone, but you didn't. You want to be my mate? Well, open that hot little mouth and fulfill your goddam duties."

His fingers wind through my hair, rough and twisting. The action dashes any hope of getting out of this—that he's just messing with me. His cock swells, a sign that he's excited, that he likes it like this, and that's when it hits me. This is my mate. This is what he likes, and that means, by the applications of The Way, I will perform as he desires, no matter how uncomfortable or demeaning it is.

I exhale and conjure up the video, thankful that Silas had the foresight to show it to me. I mimic what Silas liked when I touched him with my hands, running them up and down the shaft. Rex is warm and heavy—wider than Silas. I feel him grow with my touch, getting impossibly bigger, and like before, heat explodes in my lower belly, burning with my own want.

"That's it, Imogene." He tilts my head upward. "Open that pretty mouth. Show me why my father picked you."

I blink, trying to understand that statement. Does he think I've done this before? With Anex? There's no time to ask—he doesn't want to know. He's pushing his cock against my lips before I can open them, smearing fluid. I lick my lips. He's saltier than Silas, his cum thicker. I close my mouth over the head, sucking the rest off with the twist of my tongue. His hand tightens in my hair and he leans back on one elbow. Groaning, he mumbles, "Goddamn. You're a greedy little bitch, aren't you? You like the way I taste?"

"Yes," I tell him, knowing that it's what he wants to hear.

I'm not sure how to handle his talk, the harsh words and name calling. It's shocking and unlike any way anyone has ever spoken to me before. It's not like it was with Silas. It's humiliating. Shameful. In contrast to his words, his movements are slow, precise, different from the video. Pushing the tip past my lips and slowing inching further down my throat. "Ah, mmmm... yeah..." he exhales. "Thatta girl."

It's a morsel of approval, and I grab onto it, willing to do anything to make this end. I use the moves I learned from the video, running my hand and tongue up and down his length. I fondle his balls. I lick the head. I refuse to look him in the eye as I take him deep and try not to gag, but he's not satisfied, and his big hand slides down to the back of my head holding it in place as he picks up the pace, pounding his cock into my mouth. I try to squirm away but he tightens his grip.

"Don't even think about it," he threatens, hips slamming into me, "don't stop. Don't you goddam stop. You want to play with the big kids, well suck it." He fucks harder, erratic and holding me by the neck. I don't think I can take it anymore, when it grows faster, and his movements turn erratic. I know that the clench of his jaw, and the loss of words, mean that it's almost over. I just want this over. Please let it be over.

My prayers are answered when a groan rumbles in his chest and his hips lurch forward, and hot, salty, come pools in my throat. I jerk back, nausea rolling over me. He glares down and says, "If you puke that up, I'll just do it again."

Closing my eyes, I force it down, fighting the urge to expel every drop of him. When it's settled and I look back at him again, he's tucking himself back in his pants. "I shouldn't be surprised daddy knew how to pick a girl that could service a man like that. How many times have you done that before?"

I cough and fight a wave of nausea. "None. Never. I swear."

His eyebrow arches skeptically. "Well, that's some outstanding beginner's luck." The sound of his zipper echoes in my ears, and he adds, "Get her the fuck out of here."

I turn as he passes me and spot Elon in the doorway. His eyes are dark, and his mouth set disapprovingly. How long has he been here? How much did he see? The humiliation I feel multiplies and the semen in my belly threatens to come back up. The tears I've held back this whole time let loose.

"Elon?" I say, my voice small. It was one thing to experience that embarrassment, the violation, with the person inflicting it. It's a whole other one to know that someone was watching. Especially, for some reason, Elon.

"He—" I start, but he strides over, lifting me off the ground with a jerk. I wiggle away. "Did you know that was going to happen? Is that why you brought me here?"

His lack of response is all I need to know the truth. He dressed me, fattened me up and delivered me like a lamb to slaughter.

23

Rex

"My apartment is a few blocks away if you want a little privacy," the girl says, her breath tickling my ear. Her hand lays flat on my stomach, and her breasts press against my arm. I wait for the stir of arousal. It doesn't come, not like earlier when Imogene had me in her mouth, tongue gliding over my shaft, swallowing me whole.

That memory causes a twitch.

"How about you get me a fresh drink," I say, pushing her off my lap and shoving my glass at her. She frowns, and I give her a quick grin. "Thanks, babe."

She walks off, hips swinging, her skirt so short it gives me the barest hint of the curve of her ass cheeks underneath. I tilt my head to get a better glimpse, but a figure steps between us, blocking my view. I look up and see Elon glaring down at me.

"You're back," I say, making a show of looking behind him. "Come alone, or did you plan another ambush?"

"She's your Mate," he says, dropping into the leather seat across from mine. "I figured since you weren't coming home, I'd bring her to you."

"As unexpected as it was, I admit it did turn out pretty pleasurable." I throw my arm over the back of the chair. "She did better than expected."

"You had expectations?" he asks doubtfully.

"Although the submissive streak usually turns me off, with a pretty mouth like that, it was hard to resist." I shrug. "I needed to see what she would do."

Elon snorts. "A test. Father like son."

"A test she failed, Elon." My short-skirted friend returns with my drink. I take it from her, and she moves to perch back on my lap, but I wave her off. "You dressed her up like one of these bitches, but she's got no more spine than anyone else in Serendee."

"You mean like that girl you just brushed off? She'd let you fuck her right here, in front of the whole club." He cuts his eyes over to her, where she's dancing by the balcony railing. "You pretend like you want a strong, secular, female, but what you really want is to piss off your father."

I tip the glass back and consume the drink in one swallow and slam it on the table. "You're right. That girl over there will do anything I ask of her, but the difference is that she doesn't know Anex. She wouldn't be doing it for Anex or for some higher calling to The Way. She'd do it because she thinks I'm good looking, rich, well hung." She looks over and I wink, causing her to smile back. "With her it's just fun—not obligation."

"A Mate isn't an obligation," Elon says. "It's a gift—and Imogene..." he camps his mouth shut.

"Imogene what?" I ask, narrowing my eyes at him.

"She deserves better than you."

I laugh. "Ah, is that what this is about? You want to fuck her."

He shakes his head. "You're pathetic. Get your shit together, Rex. You can't run away from this, from her, or your father for much longer."

"No?" I ask, waving the girl over and making space for her to sit on my lap. "Despite what my father has implied, the end of the world isn't coming any time soon."

He stands. "No, but your world is. Your play time is up. It's up for all of us and the sooner you figure that out, the better."

He walks off, heading back down the stairs. The girl leans in but once he's gone; I push her aside. I don't care what Elon says. My father will not control my life—not the way he controlled my mother's and everyone else under his thumb. If he thinks a skinny little girl with puffy lips and shiny blonde hair is going to bring me back to the fold, Anex is dumber than I thought.

24

"Oh my," Margaret says, opening the door to her suite. She's wearing all white and her blond hair curled just over the top of her shoulders. "What happened to your eyes?"

"Allergies," I lie, sniffing for good effect. "Stuck my nose in a bunch of flowers yesterday. I've been a mess ever since."

It's a lie, obviously. I'd tried to beg off when Levi appeared that morning with the handwritten invitation. Margaret wanted me to come to her rooms for tea. I almost blurted that I'm going to need something a lot stronger to wash the taste of Rex out of my mouth, but bit my tongue and said yes.

You don't say no to one of Anex's spiritual mates.

"Well, let's get something to ease that irritation."

I follow her through her apartment. It's in the main house, just like mine, only a floor beneath. I'm starting to think this place is filled with little suites, one for each of Anex's inner circle. It's obvious that Margaret decorated her own—the colors are light and breezy. Her back windows are open to let in the fresh spring air. I'd spent the night crying and trying to reconcile what'd happened

147

between me and Rex. What he'd forced me to do in the cover of darkness. What Elon saw. Margaret's world, filled with brightness and light, is the opposite of that dark, gritty, confusing pain.

In the bright kitchen, I watch as Margaret opens the freezer and pulls out a few chunks of ice and places them in a bowl. "Fill that with water," she instructs. When I finish, she's standing at the island in the middle of the room, cucumber lying on the cutting board. Her hands move quickly, cutting the cucumber into slices. "Drop those into the ice." I do as I'm instructed, and she grins. "That should do the trick."

"Cucumbers?"

"For your eyes," she replies, strolling back into the living room. She crosses out to the balcony where there are lounge chairs and a table set up for tea. A plate of bakery cookies sits next to the tea service. "Lie back on that chair." She points to the one with the back that falls back. "Place the cucumbers on your eyelids. It'll take away the swelling and irritation."

It's an awkward position, lying out here with my eyes covered, but it feels good. I hear her sit in the chair next to mine, then filling our cups with tea. She asks if I like milk or sugar, offering honey from the hives down by the lake. Her voice is soothing and for the first time since I entered that club with Elon the night before, I start to feel better.

"How is your training going?" Margaret asks.

"It's... challenging," I admit, feeling the heat of tears building in my eyes again. Any fresh tears can be waved off as water from the cucumbers. "I'm definitely being tested."

"I'm sure you are."

I exhale and sit up, peeling off the cucumber. "May I speak freely?" I ask. "Confidentially?"

She nods. "Of course."

"I saw Rex last night."

Her eyebrow rises. "How did that go?"

"It was..." I have no idea how to even begin to describe what happened between us. He'd violated me. Used me. Made it very clear that he didn't want me. "It was complicated."

"Most powerful men are." She takes a sip of tea. "Did you try to make progress with him?"

"I tried. He was… aggressive. I don't think I was very effective."

"He's angry."

I sigh. "All the time. And distant. Even if I give him what he wants, he makes it very clear that he dislikes me and everything about me. Dislike is probably not a strong enough word. I'm doing my training—everything that's asked of me—but none of it seems to work."

"Anex would never set you on a journey without anticipating success. You know, it's my understanding that it was after Rex's mother died that he became so withdrawn and discontent. Over the years he rebelled against his father, and Anex gave him a little too much leeway in an attempt to soothe his pain."

I blink, stunned that Margaret would criticize Anex at all. "I doubt Anex could have managed it any differently. He was in pain, himself."

"True," Margaret says, tightening her finger around the handle of her cup, "but parenting children isn't the same thing as leading a flock." Her mouth forms a line. "If I may offer some advice—"

"Please," I reply, a bit too eagerly.

"Anex may think he knows what his son wants, but they've never seen eye to eye. I would focus on getting Rex to see you as a person—a mate—not just an obstacle. Rex is rebellious. Oppositional. He actively seeks the secular world and its women." She lifts her teacup to her mouth and says, "Giving him what he wants may not be the way to his spiritual truth."

"What does that mean?"

"Maybe you need to be a little less compliant. Maybe the way to win him over is by not being what his father wants, but by truly being what he wants."

"The clothes, the makeup and hair… I'm doing all that."

"It's not just the outside, Imogene. It's the attitude." She sets her cup on the table and picks up a cookie, nibbling on the edge. "Believe it or not, at first Anex and I didn't exactly get along."

"You didn't?"

"Nope. He totally rubbed me the wrong way. I thought he was pretentious and kind of full of it." My eyes widen in shock and she just laughs again. "I didn't understand him and, honestly, he didn't understand me. So, we started meeting up, taking these long walks and discussing—well, arguing—almost everything. Over time, we came to realize how charged the energy between us was. This difference fueled our relationship."

"That's amazing."

She reaches out and takes my hand. "I don't think the training you're being given is about just being able to meet Rex's secular desires. I think that there's more to it—something that will require you to dig deep and find your true self. Men like Anex and his son do not want the easy route."

I nod, finally understanding a little more. Going to Rex and giving in, caving to his demands and begging him to accept me. God. It was probably the exact thing he hates. Despite my clothing and hair, that was the behavior of a woman from Serendee. Not from the outside. No wonder he forced me into such humiliating submission. It was a test, and I failed.

"They seek strong women," Margaret continues. "They need that energy to balance them. They must be challenged to become better men, to be powerful leaders."

"I understand."

"You do?" she asks, head tilted in curiosity.

"Yes, I really think I do." She picks up the bowl of cucumbers and offers it to me, but I wave her off. "I'm good," I tell her.

If Rex wants a challenge, a woman that can meet his needs on a whole other level, I can be that person. I will be that person. I just need to figure out when and how.

As if she can see in my mind, Margaret says, "Anex's birthday celebration is next weekend. Rex should be there."

The birthday celebration. I'd forgotten. It's a full weekend of camping out in the back pasture. They put up tents and the adults spend the night. There are games and bonfires. Dancing and cake. Anex's birthday weekends are legendary, and it'll be my first year. "You think he'll come?"

"I know he will. Anex will demand it and since he's your Ordered, he will be required to stay in the tent with you." She grins. "All weekend."

"That gives me a week to prepare," I say, my mind already spinning with ideas. "I'm definitely going to be ready."

25

His fingers are somehow both delicate and strong. Firm but gentle. I watch, enthralled as he touches himself and then commands me to touch myself. I stare at him, confused, as warmth rushes across my skin.

"I can't do that."

"You can," Silas says propped up on his elbow and gazing down at me, his erect member hard between us, "because it is very important for you to understand what makes you feel good."

I'm lying next to him in his bed. I'd come to him for a lesson—something specific. Rex obviously doesn't respect a woman that simply obeys. That he made perfectly clear. He wants a woman of her own mind. I want to be that woman during the camping trip next weekend. I'd told Silas what happened at the bar. Every humiliating detail. He didn't seem surprised. Maybe he wasn't. Maybe Rex already told him or Elon.

God.

Silas just nodded his head and asked me to take off my dress, then instructed me to get on the bed. He'd then removed his own clothing, down to his shorts. I can't help but stare at his flesh—soft looking skin covering hard muscle. Silas' lean but fit body is a marvel of genetics. He's pretty, but handsome. Delicate but strong. It's his confidence that intrigues me the most.

"Touch yourself, Imogene," he repeats.

"Seeking pleasure is indulgent," I remind him—or maybe myself. "I'm happy to do whatever you need to feel good, but I can't do that to myself."

"What if watching you pleasure yourself makes me happy? What if you're being indulgent by not giving me what I need?"

These are common questions used to process The Way. What is the real meaning behind your thoughts and actions? Why are you hesitant to do something? Why do you resist?

"Do you know how often I touch myself?" he asks, running his hand down his shaft. It bobs lazily in response. "Daily."

"Daily?" I repeat, eyebrows shot up my forehead. "Once a day?"

"Several times," he says with a shrug. "Men's bodies want to spread its seed. We're always seeking a partner to thrust into, but that isn't always possible. We must find release and we do that by taking care of it on our own." He rolls his balls between his fingertips and swallows thickly. "That experience is how I know what makes me feel good and how it can make others feel. You need to do the same. Knowing yourself—your true self—will allow you to be a better mate to a man like Rex. A man that wants a partner, an equal."

It all sounds logical, and as Silas continues to fondle his cock, bringing himself closer and closer to release, I can see what he means. Silas knows what feels good. And he can show me. Seeing the pleasure on his beautiful face, watching the ecstasy undulate the ladder of muscles on his stomach—it's thrilling. It sparks the fire in my belly and ignites the heat between my legs. Just watching him makes me want him and I consider that if I can make Rex feel about me, the way I feel about Silas right now... well, that would make this practice worthwhile.

"Touch yourself," Silas commands. I place my hand on my belly and he shakes his head. "Start with your tits.

I reach for my breast, covered in the soft cotton of my tank, and run my palm over my nipple. Silas watches me, licking his lips, and continuing his own ministrations. Watching him has already pushed me closer to the edge. I'm already hot, horny, and touching my breasts only fans the flame.

"Now your pussy."

I swallow but obey, my other hand inching down my belly and between my legs, pushing aside my panties. I feel the cool air hit my core. It feels wrong to do these things to myself—the opposite of the self-control we'd strived for since entering the girl's domum. That's when we started learning that our bodies aren't our own. Aren't for our own indulgence. We were to save them for the Ordering and our mates.

That deep-seated notion is hard to shake, but Silas bends over and kisses me on the mouth. His tongue slips between my lips and my fingers explore, moving at the same slow pace as his kiss. I find the slow rhythm more appealing, and I lazily massage the bundle of nerves he'd helped me find. The motion shoots sparks of fire up my body. I groan into his mouth and his jaw slacks, breath panting in return.

"Take your time," he tells me. "Figure out how you like it. Hard. Soft. Gentle. Wet..." he continues, suggesting things I'd never thought about. I don't need any of it. Just his words and his closeness, the heat of his body and the sweet taste of his tongue, spurn the coil in my lower belly to twist tighter and tighter. My brain fogs and my resistance fades, leaving my body to take over.

"That's it," he says. "How does that feel?"

"Good," I blurt, then I open my eyes. I start to remove my hand. "This is wrong. I should save this—"

His fingers circle my wrist. "Don't you dare stop, Imogene. God gave you this body, these nerves and feelings. It's a dishonor not to learn the purpose of it." He forces my hand to move again, stroking against the heated, wet nerves. With his eyes holding mine, he asks again. "Tell me, how does that feel?"

"Amazing." I swallow back a sigh. "Heavenly."

"Then keep going." He releases me, watching to make sure I'm still pleasuring myself. He goes back to his own needs, resuming the lazy strokes up and down his shaft. My jaw slacks, and my breathing turns embarrassingly erratic. I don't stop, even though I still feel awkward and unsure. "That's right. God, you're beautiful."

My body reacts to his words and the urge for more propels me forward.

Silas' eyebrow arches and he says, "Climb on me. Ride me."

"I c-can't," I start, but he's pulled me onto his lap. His hard, slippery warmth glides against mine. "I can't let you enter me."

"I won't," he says, holding onto my hips. The position feels powerful—controlled. My tits rise and fall, and he captures a nipple between his teeth, biting down gently. I cry out from the feel of him—everywhere. Below, above, wet, sharp. He thrusts against me, friction building and it's not long before a spasm ripples through me. It's not fast or intense, it's slow and like riding a cresting wave. It feels good and warm, spreading through my limbs until I'm a puddle of goo.

Silas holds me upright, hips pounding against me, his eyes holding mine, until he jerks to a stop, a groan rumbling deep in his chest. He falls back, and the room filled with the two of us trying to catch our breath.

"How did that feel?" he asks, easing me to lie against his chest. "Pushing through your limits."

"Scary," I say. "But fulfilling. Powerful."

He nods and pulls my hand to his mouth, kissing the flat skin on the back. "You're very sexy, Imogene. And very powerful. Never underestimate that."

My cheeks are already flushed from the orgasm, but I feel them heat from the compliment. "How did you get so comfortable with this? Did it always come easily to you?"

"Not at first," he admits, rolling me off and settling us so that we're facing one another. "I had to work through some of my own hang-ups. Granted, I was sixteen when I started my training and a horny teenager, anyway. It wasn't a huge hardship."

"You were trained at sixteen?"

"I came into my gifts early. Anex saw my potential and encouraged me to start exploring them."

"Anex trained you?" This question makes me uneasy, but for some reason I need to know.

"No. Not directly." His lips form a line. "There are others in the inner circle that have gifts like I do. Together we explored these skills and learned how to use them to further the glory of The Way."

"What exactly is that gift? Sex?"

He grins, and it lights up his face. "Well, that's part of it, but only part. There are certain people that struggle to accept all aspects of The Way. They aren't like me and you. They didn't grow up here. They weren't raised within the walls of Serendee understanding the joy of this experience. They're caught up in the secular world, but Anex sees something in them—he can tell they want more. I, along with a few others, have the ability to reach them on that secular level. A physical level."

I nod, pretending I understand, but I'm not sure I do. Not completely. "So you connect with them and then..."

"And then once they have let down their guard and relax, they are ready to take the next steps toward following Anex and the visions of Serendee."

"So you're like a conduit of The Way." I've heard of these people. They're very special. And to learn there is one next to me now, teaching me his ways. I'm honored.

He smiles again. "A link between the outside and the inside."

"I bet you're good at your job."

"Oh, I'm very good." He runs his finger down the column of my neck. "Anex rewards me handsomely for my service." He kisses my shoulder, and it sends a cascade of butterflies down to my lower belly. "When he asked me to work with you, it was the highest honor."

It's hard to think clearly while Silas is touching me—or just near me in general. He's handsome, confident, charming. Sexy. He's like no other man I've ever met before. I can see why Anex would find him useful in easing the concerns of new members. Just talking to him has eased my worries.

"Thank you for the lesson," I tell him.

"I want you to continue practicing—really explore your desires."

"I will."

He kisses my forehead. "Rex is a lucky man. I know in my heart you'll please him and bring him back on the right path."

"He is lucky to have you as a devoted friend."

"He's lucky to have all of us," he says, allowing me a moment to curl into his side, "and one day he's going to realize it."

26

I WAKE on the second note, the deep strains of classical music filling the air. Clair de Lune. It's the same song every time, although no one knows when it will come; morning, noon, or night. I grapple for the bedside clock and look. 2 AM.

I get up quickly, not taking the time to change or brush my hair. When the music plays, we are to go immediately to the community center. No questions asked. No dilly dallying. Once Clarissa had a cake baking in the oven. She shut it off and ruined the cake. It's a testament of faith, of obedience. When Anex calls, we come.

Elon, Silas, and Levi are in the living room when I walk out. Even the inner circle is required to attend. Well, except maybe one.

"He's not here," Elon says, answering my question before I ask it. He shoves his arms into his jacket and holds the door for everyone.

"Will he be?" I ask, already worried that walking into the meeting without my Ordered will look strange. People will notice. I know I would. We haven't been seen at a public event yet and gossip will start.

"Your guess is as good as ours, Little Lamb." The look exchanged between the men is an indicator they aren't happy about it either.

The meeting house is down the hill—and a cool breeze kicks up as we walk towards it with other residents of the Main House. I shiver in the thin nightgown. I see the healer that examined me before the ceremony, and a few of the women that clean the apartment. A drumbeat greets us as we enter. Anex thinks the sound of the drum mimics the heartbeat of the Earth and begins and ends each lecture with rousing music.

When I walk into the big room at the community center, I see Margaret on the platform, curled up by Anex's side. His other spiritual mates are there as well. Our leader is at center stage, sitting in a cushioned chair. Members of the community spill in, settling on the floor. I follow Elon, ignoring the eyes watching me, wondering about my mate. Maria catches my eye and waves. She sits with her Ordered, and they lean their shoulders together in support.

I wave back, but divert my eyes quickly, not wanting her to see the worry and grief I have over the failure to please Rex. Instead, I lock eyes with Anex. His gaze is critical, assessing, but jumps from my face to the space next to me. I sense him immediately, his figure eclipsing everyone and everything else in the room. Before I can look up, his fingers interlock with mine and he tugs me to a corner of the room where a second chair has been set up. The guys take their positions among the Chosen. Levi with the other Guides. Silas with the beautiful men and women, Anex surrounds himself with and Elon, just to the back of Rex's chair. Always on guard. Rex sits and just as I am about to take a cue from Margaret and sit on the floor, he pulls me onto his lap. I start to protest, but he holds me still. That's when I realize he managed to get the back of my nightgown pulled up and the bare backs of my thighs are against his.

"Play nice," he whispers in my ear. I'm frozen, unsure of how to act or even how to 'play nice' with this man I barely know—the man, that the last time I saw him had me down on my knees forcing me to pleasure him while he mocked me. "Unlike my father, I won't require my mate to sit on the floor."

"No, you'll just push them to their knees and force them to service you," I grind out.

His eyebrow raises, and a small, smug smile quirks at his lips. If he wants to say something back but his father's voice booms through the room, cutting across the drumbeat and forcing it to stop.

"Thank you for coming so quickly and efficiently," Anex says. "It's never my goal to wake you from your well-deserved sleep, but you know how I am when The Way speaks to me." He smiles, and the crowd smiles in return. "I have to share it with all of you because it's never about me. It's always about you."

"Here we go," Rex mutters, "get ready for a long one."

As always, his words catch me off guard. So full of contempt. Despite that, he settles in like the rest of us, adjusting his position so we sink closer together in the chair. I stiffen, not just because of the proximity, but because the focus of the crowd isn't just on Anex tonight. It's on me and Rex.

"You need to relax," he says in my ear.

"It's hard with everyone watching," I reply, keeping my eyes on his father. "And with your hand on my thigh."

"Does that distract you?" His fingers splay over the top of my leg. "Isn't this what you wanted? To be my mate?" His voice is low. I assume no one can hear him other than me. But, when I spare a glance at Elon, I gather from the tight set of his jaw that he can hear us as well. "That title comes with scrutiny."

With the hand above the folds of my dress, he takes my hand and rests them both on his lap, inches from his crotch. He rubs his thumb up and down the side of my hand. It's firm but soothing. I feel his breath on my neck and the strength of his body pressed against mine.

Heat boils under my skin.

"What are you doing?" I ask, unable to focus on Anex's lesson. I shift uncomfortably and am met with the hard press of his erection against my backside.

"Whatever I want, Little Lamb." He glances up at Elon. "Give me your coat."

With his dark eyes darting between us, Elon shrugs out of the jacket. It's heavy and black and I'm accosted by his scent when Rex drapes it over my lap.

"That's better."

Underneath the coat, his fingers move, dipping between my thighs. Warmth spreads at my core. It's not unfamiliar now. Silas has taught me how to understand my body, but the intensity is still surprising.

"Spread your legs for me."

"I should listen," I say weakly, trying to regain control, but he brushes his knuckles against the inside of my knee and they part like the Red Sea.

"Why?" he asks, brushing the pads of his fingers against the nub of nerves. My clit, Silas told me. The most sensitive place outside a woman's body. "You know why my father does these late-night lectures?"

"Because he's been given inspiration by The Way and he's excited to share it with us."

He chuckles softly in my ear and circles around my clit, sometimes too far away, sometimes dangerously close. I can't decide which I want more. "He does it to keep everyone off balance. Exhausted and tired. Sleep-deprivation keeps everyone in line."

"That's—" I start, but his finger pushes under my undergarments, touching my clit dead-on. I shudder and curl against him, biting down on the moan of pleasure. "Stop."

"I thought you liked being manipulated by men in power."

His tone is mocking and mean, the one I'm most familiar with. I lamely attempt to separate myself from him. "You're wet. You like this." He presses his fingers against my core and pushes past the entrance. "Tight, too," he says. "No man has entered you before, have they?"

"Of course not. I am yours and yours alone." My eyes flick to Elon as I say it, knowing I am skirting a line of truth.

He curls his finger inside, applying the most wonderful pressure. I want to plead for him to stop and beg him to keep going. At some point I shut out Anex and all I feel is Rex. I feel his hitched breathing against my ear, his heartbeat thrumming against my back, and his invasion inside. I feel him everywhere.

Across the stage, Anex pauses on stage and looks to the upper windows where the faint streaks of the sunrise brighten the sky. "Let's greet the new day with the song of The Way," he says, urging his musicians to start playing. Everyone around us rises, swaying to the beat, clapping and humming with song. But not us. Rex's hands hold me in place and under the cover of celebration he applies pressure against both my clit and something deep inside, causing my body to spasm with the growing drumbeat. It's not just an orgasm, it's so much more. Earth shatteringly more and I cry out, my voice just another in the cacophony praising his father.

I heave against him, hips rising and falling with the rush of euphoria. I tilt my chin upward and touch the side of his face. "That... that was incredible."

He scrapes his teeth against my ear and whispers, "Every time you think that man is a god, Little Lamb," he holds me against his chest and slowly removes his finger from inside, "you remember that I'm the one that made you feel like that."

He sits me up right and sets on wobbly legs, pawns me off on Elon, who catches me by the arms. Rex steps off the platform and vanishes into the crowd.

"Where is he going?" I ask, leaning into Elon's side.

He shakes his head, but his eyes dart over to Anex. I see that he's watching us, a twisted, knowing smile on his lips. Something just transpired—something deep and sensual and complicated and vindictive. Something between a father and son, and I'm right in the middle of it.

27

———————

Silas

I'm walking down the road toward the market when I see a woman ahead. Her narrow shoulders taper down to a small waist, partially obscured by a baggy dress. Nevertheless, I recognize the swing of her hips and the pale blonde hair braided down her back. I jog to catch up, tugging her braid when I reach her.

"Hey!" she shouts, spinning in a circle. She grins when she sees me. "What are you doing out here?"

"Headed to the market. What about you?"

"Same." She lifts the empty basket in her hands. "I thought I'd find something for dinner tonight."

One of the perks of growing up in Serendee is the fresh food and natural products. All of the oils and lotions I use in my massages are locally made. "I thought you had to work today," I say. "Playing hooky?"

"Anex gave us the afternoon off." I raise an eyebrow. Afternoons off are not something that happens here—at least not sponta-neously. She laughs. "I know, right? He had some kind of official meeting and didn't want anyone around."

"Well, that works out for my benefit. Now we can go together."

She hesitates. "Are you sure that's a good idea? For us to be alone?"

As much time as I spend with women up at the Main House, as a single, unordered man, walking with a female alone in the middle of Serendee is against the norm. "Do you think anyone would question me?" I ask, flexing a little. People are aware of my position in the inner circle.

"I'm less worried about you and a little more concerned with my reputation," she says. "You may be Rex's best friend, but I'm not sure that clears the way for us to be so familiar."

"I assure you, Little Lamb," I say quietly, as we pass a woman walking by with a small child, "they have no idea how familiar we've been at all."

The comment makes her cheeks flush pink, and it makes her even more beautiful. How Rex can turn this girl away is a mystery. To have her in my bed every night, waiting for me with those soft lips and her hungry mouth. Well, that is the kind of dream it's best not to have.

"You're bad," she mutters, entering the open-air market. "Terribly bad."

"You really have no idea," I reply, splitting apart. She's right. Walking around together in here would turn heads and elicit questions, less about me and more about her. The last thing I want to do is tarnish her reputation. I locate the woman that sells the oils. I purchase two and then add a bottle of lotion and lavender soap from another merchant. Imogene takes her time, looking through the organic fruit and vegetables. She's confident here, bartering with the other women or smelling and testing the skin of fruit. It's a different side of her from the woman I know at home. Less timid. More assured. She's trained for the life of a mate for years—I've only been training her to please a man in bed for just a few days.

While she pays, I linger by the fresh flowers, drawn to a bunch of daisies. Imogene would probably love these on the dining room table.

"Silas!"

I turn to the voice and see Kayla. I've had two more sessions with her since the first. Anex is pleased with her progress. I plaster on a warm smile and say, "I see you found our little market."

"It is adorable," she says, holding up a basket of items she's purchased. "My friends back home would die for this type of organic product."

"Well, your friend's back home aren't special like you." Unless they are. Wealthy. Impressionable. Anex will find out soon enough if it's worth pursuing. I spot Imogene walking our way over her shoulder and grab the bunch of flowers, paying for them quickly. "It was nice seeing you. I should let you get back to your shopping."

She digs into her basket and holds up a bottle of honeysuckle wine. She leans in and says, "I thought maybe you and I could crack this open tonight and spend a little more time together."

Imogene, who is now admiring the same daisies as the ones I just bought, flicks her eyes between us. Now I'm the one that has to play the part of living in two worlds. My job is to be available to the recruits as they need me, but none of the people around me have any idea. But a woman like Kayla is special. Even with Anex's directives for training Imogene, Kayla comes first.

"How about this?" I say, voice low. "I need to do a few more things, but you head back up to the house, slip into something comfortable, and I'll meet you in your room after dinner?"

"That sounds wonderful." Her hand lowers to my butt and squeezes. I step away, carrying my things and heading back to the road. A moment later, Imogene appears.

"I can explain—"

"There's no need," she says, walking past me. "I'm well aware that you and the others live by your own rules."

"It's not that." I feel the need to clear things up. "It's not something I want to do."

She looks back at the market—back at Kayla, who is standing by a table of strawberries. There's no doubt she's a beautiful woman; poised and cultured. She sticks out among the other women in the community—yet I know all she wants is to belong. She thinks she's found Utopia.

Imogene laughs and continues down the road. "You don't want to spend time with a woman like that? Drinking wine and... well, doing what I know you're very good at."

"That's not fair. It's my job."

She pauses. "I'm not judging you, Silas. And I don't expect exclusivity in this arrangement. We've been given a directive by Anex and it's our duty to fulfill it."

She hitches her basket in the crook of her elbow and starts back up the hill toward the Main House. Everything she said is true. I'm doing what Anex asked me to, the same way she is. The problem is that I'd rather spend the evening training her than Kayla.

Or, I realize, the further she gets away, I want to spend my time with Imogene over anyone at all.

28

"You know why my father does these late-night lectures..."

The memory of Rex's voice draws me out of sleep.

"He does it to keep everyone off balance. Exhausted and tired. Sleep-deprivation keeps everyone in line."

I toss and turn, pushing the questions out of my mind. Rex is a liar. A troublemaker. He said it himself; he manipulates.

Then why does what he said make my stomach hurt? My chest pound with anxiousness? I know it's just my lack of faith talking. My Indulgence. My belief that I need to control everything. The Way will guide me. Anex is in control. I am nothing but a speck in the bigger plan. I repeat this to myself, over and over, hoping it quells my nerves, but it doesn't.

Only one thing will.

I sit up, feeling the cold sweat along my back, and open the drawer of my bedside table. I feel around in the dark for my journal and pull it out. I sit with it on my lap for a long time, feeling the heaviness of the leather and the weight of what's inside. Taking a stunted breath, I flip it open and search for the sharp metal tool shoved in the spine.

The end pierces my fingertip, giving me a sharp stab of pain. A small rush of release flows through me. Correction. That is what I need. To be corrected.

I stare at the tool and already know it's not enough.

Leaving the tool and journal on the bed, I step into the hallway, stopping at a closed door. I rest my hand on the doorknob. Do I knock? What if he doesn't hear? What if Elon or Silas do? Understanding that this is between me and Levi, my Guide, is what pushes me to twist the knob and enter his darkened room. The door shuts behind me with a soft click and I stand over the bed, shaking him by the arm.

He rouses slowly, rubbing his eyes. "Imogene? Is that you?"

"Yes," I say, my eyes adjusting to the dark. He shifts to a sitting position, and the faint light from under the door reveals he is shirtless. His upper body is exposed, down to the pooled sheet at his waist. He's lean with tight rows of muscles. A faint hair scatters over his chest.

"You should be in bed."

"I know." I wring my hands. "But I woke up, and I couldn't go back to sleep. My mind kept racing. All the things I've been doing, the extra calories, the urge to defy with questions and judgments... the Lapses." I still. "I was going to seek release."

"You were going to Correct yourself."

"I wanted to, but I stopped myself. I came to you for Guidance." As I talk, he sits up and turns on the light, giving me a better view of his body. Butterflies churn in my stomach. Not the kind of anxiety I was feeling in bed. Something different. I drag my eyes away from his flesh and blurt, "I'm sorry. This is inappropriate."

"No," he says, swinging his legs over the edge of the bed. "I'm your Guide, and you need my help. You did the right thing by coming to me."

I exhale in relief. "I'm ready."

He looks around the sparse room. Along with the bed, there is a dresser with a mirror and a small desk. He nods at the dresser. "I think that will work."

I face the dresser, getting a full view of myself in the mirror. I look a wreck. My braided hair is disheveled. Dark smudges mar the skin under my anxious, red eyes. I look tired. Exhausted. Levi is probably horrified to see me in such a state.

"Bend over," he says, placing a hand on my back.

I do as he says, flattening my palms on the wooden surface. My body tenses and tingles, knowing what is going to come. I want it. I need it. A strange flicker warms my lower belly. In the mirror, I watch as Levi opens a drawer and pulls out a white T-shirt. "You're going to have to be quiet, so the others don't hear." I nod in understanding. He holds up the shirt. "Bite down on this."

He pushes the cotton in my mouth, and I face the mirror, watching as he lifts up the back of my nightdress, pushing it to my waist. He stares at me for a long moment, so long that I think he's about to change his mind, but then he moves, hooking his fingers into my underwear and dropping them to the floor. I feel a tap on my inner knee, and he says, "Brace yourself."

Anticipation bubbles in my chest: fear combined with want. I want to rid myself of these Lapses. Of these Indulgences. I want to feel the pain of Correction. Levi and I make eye contact in the mirror, his jaw tight and determined. I'm looking into the grass-green of his eyes when his hand comes down hard on my backside, lurching me forward. The cry is trapped behind cotton.

He spanks me again, palm flat and stinging. The pain and heat shooting across my skin, building in my core. I know I should look at myself in the mirror—reconcile my Lapses—but I can't look away from him. Not away from the conviction on his face, and the fire burning in his eyes.

"It is not your place to question," he says quietly, between spankings. "It is your role to follow. To uplift. To reflect."

His hand comes down harder, and I fall on the dresser, landing on my elbows. I bite down on the cloth and shift to rise, but his hand comes down flat on my lower back, holding me in place. "It's my job to Correct the wildness out of you." Smack! "The Regression." Smack! "The doubt and distraction." Smack! The spankings come faster now and the pain spreads across my nerves. I feel it in the sharp points of my nipples, in the slick heat between my legs.

He reaches around and yanks the shirt out of my mouth.

"Confess, Imogene. Everything."

"I eat too much. Fatty foods. Even sugar. I let Rex get into my head, spreading doubt about this father." Levi grunts behind me and I catch his eye. He hasn't touched me again, but I sense him moving—hear him. The rustle of fabric, the jerk of his arm. "I let Silas touch me. I daydream of Elon's harsh hands, groping, pinching, and grabbing." I swallow, seeing Levi's jaw tighten, his nose wrinkle. "I fear that I Lapse so that I can come see you. To do this. Seeking this pain because no matter how bad it makes me feel, there's another side that makes me feel good. So good." The confession comes out in a rush and Levi's hand grabs my hip. His fingers dig into me, and I feel the brush of something wet hit my backside as his hand pumps up and down. I know the look on his face, the motion. Silas has done it in front of me. He's pleasuring himself to my pain.

"Spank me," I beg, catching his eye once more.

He releases my hip, and his hand comes down painfully hard, the slap of our skin against one another loud and raw. The ache between my legs throbs almost as much as the flesh of my backside.

"Again," I plead. "Please."

He does it again, and without the shirt in my mouth; I cry out.

"You're filthy. Dirty. Dangerous." His jaw slacks and his movements pick up, hand jacking up and down. "You're bad, Imogene. You're a bad girl." His assault is cut off by a deep groan rumbling in his throat, and he lurches forward, falling against me. I feel his breath on my neck as hot, sticky, fluid spills on my lower back, branding me with his come.

I'm frozen like this as he breathes heavily against me, his chest rising and falling. He reaches around me for the shirt and a moment later I feel him wiping the come from my back. Levi tosses the shirt toward the closet and lifts me up. My dress falls to my ankles. My backside burns.

"Do you feel better?" he asks, face stoic.

"Yes. Thank you for the Correction."

His head tilts, eyes narrowed, and assessing. "You're lying."

"I-I'm not."

He reaches for me, gathering the dress in his hand, exposing me. "You may have gotten what you came here for, but you don't feel better." His hand dips between my legs, brushing against my clit. "You're wet. Horny. You get off on feeling the pain."

I swallow. "And you get off on giving it."

He laughs. I'm not sure I've ever seen him laugh, although it's not filled with joy but derision. His next move is as surprising. He lifts me by my hips and places me on the dresser. He pushes aside my dress and yanks me to the edge. I wince at the pain.

"What are you—"

He drops to his knees and spreads my thighs wide, swiping his tongue along my folds. He flattens it at the apex, lathing my clit with hot, warm heat. Electricity runs up my spine.

"Oh my—Levi!"

Holding my legs apart, he kisses me down there once again, mixing intense pleasure with the slightest hint of pain. What he's doing lands somewhere in the middle—the good middle—the one I came to him for tonight, even if I didn't know this is where it would end.

The tension I woke up with melts away with each and every swipe of his tongue, every flick and suck. He's gentle in a way that's unexpected, the brutality of his Corrections not in this space. I sink my fingers into his thick, copper hair, and press my back against the cool mirror.

That diligence, the one that makes him a good teacher, a good student, keeps him focused and soon hard bursts of air push from my lungs, while my hips rise to meet his mouth. That tightly wound coil that started winding when I walked in his room, spins and spins and spins, until it snaps, unfurling in waves of spine melting pleasure. It feels so good, so very, very good, better than the spanking, better than the highest high. I reach the peak and float back down, loosening my grip in his hair. I sink against the mirror, breathing hard, and feeling warm all over.

"Where did you learn to do that?" I ask once I can speak again. It's unspoken, but unlike the others, I've had the distinct feeling Levi is not overly experienced with women.

He stands and wipes his mouth with the back of his hand. "I'm a student," he says quietly, "of everything. I make it my job to learn as much about everything as I can."

I ease myself off the dresser and wince. The pain in my backside throbs.

I want to say something, anything, but the cool, distant look that is so often on his face is back. He turns his back to me and says, "Good night, Imogene. I expect you to do better from now on."

I nod and exit his room, that same shame bubbling under the surface as I quietly go back to my own. I lie on the bed, flat on my stomach, too tired to focus on the heat radiating off my tender skin. The tension I'd been carrying has dissipated, leaving me relaxed, if not sore. I drift off quickly, easily, only waking when the light shines through my window the next morning. When I roll over, grunting at the pain, something soft and malleable falls off my still sore backside. I pick it up and blink at the object.

An ice pack.

29

ELON

THE FIRST PERSON I see when I enter The Center is Imogene, standing behind her desk.

"Have you seen Rex?" I ask her.

"The last place he'd be is here," she says, collating sheets of paper lined up on the desk into a single packet, "he spends most of his time avoiding me."

I tap on her calendar. "Any idea then? Isn't it your job to keep up with the comings and goings of the community?"

She gathers the stack of packets and circles her desk. "No. He does what he wants, you know that. Maybe he's holed up with some girl right now." She pushes past me, arm grazing mine. "Maybe some other woman is taking care of his needs."

"We have an appointment, and we were supposed to meet at the Main House, but he never showed," I say, following her down the hall. My eyes travel the lines of her thin shoulders down to the narrowing of her hips. That's when I frown. Something is wrong with her gait. She's walking tenderly, as if she's injured.

I reach out and flatten a hand over her ass. She yelps, her whole body shudders, and comes to a stop.

"I don't think that was about me touching you, Little Lamb. What's wrong?"

"Nothing." She swallows. "You just surprised me."

I reach for the nearest doorknob, open it and drag her inside. It's the supply closet, musty and smelling of chemicals. I shut the door and stand in front of it, blocking her escape.

"Show me."

"There's nothing to show, Elon." She clutches the packets to her chest. "Please let me go so I can put these in the lesson room."

"Not until I see what has you walking like a hobbled old lady."

She eyes me. "You're not going to let this go, are you?"

"Nope."

She sighs and shoves the stack of papers at me. I grab them, and she slowly pulls up the hem of her dress until it's bundled around her waist. I look down at her pale legs and see nothing wrong, but her fingers hook into those godforsaken utilitarian panties, and she pulls them down.

Using my finger, I make a swirling motion, gesturing for her to turn. I need to see exactly what is causing her so much pain. Even in the dim light, when her back is to me, I can see the red, blistering flesh on her ass. "Holy shit," I say, resting the papers on a shelf. I crouch down and stare at the imprint of a hand. Gently, I run my fingers over the skin. She flinches, cheeks squeezing. "Was it Rex?"

"It's none of your business."

"Little Lamb, don't make me drag you door to door throughout Serendee and force the person that did this to you to step forward, because I will."

"They are corrections. Inflicted by my Guide."

I blink at the hand imprint. "Levi did this?"

"Yes."

"He marked you." I run the back of my hand over the heated welts. "He went too far. It's unacceptable."

"No. I asked him to do it," she confesses, looking over her shoulder. "He's helping me deal with my Lapses. He isn't doing anything to me that I don't deserve."

I narrow my eyes at her. "Nothing you are doing deserves this sort of Correction. You are obedient and devoted. I've seen it with my own eyes."

"I struggle with defiance. I have questions and judgements."

"You are human." I lift the undergarments from around her ankle and slowly drag them back up, being careful as I cover her swollen cheeks. Her dress falls and I stand, turning her around to face me.

"I'm bad," she whispers.

I touch her chin. "Because you have a brain? A mind of your own? Remember, this is who Rex wants."

"No," she says, turning her face away, "because I like it when he hurts me. I am not only getting Correction, I'm getting pleasure."

My eyebrow raises. I have a feeling she's not the only one getting off from these sessions.

"It's not wrong to want to feel something when you're having sex," I tell her, "even if it's rough and hard. But you don't need to punish yourself for it. Do you think Rex punishes himself? Silas? Or even me?"

"You're different."

I run my fingers down the side of her face. "You're one of us. Different rules. Different desires."

"But what about Levi?"

"Levi is fucked up. He buys into all of Anex's bullshit, and like you, he's twisting things up."

Her expression clouds with confusion and it strikes me how much mental endurance it must take to be in her position. She's got all four of us, plus Anex and herself, coming at her from all angles.

I open the door. "Come with me."

She grabs the packets off the shelf. "I have to work. A class is coming in and—"

"And someone else can deal with it. I'm overruling it. You're sick and you're coming with me."

She opens her mouth to argue, but I give her a stern look. One she knows means to shut up and follow directions. "Let me drop these off and get my things."

"I'll meet you out front."

I watch her walk down the hall, now fully aware of why her gait is so stilted. It's not my place to interfere with Levi's Guidance. That's his role in the community, but I can make sure she's taken care of. I wait for her outside and pull out my phone, sending a message to the one person that will know how to treat this kind of wound, and when she meets me outside, her blonde hair shining in the sun, I take her there.

30

———————

IMOGENE

It WAS bad enough having Elon see the marks from Levi's spankings, but this was worse.

"Ouch," Silas says. "These do look painful."

Elon took me to the guest cottage behind the pool, apparently where Silas has a studio for work. Foolishly, I stood outside while the two spoke, no doubt discussing the wounds on my backside. I can't even describe the feeling I had when Elon left, handing me over like a child that needs supervision. Silas instructed me to remove my clothes and lie on a table in his studio, covered only with a sheet. I've never quite understood what he does for Serendee, other than working with recruits, and now that I'm in the small room filled with candles and incense, doesn't clear things up much.

"Are you a healer?" I'm naked and flat on my stomach on the table. It's not sterile like the healer's offices, but I understand now that things are different for The Chosen.

"Not exactly," he says, "although it's not totally wrong. I help people relax and get to know their bodies, using massage and other techniques." He walks over to a shelf and removes a small jar. "You know, like I've helped you understand your body better."

I bite back a laugh. "Then maybe you can let me know why I want Levi to Correct me like this. Elon says I shouldn't."

I hear the scrape of the jar lid as Silas unscrews it and a moment later, a cooling sensation spreads across my buttocks. "Oh," I exhale. "That feels good."

"I thought it would."

His fingers knead and glide over my skin, working away from the painful area to my lower back. The sensation is firm but gentle, and I sink into the table. "Do you know why?" I ask, serious now. "Why do I like it?"

"It's not wrong to want things a little rough," he says, continuing up my back. "People like things differently. You're a strong woman, Imogene, I'm not surprised you can handle more than most." He moves to my shoulders, working against my muscles. His moves aren't sexual but sensual. With every passing second, I'm putty in his very skilled hands. "You're one of the Chosen now. Correction is relative. You have permission to indulge more than you used to. You're still behaving like a normal member of the community."

"I don't understand."

His fingers prod at my neck, teasing out the knots. He leans close to my ear and says, "If you want to enjoy rough sex, go for it, but it doesn't have to be a punishment. Unless, of course, you want it that way."

What I want doesn't matter in the grand scheme of things. It's not part of the principals of The Way, and Rex certainly doesn't care. Everything in my mind is muddled. I feel less in control than I did when I was in the domum. Did I want Rex to shove me to my knees? Or Elon to touch me harshly. Did I go to Levi in the middle of the night to get what I wanted, or to do what was right?

"It's going to take time," Silas says, "but until then, we need to make sure you're healthy. Ultimately, our goal is to make you Rex's mate—one that can handle anything thrown at her."

"If that's the goal, then I guess you're training me correctly."

He squats down so that our faces are level. "From now on you come to me if you have any injuries, worries, or concerns about this, okay?"

"I will."

He leans forward, kissing me softly on the lips, tongue licking against the seam. I'm spun with a whole other kind of heat.

When he pulls away, I sit up. "I do have one thing to ask you. A favor." I grab the sheet and cover myself. "For Rex."

* * *

"As you know, this weekend is Anex's birthday party. Rex should be there, and I want to take the opportunity to show him I can be a good mate."

Silas' face brightens as we exit the cottage and step onto the deck that surrounds the pool. "What do you have in mind?"

"The things I was taught growing up about how to make my mate happy are not the things Rex wants. He doesn't just want a submissive, doting female from Serendee. He wants a strong companion, but I don't always know what that means and," I exhale, "I thought maybe a little insight into his private life could help me get a better grasp."

"You want me to tell you about him? Personal things?"

"I know nothing about the man, and he certainly isn't telling me. I don't even know where he lives."

He studies me closely, like he's trying to figure out a puzzle. "He lives in the Main House. With everyone else in Anex's inner circle."

"Obviously, but I thought maybe you could show me his quarters."

"You want to go to his suite?"

"I want to see how he lives. What he eats and drinks. How he arranges his furniture." We stand near the pool. The water is crystal blue and I wonder what it feels like to swim in it. "I think if I can understand him a little better, I can make things go a little more smoothly. Especially if we have no choice but to spend the weekend together. The last thing I want, and I assume Anex wants, is for him to run off and reject me. Again."

"None of us want that," he says, taking my hand in his. "I'll take you there."

He opens the back door that enters the house library. It's filled with books and papers—many penned by Anex. A few, I suspect, were written by my mother.

"Do you know why he rejects The Way?" I ask, as we go up the backstairs.

"I've heard his arguments," he says, slowing his gait. "He has a lot of anger directed at his father, and in all fairness, he has had his faith rocked more than once."

I nod, trying to process it all. I can understand that. When my mother was determined to be a Regressive and left Serendee my faith wavered as well. "But you don't think he's lost, do you?"

His mouth is set in a grim line. "I hope not, which is why I'll assist you in whatever way you need, even if it means violating my best friend's privacy." I hadn't thought of it that way. "Being Anex's son isn't easy. He's forced to share his father, his only parent, with the rest of the community."

"That had to be hard."

"It was, and it's one reason Anex encouraged him to become so close to me, Elon, and Levi. He needed support and over time we grew to be like brothers."

I grab his forearm and look into his eyes. "You're very devoted to him. It shows. And I appreciate how that devotion has spread to me. Once Rex and I are mated, I hope that you feel the same toward me—like family. Until you get your own mate, of course."

He looks down at my hand and then back up. His eyes are so clear, but they are filled with something deep inside that I can't reach. "That would be nice."

He continues forward, easing his arm out of my grasp, and I follow him through the maze of hallways and staircases. All I know is how to get from my room to the foyer, but generally it's not necessary. One of the guys usually escorts me to and from work, or someone from the house walks me up when I return. No areas of the house are barricaded or blocked off, but everything looks identical to the clean white paint and the modest décor. There are no identifying traits and more than once, I've gotten turned around. Silas confidently walks the halls until he stops at the door and unlocks it with a key, but I pause before I cross the threshold. "Are you sure he's not here?"

"He's with Elon, remember? They had business to take care of today outside of Serendee." His eyebrow arches. "Are you having second thoughts?"

"No," I say, as much for myself as him. Snooping into people's things isn't something I'm accustomed to. I've never had secrets and as far as I know, no one I've known has either. Well, other than my mother.

The layout is similar to my suite, but the contents are very much male. Secular male, from what I've learned during my TV watching.

The living room has comfy leather couches and a massive television. There are electronic devices that Silas explains belong to the video games Rex likes to play. He describes the games and they run through different themes; sports, mazes, battles, military. I don't understand any of it, but that's okay. At least I know.

I wander into the adjacent room—the kitchen—and feel more at ease. This is what I know about serving my mate. Feeding and nurturing him. I open the refrigerator and see well organized food, plenty of fruits and vegetables from the Serendee market, but I also notice the soda and sugary drinks. A box from the bakery is on the counter. Bags of chips and crackers are lined up against the backsplash.

"Did he do this himself? Buy these things?"

"There's a maid and a cook."

I nod. It makes sense. "Do they live here?"

"In the house, not the suite. There are servant quarters somewhere," he says, opening the box and taking out two cookies. He hands me one. "Eat."

I look at it guiltily, but he nods in encouragement. I take the bite and sugar rushes into my taste buds.

"How long has he lived here?" I ask.

"We all moved in when he turned sixteen."

It's a different journey than my own or the others in the

domum. The non-chosen. Further proof Rex and his friends grew up in a totally different world. One I have to acclimate to.

Silas leads me through the suite, pointing out the different bedrooms; his, Elon's, Levi's. They're bare—empty, having moved their things to my suite instead. I stop in the doorway of Levi's room and stare at the empty walls and the neatly made bed. There are a few books on the shelf, but I know most of them are at my place.

"Do you miss living here?" I ask.

He glances in and shrugs. "Not really."

"But it's been your home for years."

"'Home' is a construct," he replies. "An emotional attachment to the physical. The Way teaches us to focus on spiritual growth. Who we are, not what we possess."

"Of course," I reply, knowing he's right. It's another reason for our simple clothing, our clean eating, our lack of materialism. It hammers home how much they sacrifice for Anex and Rex. They live in transition—their whole lives centered around these two important men. They aren't Ordered and they bear the weight of Serendee's secrets. Maybe I'm not the only one that struggles with following the right path.

"You're very strong for maintaining these values despite living in the center of opulence and a friend that insists on pushing the limits."

He looks down at me. "It's a gift to serve Rex and his father."

"I agree."

"I know, Imogene." His hand moves. Up, then down, finally tucking my hair behind my ear. He's so good at these intimate moments, so at ease. "I have no doubt you are perfectly Chosen for Rex."

He turns and continues down the hallway and I pause for a moment, letting my heart slow its pace. His touch kicked it in gear. My body responds so differently now to the slightest affection. It's not satisfied with a simple touch. It wants more.

Rex's scent hits me before I even step into his room. It lands like a punch to my gut—the memory of him pushing me to the ground, the way he tasted in my mouth, comingled with the clean soapy scent and masculine cologne. The feel of him under me during the lecture, invading my body with his fingers, drawing me to the edge.

I push the emotions back—like we're taught with The Way. Females all too often let emotions rule, instead of accepting it like a man would. The incident was nothing more than a power play in an attempt to prove his father wrong. It had nothing to do with me.

His bedroom appears more lived-in than the others. There are a few things on the dresser. A couple of framed photos. I recognize his mother from the portrait at the Beatrice House. There are none of his father. Other items; a small carved wooden box. A jar with coins. A sleek tablet.

There's a stack of books on the bedside table. None authored by his father. The titles are in bold: Escape. Infidel. Educated. Witness.

Silas is silent as I comb the room, opening both closets. One for Serendee. One for the secular world. On the floor are sneakers. Sports equipment.

"He likes sports?" I ask, trying to glean something. "Does he play basketball like his father?"

Silas shifts in the doorway, arms crossed over his chest. "No. He likes to watch football. But he plays soccer."

I nod. There are sports teams in Serendee for the children. Athleticism is encouraged. A healthy body is a temple to The Way. Anex has frequent basketball games late at night. I've seen the hard lines of Rex's body. The broad shoulders. I'm not surprised he's athletic.

Even though it's overkill, I enter the bathroom and peer into the shower. Bottles of soaps and gels line the tiled shelf. A razor sits on top of a can of shaving cream next to the sink. I pull open the drawer and it glides out easily. A box of condoms sits on top. I know what they are. We have sex education. I also know that men prefer not to use them—it's best for women to take care of birth control on our own. Males are ruled by biological need. Seeing the box does make me wonder... does he bring women here?

I don't expect the twist of jealousy swirling in my gut.

That thought propels me out of the bathroom. I stare at the bed. It's comfortable looking, stacked with pillows and a soft, worn quilt.

A T-shirt and sweatpants lay at the foot of the bed. On the small table I see a black leather journal—a thin cord is wrapped around it.

"He logs?" I ask him.

"I suppose. It's a hard habit to break, even for him."

What I'd give to read between those pages, but I don't dare. It would be unforgivable.

But I do open the drawer and see two things. A few other journals. One with a pink cover. Also, money. A lot of money. Curled into tight rolls. I pick it up and study it. There are dozens, if not hundreds, of bills tucked inside.

Glancing over at Silas, I find him staring back, stone faced. After a moment he says, "We should go."

I place the cash back in the drawer exactly how I found it and shut the drawer. We exit the suite quickly. In the hallway, Silas asks, "Did you find what you were looking for?"

"Maybe," I reply, still processing everything I saw. My mind is mostly on the money. Why does he have so much? What does he do with it? Does Anex know? Although I do feel like maybe I learned a little more about Rex today, I definitely feel like something is missing. Something about Rex that I just don't understand. There's one other person I want to talk to before I make my final plans for the weekend.

Elon.

31

IMOGENE

It's dark when Elon returns home, his jacket smelling of smoke and his eyes rimmed red. I'm in the living room. Silas and Levi are on the basketball court with Anex.

"What are you doing up?" he asks, tossing the jacket on the chair. "Shouldn't you be in bed?"

"I'm waiting for you," I tell him. "There's something I need."

"Really?" His eyes rake over me, and I shift anxiously. Does he think I mean sex? He could be stoned or drunk enough to consider it. Would I consider it? Whatever brief desire I see in his eyes—or think I see—shutters and he says, "It'll have to wait until tomorrow. I'm beat."

"Wait." I hop from my seat and jump in front of him. If he wanted, he could pick me up and move me. Instead, he stares down at me impatiently. "I want to know what I'm really dealing with here."

His eyebrow rises. "Dealing with?"

"With Rex. You took me to him at the club, and he showed up that night for Anex's lesson—neither encounter did much to improve our relationship. You've taught me how to dress and act.

Silas has attempted to teach me how to attend to his needs," his other eyebrow lifts and I quickly add, "at least on a basic level."

"Then you're good." He starts around me, but I hold my ground.

"I'm not." I hold. My. Ground.

He notices.

"I need to know about the business. What exactly does Rex do for Serendee? What does Anex pay him all that money for?"

He runs his hand through his dark hair. "That's not possible."

"Says who? You?"

"It doesn't matter. It's not happening."

"Make it happen, Elon." I rest my hands on my hips. It feels strong, even if I'm quaking inside.

"And if I don't?"

"I guess I go ask Anex on my own." I tap my finger on my chin. "Do you think he knows Rex has all those rolls of cash in his bedside table? He may be curious about that."

His steel-gray eyes pin mine, but I don't falter. Finally, he grimaces and says, "Fine." Then takes in my outfit. "Get out of that dress. Jeans. Black sweater. Sneakers."

"Sneakers?"

"I know I bought you some."

"You did."

"Well, put them on."

I don't hesitate, changing quickly, sliding on the stretchy but tight jeans and a dark sweater from the back of the closet. When I return to the living room, I see that he's in a similar outfit.

"Are you sure you want to do this?" he asks, zipping up his hoodie.

"Yes."

His head tilts slightly, like he's gearing up to talk me out of it, but he ultimately says nothing, and we head out of the suite. The Main House keeps a constant rhythm, open all day and night because Serendee runs on Anex's time. Basketball all night. Sleeping late. Courses and training go as long as needed. Even so, we don't pass anyone on the way out, and although I assumed we would go down to the garage, we don't. Elon takes me out one of the back doors, along the back driveway, until we reach a path that I know leads behind the school.

The gym lights glow a block away, and I notice Elon places himself on the outside of the path, blocking me from the street. We pass the playground and suddenly he announces, "That's where I first saw you."

I glance over and stumble over a root. His hand shoots out to catch me. "What did you say?"

"Remember when we were kids, and everyone would pile onto that merry-go-round and an older kid would come around and spin it really fast?"

"Yes," I say, the memory flooding back. A dozen kids would climb onto the flat surface and hang onto the bars for dear life. It was thrilling and exciting and even though it made my stomach twist anxiously, I always wanted more. "You were there?"

"I was the older kid."

I look up at his face and try to place this Elon with one that's much younger, although still strong and using that strength to make everyone on the playground happy. A flash of color bursts through and I see him. Bigger than everyone else, laughing and enjoying the game. "Wait. You always wore that soccer jersey, right?"

"Yeah," he smiles. It may be the only genuine one I've seen. "I loved that jersey. I had to give it up when we moved into the domum."

"Same, but mine was pink overalls. I loved all the pockets."

We walk a little further, veering away from the school and taking the path that leads to the agricultural sector. "You really remember me from back then?"

"Yes. You were small but always had a big smile. Bossy." He laughs. "You'd scream, 'go faster! Make it faster!'"

"And you'd do it." I can almost feel the wind on my face. "It felt like flying. Sorry I was so demanding."

"It was worth it to see you happy." That's a revelation I'm not sure how to handle and I stay quiet as we cut through the woods until straight ahead is the big red barn. Elon stops. "I miss those days," he says suddenly. "Just being a kid."

"It was easier," I agree. Of course, back then, my mother was still living at home. My family was intact, and I wasn't connected to a Regressive. And Elon, well, he hadn't started on the journey that led us here—out by the barn in the middle of the night. When he doesn't say anything else, I point to the building. "Is this what you're showing me? The barn?"

The tension returns, tugging at his eyes, and I regret breaking the spell. "Not the barn exactly." He starts down the hill and grabs my hand, pulling me along with him. He's quiet, and I try my hardest to be the same. We reach the storm door on the backside of the building. Flat doors that open outward. "We're not going in the barn, but under it."

There's a keypad, and he punches in the code. A moment later, the doors unlock, and a dark staircase is revealed. Apprehension rolls in my belly. Is this a trap? A trick? Suddenly, fluorescent lights flash on, illuminating the stairway. My steps falter when I see what is stretched out before us: rows and rows of tall, leafy plants.

"A nursery?" I ask, trying to process the enormity of what I'm seeing. It's clean, the rows are orderly. Complicated light and sprinkler systems are attached to the ceiling.

"Of sorts, yes."

I touch the plant closest to me and sniff the leaves. The odor is herbal, woodsy, and a little skunky. "Is this...?" I don't want to ask, but I have to. He's showing me for a reason.

"Three acres of specially cultivated marijuana." He nods down the row. "It's longer than the building."

I frown. "What does specially cultivated mean?"

He gives me a look. "You definitely don't want to know that."

I stare out at the rows of plants. "So this is the business Rex carries outside the community."

He walks over and tugs a leaf off and smells it. "Yep. The farmers grow it. We sell it and the money flows back to Serendee."

Pieces click together about my betrothed and his friend. The hours working outside Serendee. The mingling with secular people. Their secretive nature. And, of course, the money.

"Rex is a drug dealer."

His face twists up in displeasure. "Rex is a salesman. Of Serendee and the product that keeps the community running. He's the face of Anex's world."

"And you?"

"I'm his bodyguard. I protect his very lucrative face."

My mind spins. Anex believes in the healing qualities of natural supplements—or drugs. It's preferred to other toxins. Marijuana. Herbal extracts. Natural potions. It's common. I knew we even had products made of hemp. But to be involved in it to this extent—to this level of secrecy is shocking. There's so much I didn't know about Serendee and most of it conflicts with everything I've ever been taught.

"Isn't this illegal?" I ask.

Elon shrugs. "You know, Serendee does not always prescribe to the laws of the secular world. We don't believe in government bureaucracy and regulation. Marijuana is grown naturally."

I nod. I do know this. We're Ordered and mated. There's no official wedding or paperwork. Women have children at home. We work for ourselves, without the use of social security numbers or even identification. Anex thinks the government will want to shut us down if they know how efficiently, how sustained we are living.

I glance into the cavernous warehouse again and realize that Anex is more prepared, more serious, than I ever could have expected. Rex is an important leader in all of this. He is definitely not expendable. No wonder he has to keep him close.

I have more questions, like, what does Rex do with all the money besides stash it in his bedside table? Who knows about the farm? Has there ever been trouble? But the sound of footsteps and voices echo off the cement floor, cutting off my thoughts. I've barely processed that they're coming or that maybe we should hide, when Elon grabs me and pulls me into a dark corner behind oily smelling machinery. The people pass us, talking quietly to one another as they take their time walking down the rows.

My heart pounds, both in my chest and in my ears. It's hot back here, near the generators, and I'm tucked against Elon's large frame. His arms are wrapped around me like a shield, and my ear is pressed against his chest. My heart isn't the only one beating like a drum.

Neither of us speaks as the voices drift farther away, although Elon shifts out of discomfort. The space is cramped, and the movement pushes us chest to chest as his hips brush against my lower belly, revealing the hard bulge in his pants.

I suck in a gasp. Oh.

Elon has been more abrasive to me than Rex. He's insulted me, groped me, belittled and watched as his friend humiliated me. He doesn't like me. It must be the proximity. Men can't control their bodies, which is why we're taught it's up to us to take precaution. It's my fault for putting us in this situation. For demanding that we come here.

We're frozen like this, his cock drilling into me, and my body tunes in to the fact that on some primal level, he wants me. Heat spreads through my limbs and my pulse changes, thrumming in a steady beat; less fear, more desire. Just when I think I'm making it up, Elon's hand slides down and cups my backside. In one swift move, he's lifted me off the ground and spun us around. My back is against the wall and our bodies fit together. Nose to nose, he stares at me, eyes dark and hard.

An apology for being a woman, for pushing him to bring me here, for dragging him out in the night, sits on the tip of my tongue. "Elon, I—"

He cuts me off with a kiss. It's not our first that happened at Anex's will, but this—it's all him—us. There's no hesitation, only lust. I taste it on his tongue as he parts the seam of my lips. I feel it in my core, where he rocks his hips against mine. It burns in my belly, my spine, my ears. His breath is warm, his hands greedy. He holds me against the wall, like I'm light as a feather, and slips a hand up my sweater and palms my breast.

My legs hook around him, anchoring me in place. We're clothed. We're cramped. We're caught in this moment alone. The people we're hiding from are long gone, and it's dark enough that I can barely see his face. I'm glad, because I don't want him to know how good this feels, because is it any different from Levi's Corrections? Isn't this just me wanting something that hurts? A man that loathes me?

But I am that person—that woman—and I grind into him. He pushes back, a growl rumbling in his chest. It reveals that sensation I felt with Silas—power. Anex tells us that to get what we want, women need to be more like men. Less emotional. More demanding. I want what's happening right now as much as Elon. My body demands release. I push into him again, and he ruts against me in return. Back and forth we go, rubbing, grunting, allowing our needs to take control.

It hits me hard—harder than with Silas or on my own. As hard as it was when Levi placed his mouth on me, which seems crazy, with the barriers surrounding us. It comes down like rain, sweeping over my body with such intensity that I have to hold on to Elon. My teeth bite into his shoulder—holding my groan inside. His movements stop abruptly, hips jerking upward as he buries his face in my neck. "So good," he mutters. "So fucking good."

It's the only thing he's said since he dragged me back here. I almost think I made it up.

Elon shudders and exhales and steps back, slowly unpinning me from the wall. He grimaces down at his pants and mutters, "Jesus," while I straighten my shirt. My panties are wet and sticky, but I assume it's nothing compared to his.

He eases around the generator and then glances back. "It's clear," he says, jerking his head for me to follow. "We need to get back."

I nod and slip back up the staircase and out into the night.

Elon showed me a lot in a few hours. The truth about Serendee. The obligations of my mate. The ties that bind him here. The power that I hold.

He also revealed that he's a man that takes what he wants, even if it doesn't belong to him.

32

I toss a jacket into my bag and grab my journal and a roll of cash out of the bedside table. It's enough to get me through the weekend—which is how long I plan on staying away from Serendee. There's no way in hell I'm celebrating my father's birth with a three-day celebration. Fucking narcissist.

I'm not expecting company when I walk back into the living room.

"Going somewhere?" Silas asks. He's sprawled on the couch. His feet are propped on the coffee table. Levi is next to him, while Elon stands near the door peeling an apple with the blade of a knife.

"Out. Away. Anywhere but here."

"You're bailing on your dad's birthday weekend." Levi says it as a fact, not a question.

"Nailed it." I knock over Silas' legs and cut through the room. "Have a piece of coconut cake without me." Anex loves coconut cake. There will be at least twenty cakes, all in his preferred flavor. Just the thought of it makes me gag.

"Rex, put down the bag," Elon says mid-peel. I've been pissed at Elon for weeks now. Ever since, he showed up with Imogene at the club. My goal had been to ignore her completely, but he pushed that altercation. I had to do what I had to do.

"And why would I do that?"

He doesn't bother with an explanation. "You're going camping with the rest of us."

It's not often that my friends stand up to me. I eye the three of them. "Why? Because it'll hurt daddy's feelings if I'm not there to fawn over him like the other minions?"

"Because your mate is expecting you there," Silas says matter-of-factly. It's exactly the answer I don't want to hear. "The final day is Solstice. You have to show."

Imogene. God, that woman is both expected and unexpected at the same time. I expect her to follow my father's rules. I expect her to be submissive and compliant. I expect her to behave like a sheep, even when she's being led to slaughter.

I did not anticipate her beauty, or the way she would look in secular clothing when she walked in that bar. A lethal combination of sexy and sweet. I wasn't prepared to see her on her knees, to feel her mouth around my cock, to watch her swallow even though I was the one that made her do it. I thought there would be tears. Anger. Humiliation. I thought she'd run long before we got to that place. But she didn't run, and I had to follow through. She made me do that. Anex made me.

And then the night she perched on my lap, when I'd pushed my way inside of her, making her come.

She needed to know what a man—a mate—from Serendee was truly like. We take. We demand. We possess.

I snort, brushing Silas off. "Imogene is not my concern."

Elon pushes off the wall and drops the spiral of skin on the kitchen counter. He then snaps the blade shut and tucks it in his pocket. "She is your concern. You agreed to the Ordering. You picked her. Now you have to fulfill your obligation and this weekend is one of them."

"I'm not obligated to anything or anyone—at least not yet. No one will notice if I'm not at Solstice."

Even I know that's a stretch.

Elon shakes his head. His whole attitude confuses me. None of these guys has ever cared what I do. We work, we party, we live by our own rules. Why is this suddenly a big deal? I narrow my eyes. "I'm missing something, aren't I?"

"You're missing out on hanging with a sweet, sexy girl that's willing to do whatever you want," Silas says with a shrug. "I know I'd stick around."

Silas calling Imogene sexy triggers my suspicions. "That's an awfully descriptive way to talk about another man's mate."

Elon takes a loud, crunching bite into his apple. "Two seconds ago, you didn't want her. Silas says she's sexy and you get territorial? Classic Rex."

I look at Levi. "What's this about?"

He spares a glance at the others and then says, "We've been working with her."

"Working with her. What does that mean?"

"Preparing her to be the mate of an entitled asshole that hates everything she believes in," Levi says. "Training. She wasn't ready for you."

"You did this on my father's orders?" I ask, avoiding the truth behind what they're saying. I know the kind of work my father would ask of them. The kind of training they would expose her to. If I could string them from the ceiling, I would. But I can't. I repeat, "You did this on my father's orders?"

"Yes," Levi says.

"Son of a—" I swallow it back. "You had no right."

"No," Elon says, stepping forward. He's got three inches on me, and I know for a fact he can kick my ass. "You had no right to lock this girl into being your mate and then abandoning her. If she shows up without you this weekend, she'll be ruined. You know that."

"Especially with her family history," Levi adds. "People will blame her for your absence. They'll ask questions she can't answer."

"And your father?" Silas says. "You think he'll just let her go back to the community? She knows too much. She's locked in now, whether you want her or not."

"Whose fault is that? Who showed her what goes on behind the curtain? It sure as hell wasn't me." I glare at the three of them. This is exactly what I didn't want to happen. I wanted to keep her—all of them out of this. I run my hand through my hair. "Fine. I'll go. I'll stand by her and pretend like everything is fine, but it doesn't change anything."

"Give her a chance," Silas says. Levi nods in agreement. Elon, well, he won't meet my eye. "I don't think you'll regret it."

I don't respond but turn and carry my bag back in my room, holding back a scream of rage. Giving Imogene a chance was never something I planned on doing. And regrets? Picking her to be my mate, even if just symbolically, was definitely going to be my biggest one yet.

* * *

I'm not sure when Anex's birthday became a three-day weekend. After my mother died, I think, but I could have that wrong since children aren't allowed in the encampment during the party. At sixteen, after we'd moved into the main house, we still weren't invited, but the continuous drumbeat lured me, Elon, Levi, and Silas through the pastures to get as close as we possibly could. During the day, the adults participated in field day—traditional races and matches. At night, it turned to dancing and feasting. Each day was a celebration of my father's existence—a way to show thanks for his sacrifice to Serendee and his devotion to The Way. There are birthday cakes, and musicians, drinks and the wafting of smoked herbs. Back then, I'd been enthralled by the mystique of my father. Only a man of extreme worth would deserve a celebration like this.

Now I know better.

This year it's even more of an event—the final day lands on the Summer Solstice and the Ordered will gather in front of Anex for a blessing, and the couples will gift their mates with a token of some kind. In the secular world, rings are the traditional gift, and that is acceptable here, but since material possessions are not coveted here, it can be almost anything. I walk through the campground, past the small tents and makeshift circles of friends and family. There's a hierarchy in Serendee. My father and his inner circle establish the order—the outside is filled with those who contribute less. Less skill. Less devotion. Less access. Less money. The next ring is for people diligently working their way through the lessons, whose logs are in order and their dedication clear. They attend late night basketball or sit at his side during lectures.

Then there is the ring of tents occupied by the Ordered. Each newly ordered couple gets a tent of their own—a gift from Anex in support of their mating. My tent isn't there. I am in the inner circle —usually in an encampment with my confidants. This year a volunteer points me in the direction of my lodgings and I see that it's an angular yurt perched on the edge of the circle. Imogene and I have been given privacy.

Another of my father's manipulations.

I push past the flap of the tent and step inside. I've come to this event for four years and not once have my accommodations been like this—even as a member of the inner circle. The yurt is draped in colorful fabric, and a mattress has been brought in and covered with soft quilts. Pillows are stacked on the bed, as well as on the floor, which is also covered in a thick rug. I'm taking it all in, spinning in a circle, when I see her standing in the doorway. She's in a loose white dress, the neck scooped out, revealing the hint of the soft flesh underneath. Her skin looks healthier than before—her cheeks plumper. The weight gain makes sense. Levi, or one of the guys, has been feeding her better.

"Hi," she says. It's the first time I've seen her up close since that night, and as much as I try not to, the first thing I look at is her mouth.

Jesus.

"Imogene." I clutch the strap of my bag over my shoulder. "I guess my father went all out this year."

"The tent, yes," she says, "but I brought most of the furnishings."

I eye the flickering lanterns hanging from the tent poles. "Did you?"

"I figured that if you showed, it would be our first weekend actually together. I should make it special."

And there it is. The need to make everything more. To push and manipulate. I hold back my criticism and nod at the door flap on the other side of the room. "Where does that go?"

"A separate room for Levi, Silas and Elon."

"You invited them?"

"Of course. They're your family."

A family of betrayers, I think, wondering how much they had to do with this. I know they mean well. I do. We've been through everything together. But we're talking about an outsider. She's not an outsider to Serendee—far from it. It's clear she's devoted to The Way, but she's an outsider to our tight group. They know how I feel about bringing in anyone new, particularly someone on my father's radar. There's a reason I only see women outside the community.

"Well, it's nice." I'm trying to be polite. "Far more comfortable than I expected. You better not let my father see this or he'll get jealous of my special treatment."

She smiles and blushes, pleased that I've complimented her. "I tried to remember everything we may need for the weekend, but I'm sure I've forgotten something. Don't hesitate to ask if there's something you want or need."

Irritation flickers under my skin and my response comes out harsh. "You're not my slave, Imogene."

"I know."

"Then stop acting like one."

"I'm just—"

"Behaving the way you were raised. I know that. I'm not my father. This isn't the kind of relationship that I want."

"Then what do you want?"

I laugh, and I know it sounds meaner than I intend. "What I want isn't an option. Not here. Here I live with what my father wants for us. Everyone does. You know that." I tilt my head and study the woman next to me. "I doubt I was what you expected."

"No," she admits. "I never considered being ordered to someone of your position. Not with my family history. But then, I guess that explains a lot of what's happening here. If you wanted a true mate, you would have been Ordered to a more worthy female."

Her statement lands hard. Truthfully. We stand across from one another for an awkward beat. She's right. I chose her for her flaws.

"You can leave," she finally says. "Or I can. I don't want to ruin the weekend by forcing you to be around me if you find me so unappealing."

I drop my bag and step closer, reaching out to touch the side of her face. She flinches. I can't blame her. Not after what I've made her do the times, we've been together. She's trying. I can see that and although it doesn't make a difference, I do feel compelled to say, "Your appeal has nothing to do with this, Imogene. If you understand nothing else, understand that."

Her big eyes hold mine and again I can't help but look at her lips. They're pink and soft. I know what they feel like on my skin. Quickly, I drop my hand and say, "It's more of a hassle to deal with Anex's disapproval than to last the weekend. As long as we have to be here, I think we should make the most of it. Give the people what they want. Get my father off my back."

"If that's what you want."

I grimace. "What I want, Imogene, is for you to stop conceding everything to me."

"I know." She twists her hands. "It's hard to stop. My mind just snaps back to my lessons—to the things we've been taught. Even after the training with Levi, Elon and Silas, I find myself slipping back into it."

"If we have to spend the weekend together, maybe I know how we can make that a little better."

"How?"

"By doing my favorite thing." I grin cheekily. "Breaking the rules."

33

Imogene

I try to manage myself as I walk through the camp with Rex by my side. To pretend this situation is normal and that we've spent the last few weeks getting to know one another like the other Ordered mates. I hope no one can tell my heart races like a horse's hoofbeats, or that my palms are clammy with sweat. I hope no one can see that he loathes his father, Serendee, and The Way, or that his dislike of all those things trickles down to me. I desperately pray that no one knows that the last time he saw me, he forced me to take him in my mouth and swallow his seed out of spite and intimidation.

And that I let him.

"Where are we going?" I ask, keeping up with his long strides.

"To make an appearance—let my father know we're here."

I've underestimated Rex. He glides through the crowd, nodding at men he knows from meetings or other members of the community. He accepts their slight bows, their well wishes, the way the female's eyes absorb his good looks. He is respectful to me, making sure I'm by his side, and I find myself caught up in the game. These people have no idea who he truly is: a criminal, an abuser, a blasphemer. They see what he wants to show them, and he knows his role—or at the very least, how to perform it flawlessly. His behavior creates a gnawing feeling of confusion in my belly. One, I do my best to keep off my face.

"Are you ready?" he asks, as we approach the canvas gazebo in the center of the field. It's up on a circular platform, a chair in the middle, surrounded by pillows on the ground. There's a crowd bunched around the tent, but my eyes are on the man in the chair. Anex speaks in his quiet, consistent tone, captivating the crowd.

"What is the point of this beautiful life," he says, gazing down at his followers, "if you are living it inauthentically? How do you process what you hear and see and feel if you don't know how to manage that input? Authenticity is where you find the truth in yourself and in one another. It's how your soul can open up to mesh with the soul of another person. If you are inauthentic, you will never meet that other person's true self. Which is why you have to stop fighting yourself. Fighting others. You must dig deep for who you are so that you can become whole."

The group is mesmerized. I'm mesmerized, although once he stops speaking and someone asks a question, I become attuned to the vibrations rolling off of Rex. I glance over and see his profile— his jaw clenched tight and his hands balled into angry fists. I'd had him here with me for a moment, but seeing his father threatens to shatter any truce we'd come to in the tent. On instinct, I reach for his hand. Sliding my palm over the backside of his fist. He tenses further, but I don't stop. I push the pads of my fingers into the gaps of his and wind our hands together.

"Come on," I say. "We don't need to be here."

He glances down, blue eyes hard as glass. "He'll expect..."

"He'll survive." I can't believe I said that, but I tug him away. He doesn't relax as we work our way through the crowd, but he also doesn't let go. I lead him behind a portable trailer—a kitchen used to feed everyone over the weekend. There's a covered dining area filled with picnic tables and an entire counter is covered in the cakes for Anex's birthday.

"He really bothers you," I say, starting to understand this man a little better. Not much, but a little.

"You have no idea."

"Then forget him. He'll be busy all weekend, and as long as we're together, he can't complain too much. We can blame it on him—he's the one that made the Ordered."

"True." A smile tugs at his lips. "It's not our fault we're so focused on one another. We're betrothed after all." He looks at me hungrily and my belly flutters. Fear? Apprehension? I'm not sure. He glances back and forth, making sure no one is around and it builds, but he turns away from me.

"What are you doing?" I ask, trying to settle my breathing.

He sneaks over to the cake table and grabs a big one. "Hungry?"

Of course, that look wasn't for me.

"You're stealing a cake?" I whisper.

"Breaking the rules, Imogene. That's how I survive." He rolls his eyes. "Ugh, it's coconut. Of course."

Breaking the rules is something I've tried to never do. There's no leeway with my family's history. But it dawns on me that I have a new family—at least in theory. He stares down at the cake with disgust, and I wrinkle my nose. "I'm not a fan of coconut either. We can scrape it off."

"Yeah?" he asks, surprised. Not about the cake, but about my willingness to go along with him.

"Yes." I nod in the direction of our yurt. "I have a few other things that can go along with it. Come on."

This time, I lead the way, sneaking along the backside of the campground on the way back to our makeshift home. My plan for the weekend had been to feed him, ease his anger, gain his trust. I glance back at him, carrying the cake in one hand and licking an icing covered finger with the other. I may be able to accomplish that yet.

* * *

I make him stop by the tent to gather a few of the things I'd brought with me for the weekend. I have a picnic basket full of snacks, like I'd seen in his suite. I'd also added drinks and healthier foods like fruit and meat and cheese.

We settle on an area by the lake—far from the growing celebration in the center of the camp. "You sure this is a safe spot?" I ask. I'd been full of bravado near the kitchen, but the idea of being caught not participating in Anex's birthday makes me uncomfortable.

Rex watches me spread the blanket out. "Things get a little wild as the night progresses. My father will be so caught up in it all he won't notice."

From the sound of the music and laughter drifting our way, I assume he's right.

I unpack the basket, laying out a spread of food. Rex stretches out on the blanket, his legs so long his feet hang off the edge. He watches me, and I pretend not to notice the scrutiny. I know he's looking for flaws. Weaknesses. He's coming up with reasons to reject me further.

"This isn't local," he says, picking up a package of crackers. "Did you go shopping in town?"

"Levi took me," I reply. I didn't have actual money, but I suspected he did, and I was too flustered to ask Elon. I knew for certain he had cash, but after what happened between us under the barn... well, I was still processing that. The way he kissed and rubbed against me—that was not a lesson. It was not training. It just felt good and every time I look at him, my skin sets on fire and I want to do it again. I have no idea what he thinks or feels or wants.

It's easier to push all of that aside, because Rex is here and despite the intimacy I've had with his confidants, they must fit squarely in another box.

"Levi." He opens the box and shakes out a handful of crackers. "That must have been hard for him. He doesn't like to disobey the rules."

"No." I shrug and cut slices of meat and cheese on a board. "But he will do anything to support our Ordering, even if it means pushing me a little."

I arrange the food on a plate and hand it to him. Our fingers brush underneath and I wait for a spark—a flicker of something—but no, his walls are too high.

"Don't you see how fucked up that is?" he asks, taking the plate from me. "Levi shouldn't ask you to go against your values just because my father wants something. And those values never should exist in the first place."

"Following The Way means we have to challenge our notions of self every day, Rex. You know that."

"Is that why you're okay with my father having you trained? With my confidants touching you in a way only a mate should?"

My face heats. He knows. Of course he knows. They're his confidants. Did Silas tell him about how I touched myself while he did the same? Did Elon confess to what we did in the barn. And Levi... does he know about the Corrections? I can't answer his question and from the expression on his face, he doesn't need one. The flush in my skin tells him everything.

"He'll do anything to get in your head, you know that, right? To get in my head."

Everything Rex says is the kind of thing that would get a normal resident of Serendee removed for Regression. But he speaks freely, which means he's either not afraid or he wants to be caught.

"Can I ask you something?" I ask.

"Sure."

"What made you turn against The Way?"

His lips turn down. "Do you really want to know?"

"I do." Desperately.

"I was a believer—like everyone else that grows up here. I didn't just think my father was the light and the moon. I knew it. He was smart and fun. Innovative and generous." He swallows and sets his plate aside. "But when my mother died, my father changed. Everything I'd been raised to believe shifted. His ideas became more extreme, and his sense of superiority grew. You probably don't remember any of this because you were too young, but Serendee didn't used to be like this—Imogene." He lifts his chin up the hill toward the party. "It truly was a place that co-existed with the outside world. People weren't bound to this land—to him."

"I know what it's like to lose a mother—not one to death," I add quickly, "but she's gone all the same. Life changes when someone leaves. People change. Even your father."

He shakes his head and the blonde highlights glint in the light of our lantern. "You don't know him, Imogene. Not like I do."

"So your reaction is to rebel. Regardless of who you hurt."

He looks at me, eyes blazing. "I don't want to hurt anyone. That's the point. I work and I play—doing as much of it away from Serendee as possible. Bringing you and the guys into this—that is against my wishes. If anyone gets hurt—blame the one responsible. Anex."

Every response I have is tangled in the words of The Way. Indulgency. Regression. Integrated. I know it will just make him angry. So I rise to my feet, taking care not to step on the hem of my dress.

"Where are you going?" he asks.

"For a swim." I walk to the edge of the bank, the soft ground sinking between my toes. I've swum in this lake a million times—during hot summer days and long weekend retreats. There's a dock out in the middle. I lift the hem of my dress and take the first step in. It's chillingly cold, but it zaps the uncomfortable heat off my skin.

"You can't swim right now," he says, scrambling up. "It's dark. And cold. And someone may see you."

"I thought you were all about breaking the rules." I wade deeper, futilely holding the bottom of my dress in a tight fist. The cold water reaches my knees, then thighs, then I take the final step up to my waist. When I'm far enough out, I look back at the land. "What? You scared?"

The strongest compulsion comes over me, and I fling water at him. My aim is true, and the splash rains down on his face. He glares with his hands on his hips.

I do it again.

"So that's how you want to do this," he says, springing into action. He shucks off his shirt and pants. There's zero trace of self-consciousness as he strips to his shorts. I half-expect him to get completely naked. Why wouldn't he? I've already seen—and tasted—his most private parts.

But he keeps them on and lunges into the water, making waves with every step. I can't help but take in his body—mercy, he's beautiful. Hard, lean muscle ladders up his abdomen. Smooth skin stretches over his chest. It's difficult to find him threatening like this, but the wicked grin curving his lips isn't innocent.

"Where are you going?" he taunts as the threat of retaliation propels me deeper in the lake. I'm deep now, my feet no longer touching the ground. I'm closer to the deck than to the shore, so I continue deeper, even though my dress is dragging me down. It only takes him a few moments to catch up—his long arms cutting through the water. His hand grabs the back of my dress and drags me toward him.

"Wait!" I yelp. "I'm—"

He clutches me against his chest and whispers in my ear. "Not so brave with me right here, are you?"

My legs swirl beneath me, trying to tread water, but they keep getting tangled in the folds of my long dress. I reach behind me and grip his side. "My dress." I dip below the surface. "It's too heavy."

He believes me, thankfully, moving into action. With his arm around my stomach, he swims one armed to the dock, lifting me up on the wooden boards. Lake water rushes from the hem of my skirt, and he hoists himself next to me, and mutters, "I hate these fucking dresses. It shouldn't be a surprise it could kill you."

It feels like a fifty-pound weight hanging off my frame. Ignoring the chill on my skin, I gather the hem and twist, squeezing out as much water as I can. Sitting, I ask, "What are you talking about?"

He touches the lace around my neck and goosebumps rush across my skin. His eyes dart down to where I know the fabric clings against my breasts. My nipples are hard peaks, surely visible through the sheer, wet material.

"These dresses. It's basically a leash, Imogene. A fucking choker to keep you in line." He fingers the button at the top, loosening it and then the two below that. Air blows across my skin and his touch is so gentle, I'm not sure how to process it. Gentle isn't a word I associate with Rex, but here he is. Here we are. "My father wants you afraid of your body—afraid of the power that it wields. His group, VRS? It isn't about teaching men to be better. It's about teaching men to be animals. To take what they want. To cave to their primal instincts, while you've been raised to let men do what they want."

I swallow, burning at his touch—tentatively, I brush the wet hair off his forehead. "Is that so wrong? For men to get what they want."

"You should think so." He laughs darkly.

"What if I'm not afraid?" I trail my fingers down his neck and place my hand on his chest. I'm acting bold. I'm really terrified.

"You should be scared." He exhales as my hands explore his chest. His skin is surprisingly warm. "Of my father, of his inner circle, but most of all, me."

He keeps saying this. Threatening me. Hurting me. But something rings false. A different idea pops into my head and I blurt, "Maybe you're the one that's scared."

His entire body tensed with that accusation. He doesn't like the tables being flipped back on him. His response is physical. Moving quickly, his hand grips the back of my neck, pulling me to him, crashing our mouths together.

Startled, I rear back, but he doesn't let me go. His strong hands keep me in place, his lips controlling the pace. His tongue licks at my lips, parting them, invading my mouth. I fight, pushing with all my strength, and he only tightens his grip.

"This is what I want, Little Lamb." A wicked smile tugs at his mouth. "I want to bury myself inside of you. I want to feel you quiver around me. I want you to cry my name out—in pain or desire. I don't care. As long as it's my name on your lips and no one elses."

His words are mean. Terrifying. Far beyond what the men prepared me for. He's meaner than Elon. And the pain he inflicts when he touches me is harder than the ones Levi inflicts in secret.

"Stop," I tell him. "Stop!"

"I won't. You belong to me, Imogene. This is what you wanted, and I tried to warn you. I tried. But you wouldn't fucking listen." His lips drop to my neck, and he scrapes his teeth down the tender flesh.

His powerful hands lift my dress over my head and drop it on the wooden planks. His warm hand palms my breast, and he kisses me painfully. That ticking desire, the one that I've felt with Levi, surges through me, ebbing with every kiss, every touch. But there's no limit here. I can sense it—it does scare me. So much that when the swelling between his legs grows harder, more insistent, I try to fight him off. The rules about consummating an Ordered relationship are clear; once the Order has been given, couples can explore one another freely, but we should not have penetrative sex until after the mating ceremony at the fall equinox. After Anex gives his final blessing.

Rex is not a man bound by rules, and it becomes clear in the way his fingers pull and prod. I make a break, rushing to the opposite side of the platform, lake water sloshing on the floating dock. He grabs me before I get to the edge, arm wrapped around my waist and throwing me roughly to the platform. I cry out when I land with a thud, the hard planks scraping my backside. "Rex—"

"Shut up." He stands over me and removes his shorts. His cock is erect and stabbing at the air. He's a god, I know this, and I know then he's not going to take no for an answer. "You asked for this."

He bends before me and yanks away the lace panties I wore just for him.

"You're beautiful," he says, eyes roaming over my body. "I'll give you that, but you're not enough to bind me to this place, Little Lamb." He crawls over me, twice my size. When his face is above mine, his expression is cloaked in darkness, pain. "You need to understand who I really am. Who my father created me to be."

"You're a good man," I try to tell him, but his blue eyes glaze over and he wrenches my legs apart. "Don't do this, Rex, it's not The Way."

I never expected my first time to be good, or even gentle.

Clarissa warned us that it was about a man's need over anything at all, but I thought it would be inside the realm of The Way. That it would be done right, with Anex's blessing, and at the very least in a bed with a man just as nervous as myself.

But I don't expect large hands holding me down, or strong knees pushing my thighs apart. "Tell me you didn't let them fuck you."

Them. His friends. Elon, Levi. Silas.

"N-no."

"But you let them do something, didn't you Little Lamb." His nose is inches from mine, and I feel the tip of his erection prodding at my entrance. "Did you let Silas con his way into your boring little panties? Or maybe Elon humiliated and belittled you until you caved, just to get him to stop?" He laughs darkly. "Levi? Did he guilt you into it? Telling you it's the road to Enlightenment?"

"It wasn't like that," I promise, but he doesn't believe me. I see it on his face. I see it when he wrenches my legs apart, barely giving me a moment to catch my breath before he stops nudging at my core and thrusts inside.

"Ungh," I cry, biting down on my bottom lip, the width of his cock tearing through the final barriers.

"If you fight, it'll be worse," he says, stilling for a single moment, before pulling out and punching in again.

"Please," I start, although I don't know why. He's already inside me—he's broken my barrier—he's claimed me, even if he doesn't want me.

This can't be happening, this can't be real. But the weight of him on top of me, the power of his body, there's no mistaking the invasion going on inside of me, or the man taking everything from me. I try to focus on anything else, the sound of the water sloshing against the dock, the drumbeats from up on the hill, the rising moon over his shoulder. But none of it works. Instead, because this is who I am, I narrow in on the pain, the biting grip of his fingers, the friction as he moves in and out of me. The tickle in my lower belly, the one that I feel when Levi's hand blisters against my flesh, flickers to life. When Silas pushes me to the edge or Elon pushes too hard.

The self-loathing I feel when I want it, bubbles under my skin and I seek more. My hips rise to meet his. Craving the burn of skin against skin, I fight against his hands. His brow furrows when he looks at me, confused by my actions. He should be. I'm sick and from the look in his eye, he sees it, knows it, and crashes our mouths together. I bite down on his bottom lip, and he groans with hunger. It ignites something in him, an intensity that makes his hips pound into me harder, his teeth scrape deeper and his hands bruise.

We fight like this—we fuck like this—hard and angry, until the pressure builds between my legs, in my lower belly, and his kisses swallow my desperate moans. He smirks down at me, knowing he brought me to orgasm, knowing he brought me down to his level. My muscles quiver around him and soon the movement of his hips grows erratic, and he grunts, deep and guttural, punching into me one last time.

His back arches as he spills into me, hot and wet. I stare up at this demon of a man—this hateful, terrible man, and know that he has ruined my life. Ruined me.

"Fuck," he mutters, rolling off me and lying flat on the dock, chest rising and falling from exertion. I wait, trying to separate the drumbeat on the hill from my racing heart, both intertwined—just like my desire for pleasure and pain. He blinks at me, like he's seeing me for the first time all night. Again, he says, "Fucking hell," but this time he stands, lurching forward and diving into the dark water.

The dock rocks from the wave, tossing me to the side. I should be happy to see him go—to be rid of him—but instead all I feel is cold and lost. I'd spent years as an outsider in this community, scrambling to hold my head up high. Rex just took that all away. He took everything.

34

Silas

"They're not in the tent," Levi says, walking up to me and Elon. "Any luck in the dining pavilion?"

"No," Elon says, running his hand through his hair. I've noticed he's edgy when he doesn't know Imogene's location. It may be the bodyguard in him—or something else. He holds his emotions so close to the vest it's impossible to know. "Not in the crowd around Anex either."

We agree to walk around the edge of the campground. It's not that both Imogene and Rex being missing is a problem or even a concern, the whole weekend is a free-for-all, and they are Ordered to one another. They should be together, and Imogene had this whole thing planned out, but... it's just feels like something is off.

"Wait," Levi says, grabbing my arm and pointing down the hill toward the lake. "Is that Rex?"

Our friend emerges from the water like a monster from the deep. It's dark, but the moon is high, providing enough light to see that he's bare from the waist down. He grabs his clothing and heads up the hill.

"Rex!" I call, thinking he must not see us. His expression is stormy, and he doesn't stop. "Rex, hold up!"

He stops, but only to tug his pants on. The fabric snags on his wet legs and he curses under his breath.

"Where's Imogene?" Levi asks, getting to him first.

Rex tugs his shirt on, and it clings to his wet upper body. He jerks his thumb back at the water. "She's on the dock."

I look out at the dark water. It's hard to even see the dock from here. "On the dock? She was with you?"

"You left her there?" Levi asks, already starting down the hill. "It's pitch black."

"She can find her way back. There's a lantern on shore."

Elon steps forward and grabs him by the front of his shirt. "What did you do to her?"

Rex pushes him off with both hands. "None of your fucking business. She's my Ordered, not yours, no matter what my father convinced you to do."

"Are you mad about that?" I ask, noting the tight set of his jaw. "You are, you're mad we were working with her."

"We told you," Elon says, "we're training her. There's no way you would have accepted an innocent little virgin raised in the heart of Serendee."

He laughs darkly. "You're right, I wouldn't have, but—"

"But what?"

Water drips down his face and he flips his hair back. "She's not so innocent anymore."

There's no mistaking what that means. None. Tight, primal anger spreads across my chest and I barely notice Levi take off for the water's edge. "Did you hurt her?"

"Even if I did," he winks, "I think she liked it."

Before I can make a move, Elon lunges at him, grabbing him by the shirt. "What the fuck is wrong with you? She's innocent. Naïve."

"Isn't this what you wanted? For me to claim her?" His eyes narrow at Elon. "You had the chance to break her in brother, and you didn't. I took care of it—just like daddy wanted."

The way he says it, there's no doubt that it's the truth. Elon knows it, too. "You fucked her? On the dock? Outside of the ceremony? You know what that means!"

"I don't give a shit about what that means," Rex says, his voice cold. He holds Elon's gaze. "Get your hands off of me, brother, or I'll have to make you."

"Fuck you," Elon says, shoving Rex across the grass. His chest puffs out and his shoulders widen. "I'll ruin you the way you ruined her."

Rex is a big guy, but Elon? He's a beast. That doesn't stop Rex from taking a swing at him. Elon catches his hand before it hits his jaw and pushes him back. Rex isn't finished, rushing at Elon full force, catching him in the waist with both hands. They tumble to the ground and start to pummel one another. It's not the first fight they've had and I doubt it'll be the last. This is how they communicate—with their fists. Sometimes at the gym in the ring, other times on the basketball court—this is the first time it's been over a female. I glance down at the water and see Levi is waist deep, but his entire body is soaking wet. I jog toward him and as I get closer; I realize Imogene is clinging to his side, shivering from the cold.

"Get a blanket!" Levi calls and I dart down to where they'd set up a picnic and grab the blanket off the ground, scattering food and plates across the grass.

"Hurry," I say. Imogene's lips are blue. Levi gets her to the shore, and I wrap the blanket around her quaking frame. "Are you okay?"

"I just want to get warm."

"Come on," I say, lifting her in my arms. "I've got you."

She snuggles into my chest. Up close, I can tell she's been crying. Rage swells in me as I carry her back up the hill. Rex is gone, but Elon is still there, breathing heavily and sporting a blackening eye. His gaze goes instantly to Imogene, and he walks over, holding out his arms. "I'll carry her the rest of the way." He looks at me. "Go check on the tent. Grab some dry clothes for her when we get there."

There's a deeper instruction—make sure Rex isn't there. Reluctantly, I hand her over and run through the campground. People are at the evening session—one of the designated times Anex will be addressing the group. It's not mandatory, but everyone will be there. At least no one will see us bringing Imogene back to the tent.

I don't know if Rex was telling the truth about what happened out on the dock, but he's not a liar. Even though we've spent so much of our lives together, we've never been at odds like this and definitely never over a woman. It complicates things in a way I didn't know was possible.

I enter the tent and go straight to the wood-burning stove. The perks of being Anex's son. He always has been given the best—which is part of his problem. He doesn't realize what he has when it's right in front of him.

Once it's lit, I find Imogene's bag. I pick out a dry pair of panties and a T-shirt, but nothing else is warm enough, so I go to my own luggage and pull out a sweatshirt and a thick pair of socks. I dim the lights on the lanterns and bring in two extra blankets from our side of the tent to the big bed in the middle.

Making people comfortable is what I do best. My job is to ease the people Anex has deemed worthy in to Serendee so that they'll commit to our community. Dealing with Imogene isn't what I'm used to. The more I get to know her—the deeper entrenched we all have been in making sure Rex and Anex are both happy—the harder it gets. I like her. A lot. I like talking to her, laughing with her, making her come on my fingers.

But I also know my place. She's not mine. She never will be. My duty is to The Way. To Anex and ultimately Rex. For the first time in my life, all of that makes me angry. Furious.

The tent flap opens, and Elon ducks in, carrying Imogene in his arms. Levi follows, turning a little purple himself from the cold. I wave Elon over and say, "Bring her over by the fire. Levi, go change. I've got this."

She's still pale and her body quakes with chills. I have no idea where her clothes are—she'd been in a dress earlier and now she's in nothing but a sheer bra. Her panties are missing. I reach under the blanket and run my hands down her arms, trying to warm her up. "Can I take off this wet stuff?" I ask. "I found some dry things in your bag."

She nods, lips quivering.

Elon hands me the pair of panties, and quickly I run them up each leg. Next, I pull the T-shirt over her head and then the sweatshirt. It hangs down to her thighs. Elon paces the room behind her, still furious about his altercation with Rex. He took a hard hit in the eye—it's already starting to swell. "You need some ice on that," I say over Imogene's head.

"I'm fine."

Levi rolls his eyes and Elon and just says, "Let's get you into bed."

I help her walk over and get under the covers. She balls up on her side, but doesn't stop shivering.

I sit on the edge of the bed, and her eyes open wide and she flinches. "Hey, I'm not going to hurt you."

"I-I know."

But it's clear she doesn't. Why should she? "You're going to need something else to help warm you up. Can I get under the cover with you?"

She swallows, and the shiver that runs down her spine seems to have nothing to do with how cold she is. Levi and I exchange a look. He noticed it, too. "Baby," I tell her, gently touching her shoulder. "I just want to warm you up. The best way I can do that is by sharing my body heat with you."

She stares at me, eyes guarded, and for a moment, I consider finding Rex and making him tell me exactly what he did to her. But this isn't about him. It's about getting her better. "Please?" I ask. "I promise, no one is going to hurt you."

Reluctantly, she nods, and I kick off my shoes and get under the covers. Her body wracks with cold. I wrap my arms around her and pull her tight against my chest. I look up at Levi who is also shivering, cold and wet from getting her out of the water.

"Baby, we need to let Levi in here, too. He's freezing." I whisper. "He'll be good. I promise."

"O-okay."

He hesitates—a flicker of emotion crossing his face. Imogene shudders again, and I shoot him a look. "Get in the bed Levi."

I know it's more of a testimony about how cold he is than anything else, but quickly gets under the covers. I reach underneath and wiggle the socks on her feet—they're cold as ice—and then look up at Elon who has been hovering by the door. "She's still freezing. Levi, too. Want to share some of that muscle mass?"

He glances over at us but gives a curt shake of his head. "I'm going to wait out here. Just to keep an eye out."

What he doesn't say is who he's keeping an eye out for. One thing is for certain, Imogene doesn't have to worry about dealing with Rex again tonight. Elon isn't going to let him back into this tent.

He steps outside and I refocus my attention on the woman next to me. She's gotten herself wrapped up in Levi's stiff arms—the baby spoon. I scoot as close as I can get and lift her head so that it's resting on my shoulder. I stroke her hair and lay a hand on her hip, rubbing it in circles, doing my best to generate warmth.

"Can you tell me what happened?" I ask her, when I see that her eyes are wide open and she's watching me.

"R-Rex happened." She takes a deep breath and reaches beneath my shirt. Her cold hands touch my stomach and I inhale in surprise. "We were getting along—kind of. W-we snuck off from Anex's talk, stole a cake, had a picnic, then went swimming."

"But something went wrong?"

"I don't know what happened." Her cheeks bloom a faint pink. "One minute we were fine, flirting a little. The next it was like someone else was out there with me. Someone that hates me."

Levi has been quiet this whole time. Overt affection isn't something he's used to. He has his kinks—I saw the welts on Imogene's backside, but that's not the same. I'm sure thought the first time he'd be in a bed with a woman was after Anex Ordered him. He certainly didn't expect me to be here.

"Did he hurt you?" Levi asks, breaking his silence.

"He..." She pinches her eyes shut. "He took what belongs to him."

Dread fills my belly, and I see the same emotion written on Levi's face. I knew Rex was a bastard, but I didn't know he was cruel. What he did to Imogene has consequences. Sex before the mating ceremony isn't acceptable, and Rex has made it clear he isn't mating with Imogene, anyway. He tarnished her. He made her vulnerable and now she's a target. That I understand—more than anyone else. Not only has Rex rejected her, but he stole her worth —the one thing she could give to another man. Anex will not Order her a second time and there will be nowhere for her to go. She will become Fallen and move directly under Anex's care.

A female as beautiful as Imogene? Well, Anex will not let that go to waste. He'll either put her to work, lock her up, or keep her for himself. Maybe all three.

As she slowly drifts to sleep and Levi and I continue to give her warmth, I promise myself that I won't let that happen. I won't let her become a slave for Anex's greed. I've accepted my fate, the role I play in Serendee, but that isn't what Imogene was made for and I'll do whatever it takes to keep her safe.

35

I wake in a cocoon of strong arms, bundled in warmth.

It's early morning, the campground is silent. People must be sleeping off the late-night celebration from the night before. Levi's body curves against my back, his arm around my belly. For once, he isn't tense.

Silas faces me, and I'm tucked into him, my head resting in the crook of his shoulder. He smells good and with his eyes closed, his eyelashes are thick and shiny. His leg is wound around mine and I snuggle closer, not wanting the moment to end. It's the first time I've shared a bed with someone—make that someone's—and it feels nice.

That is until I feel the dull ache below my belly and remember what happened on the dock. The reason why they're in the bed with me. Rex.

Things had been going so good—at least comparatively. He talked to me. He flirted. He kissed me. And then... well, like I said, he took what belong to him. Forcefully.

That's not all I remember about the night before. I remember Levi swimming into the lake and helping me back to shore. Silas wrapping me in the blanket and carrying me up the hill to Elon. Elon's arms wrapping tighter around me with each chilled tremor. I recall the expression on his face as he checked to make sure Rex wasn't in the yurt before bringing me in. The tent was warm and cozy, and Silas gently dressed me in dry clothes and bundled me into bed.

For every cruel mark Rex left on my body, these men soothed the pain.

Levi shifts behind me, dragging me closer with the arm wrapped around my waist. My backside presses into him, and I feel the hard insistence of his manhood. My body reacts instantly with flutters of arousal in my lower belly, craving approval after Rex's rejection.

I arch back and I feel the rush of warm air on my neck. "Oh God," Levi mumbles, jumping out of the bed. "I'm sorry. I am so sorry."

Silas' eyes bolt open. He smiles, but it fades when he looks up at Levi, who I can sense pacing behind me. "What's wrong?"

"That was inappropriate," he continues. I turn and see his cheeks are as red as his hair. "I'm—" He starts, but then he just shakes his head and stalks out of the main tent and into the small adjacent room.

I face Silas again, and he's propped up on his elbow watching me. "Any idea what that was about?"

"It seems that the only way men want me is if they're inflicting pain."

He frowns. "What are you talking about?"

"Rex only wants me when he can humiliate and hurt me. Levi has only shown his own arousal in the midst of my Correction. Elon? He certainly doesn't show me tenderness."

Silas touches my cheek gently. "And what about me?"

"Your job is to make women feel safe and cared for. What we have isn't any more real than what I have with Rex."

His kind expression falls, shifting into something I can't quite read. "This isn't easy for us," he says. "To do what I do... there has to be a level of disconnection. You're right. Sex is a not just a job, but my calling. I provide something to the men and women that come into our society that I don't get in return. It's sex, not intimacy. The line is very clear." His chin lifts toward the flap Levi vanished behind. "He has spent his whole life focused on rules and order—maintaining the disciples of VRS. He believes in those philosophies as much as you do. He woke up with your sweet, sexy body next to his and he panicked. He's probably in there listing his Lapses in his journal right now."

I reach to push the covers back. "Maybe I should do the same. I'm the one leading him to a bad place."

Silas grabs my hand and pulls me back under the blankets. He then presses my palm against his lower belly. His cock is ramrod straight, thick, and tucked under his shorts. I curve my fingers around it. "Levi didn't break any rules," he says. "It's nature. Men wake up like this every day."

"Every day?"

"Yep. It's a constant, if there is a woman in the bed or not." He swallows, forcing the lump in his throat to bob. "Which is not something any of us are used to, by the way."

I frown, pulling my hand away. "What do you mean?"

"None of us wake up with a partner in bed. Not even Rex. We may all go to fulfill our needs in one way or the other, but the construct of Serendee is hard to shake. We're all waiting for our Order." He looks down. "It's just unlikely to happen. We're too valuable to Anex as we are. When he Ordered Rex, for a brief moment I thought maybe this meant it could happen, but I see now that this was all just a test. Anex knew Rex would fail and that failure would give him exactly what he wanted."

The way he speaks, it's soft but stern. He's telling me the truth, but I don't understand what he's saying.

"What does Anex really want?"

He looks up at me, his expression twisted in pain. "You."

36

"ME?"

"I think so," he says. "It makes sense. You're beautiful. Smart. Dedicated. He's probably had his eye on you for a while."

"Then why not just claim me for his own. Make me into one of his Spiritual Mates? He can do that." He can do whatever he wants.

"Because nothing with Anex is easy, Imogene." His forehead creases. "He manipulates. Controls. He got us to break down your values, show you the dark side of Serendee. We made you complicit."

"But why? Why me? I'm devoted. I do my work. I ask for nothing. I submit to Corrections—"

"He holds grudges," Levi says, walking back into the main tent. "For a very long time."

I meet his eyes and I see the meaning behind his words. "My mother. This is about my mother."

"That's my guess," he says. "She rejected him and his ways, causing doubt in the community. Along with the death of Rex's mother, your mother leaving is what pushed him into becoming more controlling."

"So you think he wants to punish me for her Regression?" Panic flutters in my chest. I think about the girl who made the phone call, Charlotte. That was a blip compared to this. I look between them. "What is he going to do to me?"

"I don't know," Silas says. "It could be service. A dangerous job." He takes my hand. "Or he could just keep you for his own."

"For sex?" Disgust churns in my stomach. I have no doubt that Anex is aware of my sick need for pain along with my pleasure. What he'll do with that information scares me most of all.

"I suspect that you'll find out tonight," Levi adds, "when Rex does not show up for the Solstice Ceremony."

"Oh god." I hop to my feet and pace the small room. My heart pounds with every step. "What do I do?"

Silas and Levi look at me with sympathy. The answer is clear. There is nothing I can do. I have no money. No formal education. No connections outside. Hot tears build in the corner of my eyes. I have no idea how to find my mother. And even if I wanted to, I shunned her like the rest of the community. I am truly all alone.

"Come here," Silas says, grabbing my hand as I pass by, and tugging me back on the bed. He tucks me into his side. I wrap my arms around him, grateful for the familiar warmth.

"I don't want to lose myself," I tell him. "I don't want to just become an object for him to exploit."

"I understand." He smooths my hair with his hand. "You're strong, Little Lamb. You can get through this."

I sit up and wipe a tear off my face. "Will you do something for me?"

Silas glances at Levi. "Anything."

"Show me what it's like to be loved. To have a man treat me... with care and respect." I sniff. "Treat me like the men and women you service. Just for pretend."

"Of course." Silas gives me a soft smile. "It would be my pleasure."

Levi starts to leave, but I call out. "Stay. Please."

He pauses, surprised. "Are you sure?"

"Yes."

He moves to the chair across the small space, but Silas stops him. "Levi, get in the bed. Sit behind Imogene. Support her."

It takes us a moment to get situated, but I like the feeling of being cradled against Levi's chest. He's strong. Authoritative. And I know that he is always devoted to The Way. Yes, I still care about that. Too much.

"Thank you," I say, craning my neck to see him. "I feel more secure with you here."

"I just want you to relax," Silas says, kneeling at the end of the bed.

I nod, but I'm still stiff. I can't help but think of the pain the night before. The rough intrusion of Rex's body.

"Lev," Silas says, looking at the man behind me, "rub her shoulders."

I sense Levi's hesitation, but he does as commanded and massages the blades of my shoulders. The pressure is deep in my muscles, and I finally feel the tension releasing. Silas lifts my foot. He kisses the top, then my ankle, then moves to the other side. His kisses are gentle, slow, and sweet. Although every move he makes is the opposite of the night before, when he parts my legs, they tremble in anticipation of pain.

"Don't be afraid," Silas says, ever aware of my emotions. "I'm not going to hurt you, Imogene. I'm going to make you feel good."

Levi shifts my body for me, so that I'm even more reclined. I feel the hard press of his arousal against my back. He glides his pale hands up and down my arms, gentle in a way I didn't know he had in him. Beneath the sweatshirt, my nipples harden to sharp peaks. My focus is split, partially on Levi's touch and then on the man between my legs. I bend my knees as Silas moves higher, removing my panties gently, carefully. Warm air heats my core, followed by the wet flick of his tongue.

"Oh, God—" My words are lost, caught behind a building

moan. It had felt good when Levi did this to me, but to have them both touching me at once, it is something otherworldly. Again, he lathes my clit with his tongue, flattening it before drawing back. The focusing on the tight bundle of nerves is nearly too much and I writhe against Levi while thrusting my hands into Silas' hair.

"Does that feel good?" Silas asks, grinning up at me with shiny lips. I nod and he goes back to work, alternating between the pad of his thumb and the wet heat of his mouth. He works in a rhythm, one that my hips chase. He groans against me, fingers digging into my thighs. I spread wider, lift higher, push for more, until he sits up, taking it all away and I cry out. "Don't. No."

"Don't what?" he asks. There's a playful glint in his eyes. "Stop? Keep going? More?"

"Just—" I'm overcome, pressing against Levi. I grab his hands and push them up my shirt. My whole body is on fire and nothing will quench it but the touch of these men. Unmoving, Levi palms my breasts. "Touch me," I say, looking up at his face. "Please."

His hands are big, firm, and I sense his reluctance. We've only done this under the cloak of Correction. I'm about to tell him to forget it—that it's okay, when his thumbs brush against my nipples. I exhale and see Silas watching us. His fingers make lazy turns around my clit, building my arousal.

"Can I kiss you?" he asks.

I nod fervently. His mouth meets mine, tongue sweeping into my parted lips. My heart bangs around in my chest, my stomach coils. I thought I understood pleasure, but I was wrong. There's so much more out there than I realized.

Silas leans back and says, "You're wet, ready. Fuck." He licks my lips and moves on top of me, cock pushing at my entrance. "Slow and gentle. You let me know if it's too much."

He pushes in and it's so different—so good. I'm slippery and ready and his movements are firm but kind. Even while he's inside of me, he keeps his thumb on the place that sends shudders up my spine. I feel the same deep pressure, but it's not bad. If anything, it's not enough.

"Is this okay?"

"Yes." My legs spread wider and Levi cradles me as I open up. "Keep going."

He pushes in all the way, inch by inch, stretching me as he goes. I lift my hips up to meet his and he grins down. "You want more."

It's not a question, but I nod anyway. He withdraws and goes back in again, this time stretching me further. It hurts a little, but the pain is good, lost under Levi's touch and Silas' sparking touch.

"I want you to relax all the way, baby," he says, kissing me on the stomach. "I'm going to fuck you now, and I want you to let go." He rises above me, his muscular arms holding me up. He pumps in and out of me, and while I'm caught up in the movement, he bends to kiss me, saying, "Take a deep breath."

I do as I'm told, but I'm slowly losing focus. Through the haze of desire, I feel Levi behind me, his hips rocking against my backside and his breath hot on my neck. His fingers pluck my nipples, sending electricity across my skin. It's the kind of pressure I need—want—but it isn't the harsh pain of our sessions. Having two men pleasure me all at once is a new high, one that strips away the worry that I'm not enough, that I'm not worthy.

"That's it," Silas says, coaxing me toward the orgasm. His jaw is clenched tight. I know him well enough by now that it won't take much to pull him to the edge. He pumps his cock inside and Levi breathes heavy in my ear.

Their need spurs on my own and "I—oh—" I buck upward, the coil of tension that had been winding up inside springs, sending shock waves from my belly through every other inch of my body. I shudder, clamping my thighs around Silas' body and grabbing onto his shoulders. He seizes, body rigid, as he punches into me.

"Fuck, fuck, fuck," Levi mutters in my ear, his body taking a final rock behind me. Beyond the warmth cascading through my limbs, I feel damp heat spreading across my lower back.

I look into Silas' eyes and smile. "That... thank you."

I look over my shoulder at Levi. His cheeks are flushed, and he opens his mouth to speak, but I lean in and kiss him, cutting whatever apology or excuse or anxiety off at the source. His mouth is frozen at first, but he loosens up and kisses me in return.

As we part, and the taste of Levi is strong on my lips, it comes to me that this may be the last time I feel this kind of contentment—this sort of happiness—and I curl up in these men, holding onto the feeling as long as I can.

* * *

The feeling of connection follows me to the dining tent. It even dampens some of the awkwardness of walking in with Elon as my escort and not my mate. He'd showed up after we had all cleaned up and dressed. There was no sign of what we'd just accomplished together—the bed was made. Our hair straight. But the deep crease on his forehead and the suspicious look in his eye made me think he knew that something had transpired between the three of us.

"I can go to breakfast on my own," I tell him. It's obvious he's in a bad mood. As usual.

"Rex doesn't want you walking around the campground alone."

"There's a solution to that." I glance up at him. He looks tired, like he barely slept, and his jaw is unshaved. "He could do it himself."

He grunts in reply and reaches into his pocket. "I have something for you." He hands me a small envelope. My name is across the front in even handwriting. Female handwriting. Any hopes it's from my future mate are dashed.

"You're my messenger now?"

His reply is curt. "Like everyone else here, I do as I'm told."

I pause outside the dining tent and open the envelope. It's an invitation for a women's meeting in Margaret's tent for breakfast.

"Do you know anything about this?" I ask.

He scans the details. "It's for women. Why would I know?"

"Imogene!"

I turn and find Maria a few steps away. She's dressed in an apron, with her hair tucked in a bandana.

"Hi!" I give her a hug. "What's with the apron?"

"They asked all the newly Ordered to help out in the kitchen. It's tradition. I've been looking for you."

"I had no idea." I glance at Elon, but his expression is blank. "Maybe I missed the memo."

"Or maybe the mate of Anex's son doesn't have to work the kitchens." She smiles good-naturedly and then winks. "I'm sure it's only one of the perks."

The first image that comes to my mind is Levi and Silas this morning in bed. I choke back a cough and say, "Nothing more than any new mate, I'm sure."

"Well, it's good to see you. I want to catch up. Will you be at the women's session this afternoon?"

"I'm going to try. I have a few obligations first."

She gives me another hug, and just smelling her apple scented shampoo makes me wistful for when we used to live together in the domum. Things were easier then. I knew who I was and what my role was in the community. Now I'm mixed up and turned around in a world of emotions and confusion.

Elon leads me through the campground toward the center tents. Although Anex speaks from the main gazebo, several smaller yurts have been set aside for groups to meet more privately. The closer we get to these tents, the further away I feel from the rest of the community.

"Is Maria right? Did they let me out of kitchen duty because I am Rex's ordered?"

"Probably," Elon says, sidestepping a tether. "Things are different in the inner circle. There are different expectations for you."

"Like eating breakfast with one of the spiritual mates."

"Like that," he agrees.

"Is it wrong that I'd rather be working with the others from my domum?" I don't really know why I ask Elon anything. His answers are always short and limited. His façade as hard as his muscles. "I don't feel like I'm anything special. Certainly not with how Rex treats me."

He stops at a tent but blocks the entrance. "Being in the inner circle is complicated. There are, like your friend said, perks. But it also comes with the burden of knowing how Serendee operates. Anex has determined that you are worthy of knowing these things."

To hold them over my head, I wonder. To force me into compliance? "Like how the community really is funded."

His eyes dart around. "Yes."

"Am I to assume that once I enter that tent, I'm going to become even more educated in the ways of Serendee."

"I told you, I don't know." But something in his gray eyes tells me that he knows more than he lets on. Is he protecting me or keeping me ignorant? Compliant?

Every day is something new—something that chips away at my core belief system yet requires me to have even more faith in Anex and The Way. All I've learned in the last day is that there is no escaping the game.

* * *

Once again, Margaret outshines the rest of the community. Her guests, five other women besides the two of us, sit on soft padding, drinking tea and eating pastries inside her cozy tent. The tea is served in real China, painted with delicate pink flowers and rimmed in gold. The pastries are from the Serendee bakery, light and flaky. The blackberry preserves inside come from the berry shrubs that line the fencing on the backside of the farm. I eat mine slowly, methodically, mostly to keep something to keep my mouth busy.

The other women are all Anex's spiritual mates. I've seen them around him when he makes presentations—or gone to them in a time of need. They're the buffer between the community and Anex —necessary because his time is so valuable, and people crave his attention and opinion. There are men too, like Levi, who teaches the VRS classes or other instructors or founding members. But these women are important. Not just to Anex, but to the whole of Serendee.

I'm introduced to everyone; Jane has been with Anex the longest—right after Rex's mother died. She's the oldest, but the gray hair and fine lines don't detract from her beauty. She's quiet and kind. Ansley sits next to her, small but full of life. Her blonde hair is in pigtails that hang in waves over her shoulders. Her pastry sits untouched on her plate. Her food logs are probably immaculate. I set mine down and wipe my fingers, feeling gluttonous.

"It's wonderful to have you here," the fourth, Bridget, says, passing me a tiny pitcher of milk for the tea. "We've all wanted to get to know you a little better. Moving into the main house can be a little isolating."

I smile and nod. She's right. Sort of. It would be isolating if I wasn't juggling the whims and schedules of three men. It's possible that these women, outside of Margaret are unaware of that. "It's been a big change from the domum and living with so many other females."

"Yes," Ansley says. "I lived in the donum, too, and it was weird going from having a million girls around and all their drama to the peace and quiet of the main house." She curls her finger around the handle of her teacup. "Don't get me wrong, I love it. It was just an adjustment."

"Yes," I reply with a knowing smile. "Exactly. I shared a room with several girls for years. We did everything together; eat, clean, lessons, play." I think about seeing Maria earlier that day and how far apart we seemed now. "I miss them."

"Well," Margaret says with a small grin, "that's why we're here. I noticed that some women were struggling with their roles once they entered a more mature phase of life—one outside the domum. We've all left things behind."

"Friends and family," Jane says. "The structure of the domum and the support of the housemothers."

Their words strike home. I have missed all of those things. Maria, Clarissa, and the consistency. It was so very consistent.

"We started a new group." Margaret looks at me. "It's very exclusive, and the goal is to form an empowering, supportive group of women that are dedicated to both Serendee and The Way. We'd like you to consider being a member."

"Oh." I'm flattered. Incredibly so. And it sounds like what I've been missing in all the recent chaos. I've been so lost in pleasing Rex and training with the guys, I've lost focus. "That sounds amazing."

"It's not something to take lightly," Bridget says, tucking her dark hair behind her ear. "It requires a significant commitment. Part of the problem is that once we leave the domum or our old lives, some of that automatic accountability is gone. Sure, we still have our logs, but we're more independent, and it's harder to stay on the path toward self-actualization when we're also focused on caring for someone else."

"Staying true to our inner female is important while also not succumbing to indulgency," Margaret says. All four women seem excited about this group and it's infectious. I want what they have. "There are some conditions for joining the group. It's incredibly exclusive. It's also a secret. No one can know about it."

"A secret?" I stumble over this admission. Our lives in Serendee are so exposed. Logs, journals, group meetings and public expressions. "From everyone?"

Margaret takes my hand. "I know that when you bond with someone, it feels like everything should be shared, but it's important to keep a few things for yourself. It's a select group of women and anything we share between us is in strict confidence." She tilts her head. "Don't you think Rex's confidants know things about him that you do not?"

"I'm sure they do. They're very close."

"Well, you can have the same."

"And Anex is okay with this?" I ask.

"Anex is not involved, but he's given his blessing. He knows how important it is for women to support one another, but," Ansley says, "this group is not for everyone. You have to have strong fortitude and a deep understanding of The Way. Only a few women are chosen."

"Think on it," Jane says. "Meditate and journal. Search your heart. Once you join there is no going back."

"When do you need to know?"

"The summer solstice," Margaret says. "It marks a new season."

As quickly as it's brought up, the subject changes, and Jane refills my tea. I already sense the bond between these women. The solidarity of their faith and determination. They aren't the sheep that Rex complains about. They're strong and true. This group could be another way to show him that I'm different; special. A way to show him that I'm worthy of being his mate.

37

―――――――

ELON

Some things are certain in this life. Playing the annual basketball game for Anex's birthday is one of them. The entire party walks down to the gym and the spectators pack the stands. Back in the locker room, Peter, one of Anex's confidants, passes out shirts for the game. Purple, Anex's favorite color, marks his team. Orange is for the opposing. I pull the purple shirt over my head and listen to the guys talk about the weekend. Everyone seems to be in good spirits—why wouldn't they? They're having an amazing time—good food, fellowship, the honor of being chosen for the game. They haven't had to spend the past twenty-four hours dealing with Rex's mess, or carrying Imogene's shivering body back to the tent, or seeing her tear-stained face as she came to the realization her betrothed is a monster.

Something about my friend is broken, and I worry it is beyond repair. I've known it for some time, but he seemed content to take his energies out on the women in town or through the thrill of our business dealings. I figured he'd settle down once he agreed to an Order, and I assumed our efforts to make her less like the female sheep that fill Serendee's domums, would appease him. But I realize now he'll never be satisfied. Not until he has broken everyone inside this place, the same way he is.

There's a problem with his methods.

Anex may not have the guts to take out his own son, but he will punish everyone around him. Everyone that failed. Me. Silas. Levi. And especially Imogene.

I will never get a mate of my own.

Silas will never advance out of the position of a whore. Not until his looks fade and he's no longer useful.

Levi will never ascend to the higher levels of instruction.

And Imogene? She won't be let free if Rex truly rejects her. She'll be blamed for the failure. A final strike after what happened with her mother. If she is even allowed to stay in Serendee she'll end up at the whim of Anex. No mate. No home of her own. No job. Nothing.

It shouldn't bother me, and I shouldn't care, but I don't like the way all of this sits on my chest. The rest of us have had the dark side of Serendee's claws in us for a long time. Imogene? She didn't ask for this.

"Elon!" Anex calls. He's sitting on the bench tying his shoes. He eyes my bruised face. "You going to be okay for the game?"

I touch the bruised skin. "Yeah, it's nothing big. Just a little skirmish last night."

"Anything important?"

"Not enough to keep us from winning the game." I glance over at Silas, who is changing across the room. "What do you think, Silas? Twenty-point lead?"

"Twenty-five." He pulls his shirt over his head. He's a good player to have on the team. Lean but strong—fast. Levi is a quiet force. Peter is a killer center, hand-picked by Anex to fill out our team. The only weak spot? Anex. He's smart and surrounds himself with stronger, more skilled athletes. There are other second-stringers hanging around, just happy to bask in the glow of Anex's good will. No one that will outshine him. We all know our place. There's only one player in Serendee that doesn't follow those rules.

Rex.

Which is why he was kicked off the team a year ago. And why, as we walk into the gym to a packed crowd, seeing him standing with the opposing team dressed in an orange T-shirt is a complete shock. His jaw bears the brunt of my fist from the night before, and his lip is split. It just makes him look dangerous.

What the fuck is he doing here?

There are never 'big' moments in Serendee. Everything runs smoothly. If not? The fallout is not worth it. That is ingrained in us from childhood. But sometimes there are small, rippling disturbances. Rex is six foot four, with the wingspan of an Olympic swimmer. Him being here isn't a ripple. It's a fucking earthquake.

"I see my son has shown up to wish me a happy birthday." Anex's tone is light—jovial. I know better. So do Silas and Levi. "I wonder who gave him a spot on the team."

The other captain, Steve, looks across the court with apology. Anex created a complicated system. No one is to say no to his son. What was Steve to do? Tell him he can't play? Anex knows this and says nothing, but the firm set of his mouth reveals his anger. This is a fucking nightmare.

"Do you want me to talk to him?" I ask Anex quietly. "Tell him to get the fuck out of here?"

"No." He looks into the crowd. It only takes a moment to find his Spiritual Mates. Sitting with them is a new face—Imogene. She's noticed Rex as well and her eyes draw from him to mine. "Maybe he's here to impress his betrothed."

Levi grunts, but busies himself with stretching. Is Anex truly this clueless about what's happening between his son and Imogene? "Maybe, but still. There's no predicting what he'll do."

"It's fine," Anex replies with his jaw tight. "My son feels the need to test me today. It's a natural result of someone that feels weak and inferior."

The game starts off with an announcement from some of the members of Serendee. They present Anex with a new ball for his birthday—signed by Michael Jordan.

Anex grabs the microphone to a wave of cheers. "Thank you all for the touching gift. As you know, Jordan is a hero of mine. He is tough, competitive, ruthless. He doesn't worry about what others think. His goal is to win. He expects perfection from not only those around him but also himself. He never compromises." His eyes flick to Rex sitting on the bench. "I'm proud to have my son with me here today, Rex, come on over and give your old man a hug."

I cross my arms over my chest, waiting, watching. Levi shifts next to me, a tell of his apprehension. The audience has no comprehension of the animosity between these two. How close Rex is to walking away and shattering the illusion. Rex follows his father's command and jogs to center court. Imogene watches from the bleachers, conflict written on her face. She should be conflicted. Both men provide hope and a danger to her.

Rex and Anex hug in the middle of the gym, bringing a round of stomping feet and cheers. Although Rex has a foot of height on him, his father takes his face between his hands and draws his head down, whispering something in his ear. From my angle I can see that Rex responds, his features tense. It's too low to hear—it appears intimate and personal—and no one presses for more. It's just a father and son sharing a moment.

They part and go to their opposite sides of the gym. Levi, shockingly, is the one to ask. "What did you say to him?"

Equally surprising is the fact that Anex answers. "I told him that if he made a fool out of me, I would ruin everything he cares for in this life."

It's a pointed threat. For Rex as much as the three of us.

"What did he say in return?" I ask.

"Nothing," he lies, pulling a sweatband over his forehead as he steps onto the court.

We follow him onto the court and the referee, a guy named James, tosses the ball in his hands. The orange team is led by Rex, and they take their positions on the court. A moment later, the game starts with the screech of James' whistle and the ball being tossed in the air. Peter jumps, but Rex gets there first, tipping the ball forward.

It's an intentional move—one that makes it clear that he's not going to bow down to his father. Not in this game or anywhere else.

More than ever, I'm determined to stop my friend. I can't let him take us all down. Not like this. Not over something so petty and false.

I run down the court, ignoring the cheering crowd, and throw my arms up in defense. I'm bigger than Rex, both of are still sporting injuries from the fight the night before. He dribbles the ball lazily, tongue darting out at his split lip. I lunge for the ball and he spins, jabbing his elbow into my side. Silas is on him in a heartbeat, slamming his chest into Rex's. Silas does his best to get the ball out of his hands, but his arms just aren't long enough. I regain my balance, joining in to block him from the net, but Rex finds the gap he needs to take a shot. The ball arcs through the air and swishes through the net.

The crowd isn't sure what to do. Cheer for Rex? Is that okay? Hell if I know. I don't even look at Anex as I throw the ball in his direction. Rex bumps into me on his way back to his side of the court. "You're playing like a pussy. You can't hold back for him and win against me. Pick a side, Elon."

The energy escalates from there. Every ball thrown to Anex is picked off by Rex. Our leader is down on his game and Rex is right. We can't help him win by boosting him up. It's total bullshit and an allegory of our entire life. Damned if you do, damned if you don't. I leap out in front of a ball, going from the orange guard to Rex, intercepting it. I pound the ball on the court, dribbling to the net. I set up the shot ball poised on my fingers. Rex charges at me, knocking me on the ground. The ball spins loose, picked up by his quick hands, but I don't give a fuck. I jump up and chase Rex down. Shouts from my teammates, the fans, everyone bounces off of me. At the opposite end of the court, I tackle him, landing hard on top of his body. Using all my weight, I pin him down and say, "Don't do this. Not now."

I punch him in the face, the sound of my fist crashing into his jaw echoing in my ears. Before I get the next strike in, hands grab me from behind. I hear Levi shout and Silas pulling me back. Rex grins at me and gets his hands on my chest, shoving me off.

"You're just here to fuck things up," I tell him. "Get out of here."

"Why? Because I'm winning?" His eyes dart around. "Because I'm not going to play this stupid little game anymore?"

"Stop!" Anex shouts, commanding the attention of the whole room. Everyone is silent. Everyone. Anex is a man of many things, but anger isn't one of them. "Get him out of here. Now."

Rex spits blood on the floor and says, "If you want me out of here so bad, Old Man, why don't you make me."

Anex cuts me a long, hard look and says quietly. "Now."

It's all the excuse I need, and I grab him from behind. He doesn't fight me, not as much as he could and when we get outside, I shove him against the brick wall of the gym.

"What the hell are you doing?"

He runs his hands through his hair, the temples dark with sweat. "I'm done, Elon. It's over. I'm leaving."

"Bullshit," I bark, done with his theatrics.

He holds my eye. "I'm serious."

"He won't let you come back," Levi says.

"I don't want to come back. That's the whole point."

"Well, I'm glad you have that choice," Silas says, voice rising with anger. "You're destroying us, you know that, right?"

"We're men now. Not boys," he says, and I hear the sincerity in his voice. He is serious. "It's time for you to live your own life."

Levi says. "We were always loyal to you."

"If you were loyal, you'd be happy that I'm walking out of the gates of this place or," he glances at the three of us, "you'd be walking out with me."

No one speaks. No one, because what Rex is talking about is dangerous. It's Regressive. It's the kind of talk that destroys lives for real, and none of us are willing to do that—not even for him.

"What about Imogene?" Silas asks.

"What about her?" Rex's eye twitches. "Imogene isn't your concern."

I laugh. For real, laugh. "The minute you agreed to get Ordered and handpicked her to be your mate, you made her part of our lives. We can't pretend she doesn't exist or that you're not dooming her by leaving like this."

"You think she's safer with me here? Because I've seen what happens to the women I care about." He swallows. "She'll be fine."

"Are you pretending you care about her?" Levi asks. "After what you did to her last night? You just don't care about anyone, Rex. Not us, not her, not Serendee. You only care for yourself."

Rex's jaw clenches and I brace myself to stop him if he jumps on Levi. He just shakes his head and looks more exhausted than I've ever seen him. "You don't understand. You never will and I envy that." He looks between us. "I'm leaving at midnight. If you want to come with me, come. If not, this is goodbye."

Watching Rex walk off hits like a punch in the gut. We've been brothers our whole life. Groomed to serve as his confidants. He's bitched about Serendee, and wanting to leave for years, but I never thought he'd actually do it. Not until now.

38

"I'm leaving at midnight. If you want to come with me, come. If not, this is goodbye."

Rex's words ring in my ears long after he said them. Would he really leave Serendee? I, more than anyone, understand the ramifications of such an act. There is no coming back to Serendee if you leave.

I'd slipped out the back door of the gym just after they dragged Rex off the court and eavesdropped on their argument. I've never seen any of them this angry—or defeated.

After Rex walks off, I follow him. I keep my distance, taking the long walk from the campground back to the main house. He goes in the front door and although I'm not close enough to see him; I suspect he's going to his suite. His door is unlocked, and I can hear him in his room. My stomach sinks when I see him, tossing fat rolls of cash into a black bag, along with various personal items.

"So you're leaving," I blurt.

He doesn't look up, just continues to pick through his bedside drawer, picking and choosing items to toss in his luggage. "I am."

"But—the Solstice is tomorrow. We've been seen around the

campground. You chose to come and now you're just going to abandon me because... what? You want to run away? You hate your father? Or am I just not good enough for you? Even with all the sacrifices I've made for you."

He snorts. "I doubt having Silas teach you how to get off was a huge sacrifice."

I step into the room and close the distance between us. He looks up, but before he can react; I slap him hard across the side of his face that is already bruised from the night before. He doesn't recoil, not even an inch, but he clenches his jaw and closes his eyes, a sure sign he's holding back from retaliation.

I'm not finished. "I violated my beliefs for you. I went against The Way and the values instilled in me. I subscribed to the training requested of me for you, which put me in positions I never thought I'd be in. Not just sex outside my mating, but secular things. Dirty things." I glare at him, fighting the shame. "I know you may not care, but I do, and now I'm tarnished in the eyes of this community. In the eyes of your father. You've ruined me."

Now I'm finished and I spin on my heel. I'm stopped by his strong hand, clamping down on my upper arm and pulling me back with a hard yank.

"I told you up front my expectations for this relationship. I made my intentions perfectly clear. You are the one that conspired with my father and confidants. They are the ones that convinced you to go against your beliefs. Not me."

"You forced yourself on me." I say, hoping the accusation gets through to him.

His lip curls up. "You liked it. Don't pretend like you didn't." His fingers tighten around my bicep. "Did it ever—ever—cross your mind that my actions aren't selfish? That maybe I was trying to do the right thing?"

I shake him off and step back. "By assaulting me? By forcing me to my knees? By handing me off to your friends? Or do you mean when you raped me?"

"No, Imogene," his voice is a hiss, "That was to scare you off—to make you hate me. Yet here you are again, in my face, in my room, trying your damnedest to make this work." His eyes dart between my lips and my mouth. "Everything I did was for your own good."

"That's a lie, Rex, and you know it."

He steps forward, and I fear he's going to grab me again. But he just looks down at me. The anger dulls in his blue eyes and is replaced with another emotion. "My father killed my mother."

I frown. "What?" I search his face for any hint of humor. There is none. "What are you talking about?"

"My mother didn't get sick and die, Imogene. She didn't approve of the changes in my father or the direction he was taking Serendee. He wanted to open his marriage to other women— younger women who were more pliable to his manipulations. He started actively recruiting outside the community for wealthy, attractive females to become his spiritual mates and to line his bank account. He started the drug businesses, the illegal stuff." He swallows. "My mother was prepared to expose him for the fraud that he is—a charlatan."

I'd known Rex was struggling with The Way and the lifestyle at Serendee. I knew he hated his father, but I had no idea he was prone to delusions. "Rex, that's crazy."

He turns and reaches into his bag, pulling out a pink journal. "She documented everything. Hid it in a safe deposit box and left me information on how to find it all."

My knees threaten to buckle. Not because I believe him, but because all of this is insane. What will Anex do when he finds out that Rex is spreading lies about him? Or worse, what will he do to me if he finds out I know?

"I know you don't believe me." He says, returning to his packing. "Why would you?"

"It's not that I don't believe you..." The words ring hollow to both of us.

"I picked you, Imogene, because I knew your mother had similar feelings. Just like how I waited for you on the rock that night because I knew you would understand."

The rock? The memory of the night I found him on my rock,

high above Serendee comes rushing back. Not only does he remember, he'd been there on purpose, waiting for me.

"What are you talking about?"

"Your mother got away. I thought maybe she had instilled some of that rebellion into you." He tosses the journal back in the bag. "Obviously not." He zips it up. "That's why I forced myself on you last night. Hoping to ruin you for my father so that you'd finally snap out of it."

"Excuse me?" I'm stunned. "You're justifying that as kindness? As pity?"

"I gave you an opportunity, and you're too ignorant to see it!"

"You didn't give me an opportunity—you gave me a life sentence. Silas told me what your father will do to me now that you've ruined me."

"There is one other option," he says, tossing the bag over his shoulder. "I told the others they can meet me at midnight and come with me. I doubt they will. They're too afraid." He touches my chin. "I know you think I did you wrong, Imogene, but I truly was trying to protect you. I lost someone I cared for once before, and I promised myself I would never let it happen again."

He's an abuser. A criminal. A blasphemer. I don't trust him, but there's something about Rex that still draws me to him. Maybe it's because I like being hurt. Maybe I feel like I deserve the pain these men inflict on me. There's a tug at my inner belly that makes me want to follow him. To see this other life he wants so badly. But I also have to consider that a small part of me wants to follow him because I think I deserve a man like him.

"No." I shake my head. "I'm not going with you. Serendee is my home, and I'll accept my fate."

He stops before me and cups my cheek. It's intimate—sweet—nothing like how he's touched me in the past.

"Good luck, Imogene," he says, stepping around me. He walks out the door, headed toward another life, while I stay here and faithfully await the fallout.

* * *

Hours later, Levi pops his head in the bedroom. I've been sitting here since Rex left.

"We've been looking for you," he says, stepping into the room. "Are you okay?"

"Rex is gone."

"I know."

I look up at him—at his red shock of hair and his handsome face. He tries so hard to be a good servant to the community. Losing Rex must cut him like a knife. "Are you leaving with him?"

He sighs and sits on the bed next to me. "No."

"Me neither." I stare down at my hands. They feel detached. Everything is numb. "Did you know about his mother? Or, what he thinks happened to her?"

He glances over at me, surprised I guess that Rex confided in me. "Yes. We were there when he got the information and a key to the safe deposit box. It was before we had free access to go into town, and we had to sneak out. I'd never been to a bank before. I was convinced the whole time we were going to get caught and dragged back home." He picks at his fingernail. "Nothing happened, of course. No one even noticed us other than giving us a few looks for our clothing. All Rex had to do was show them the key. Ten minutes later his whole world turned upside down."

"Do you believe him? That his mother was murdered?"

"I know he believes it, but other than the ramblings in her journals, there is no evidence. I've used my position at the Center to look into paperwork about her death, to try to ease his concerns, but I can't find anything. She has a death certificate, and it states she died from natural causes—an aneurysm, not murder."

"Is there anything we can do?"

He shakes his head. "He won't listen. I love Rex like a brother, but I believe in The Way. I want to help him, but it's not possible. I believe he's lost."

"You're a good friend." I take his hand in mine.

"Not good enough." He rubs his thumb against mine. A gentle, surprising gesture. "Anex wants to speak to you. In his tent."

I bolt to my feet. "Now?"

"Yes."

"Does he know about Rex leaving? Is he upset that I didn't get him to stay?" I pace the room. "I never meant to let him down. I did everything he asked."

Levi hops up and forces me to stop. "Hey, this is not your fault, and he knows it, and if for some reason he doesn't, I'll tell him."

I look up at him, heart pounding with fear. A nervous tear rolls down my cheek. Levi wipes it away. "This is such a mess."

"You're strong, Imogene. Whatever comes your way, I have faith that you can survive."

I don't tell Levi that I want more out of life than surviving.

I want to live.

* * *

Anex's tent isn't as big as I would expect, but he does spend most of his time outdoors, celebrating, and providing lessons at the gazebo. It is large enough for a soft chair, which is where he's sitting when Levi pulls back the flap. One of the guards, dressed in black, stands just inside. A large bed takes up most of the room. It's made neatly and covered in a thick comforter.

"Give us some privacy," he says to Levi and the guard, waving them off. Levi gives me one last look before heading back outside. I wish he could stay—to be witness to whatever is about to happen, but that isn't Anex's command.

My stomach rolls anxiously as I stand before our leader. I bow and touch the center of my forehead, honoring the gift of his presence. He looks tired—but it's been a few busy days of celebration and gluttony. He smiles gently at me and says, "Tell me what the status is on my son."

I feel he already knows the answer, and this is some sort of test. There's nothing I can do but lay myself bare and pray for his mercy.

"Rex is not interested in Mating with me," I admit. "He does not feel as though we are compatible. He has rejected me. I am so sorry I've failed you."

He nods, his expression revealing nothing about how he feels about this. "There's more you aren't telling me."

How does he know? Did Levi tell him? Or Rex? Are there other spies I don't know about?

My cheeks burn with humiliation, but I know it's useless not to confess. "Last night Rex and I... we consummated our relationship."

"Before my blessing."

"Yes." I nod, staring down at the carpet. I could blame Rex and tell his father what he did, but I know better. This is my fault. My weakness. Casting blame will only make me look worse.

"I see." He taps his ring on the arm of the chair. "Do you know where he is now?"

"I don't. The last time I saw him was hours ago."

"This is an unfortunate situation, Imogene. I'd hoped that you could convince him to stay on the righteous path, but my son is stubborn." He taps his fingers on the arm of the chair. "I'd hoped that this could be your retribution—a way to clear your name after your mother's extreme betrayal."

"I know. Thank you for the opportunity."

"You're aware this puts your reputation in a precarious situation?"

"I am, and I am willing to do whatever it is needed to remain in Serendee. I am devoted to The Way and I am at your service."

A dark light flickers in his eyes. "Come forward."

I step toward him, and he gestures to the rug at his feet. I kneel and stare at his ankles until his fingers gently touch my chin and force my eyes upward.

"I knew it was possible that my son would make this decision, which is another reason I put you in training. Serendee doesn't abandon our Fallen. There is a place for you here. A place where you can work toward redemption. I won't lie and pretend it is easy, but nothing about salvation ever is. I understand that all too well. After the solstice is over, you'll move into my wing of the Main House, to a special section of rooms for other people like you." His hand trails down my throat, to the base of my neck. His fingers are calloused. Wrong. "Tomorrow night you will not attend the Solstice celebration. You will wait in your tent until the following morning, and then you will go back to your suite and pack what you came into the house with. Someone will fetch you." He takes my hand and helps me off the ground. He moves close and runs his hand down my arm, stopping at my bicep. His fingertips graze the side of my breast. A shudder of repulsion rolls through me, but I fight to control it. "This isn't the end, Imogene, it's a new path, one that I will guide you down personally."

"Yes, Anex. Thank you." I bow once again, touching my forehead, and hastily exit the tent. I inhale the fresh air, hoping to fight back the nausea rising from the pit of my stomach. I should feel honored. Saved. But those are not the feelings consuming me right now.

I am afraid.

39

SILAS

Levi and I split off from one another on the main floor as we search for Imogene. We'd gone back to the gym after the altercation with Rex and she was gone. He takes the front staircase and I go toward the back. Heavy footsteps echo off the hardwoods and I look up. Rex is coming down the stairs. He pauses when he sees me, clutching the bag hooked over his shoulder.

"You can't stop me, Silas."

"I'm not trying to stop you." I narrow my eyes. "I'm not here for you at all."

"Then you won't mind getting out of my way."

I step aside, and he moves past me.

Anger wells inside and I swing around. "You know what will happen to her, don't you?"

He pauses and sighs. "A letter will be delivered to my father in two days asking him to assign her to one of you." He glances back. "I can amend that. Do you want her as your mate? I can make it happen. He may be willing to make an exception under the circum-stances."

The circumstance that he created when he took her virginity, abandoned her, and left her in ruins.

"No," I tell him, although it's not entirely true. I just know it isn't right. "You can't. I know you think you're aware of how Serendee functions—and for much of it, you do, but your father has secrets." I frown. "We all have secrets, Rex."

"If you're telling me, my father is deceitful, I'm not surprised. He did kill my mother after all."

I inhale deeply. Rex has often stood by his conviction that his father killed his mother, and of the three of us, I know more than anyone what Anex is willing to do with those that do not follow his lead. "What do you think he'll do to your rejected mate?"

For the first time, I see doubt in his eyes. "You think he'll kill her?"

"No," I reply. "I think he'll do something worse."

His hand grips his bag. "How much worse?"

I jerk my head toward the staircase. "I'll show you."

* * *

The hallway looks like all the others, just another in the never-ending maze running through the house. But to get to this one you have to have been here before and there's no doubt in my mind that Rex has never come down to this part of the house.

There are a dozen doorways, six on each side. A small window with a sliding cover is in the center of each one. Keypad locks secure the knobs.

"What is this?" Rex asks, staring down at the locks.

"This is where your father keeps the Fallen."

"Regressives?" he asks.

"No. The Fallen. They're believers—devoted usually, but they've also had some kind of infraction and are sent here for re-education." I slide open the window covering and look inside. A small redhead sits on the bed. Her eyes dart to the window and she stares at me until I step aside and let Rex peer in.

"Who is that?"

"Her name is Bethany."

"She looks young." He glances in again. "What is she doing in there?"

"She's fifteen. She violated The Way when she snuck out of her domum and met up with a boy. Your father sentenced her to come here for punishment."

"For meeting up with a boy?"

"For violating The Way and not waiting for her Ordering. Anex believed she needed personal intervention, isolation, and training. If she submits to these things and repents, she may ultimately be allowed back into the community."

Rex looks at me. "How long will that take?"

"As long as your father determines." I slide the cover shut. "A few people have been in here for years."

I walk to another door and open it. A different young woman is curled up asleep on the small bed. Her skin is pale and her hair stringy. Rex peers in and says, "I know her. That's Charlotte Bently. I recruited her."

"Me too."

He did the work to bring her in; I did the work to make her stay. We're both responsible for this woman's fate. "What did she do?" he asks.

"She tried to contact her family, who Anex knows have been looking for her. They have resources." He nods. Her family's wealth is one reason she was targeted. "She's been down here for a few weeks."

He steps back. "Why are you showing me this? I already know what my father is capable of. All you're doing is proving the point."

"I'm showing you this because this is Imogene's fate. One of these boxes."

"I gave her a choice. Just like I gave you."

I shake my head. "Losing everyone you love and to run off with the man that abused you? That doesn't sound like a choice to me."

"Then what about you?"

I look down the hall. The guilt I feel for my participation in bringing these women here threatens to drown me. "Not all of us can walk away, Rex. That is a privilege only you have."

"You won't make me feel bad about this." He exhales. "I can't stay here."

He turns to walk away and I call out to him. "You know, I think this is exactly what he's wanted this whole time."

He narrows his eyes. "What are you saying?"

"The people down here... they're all women, Rex. Young, beautiful, independent women. Your father brings them here to break them. To use them." I stare at Bethany's door. "He claims them, because he can, and calls it "training" or "reintegrating." Imogene was a test—one he knew you would fail. One that sends her straight to him."

"I don't believe you." He shakes his head. "This is just your way of trying to get me to stay, so that you'll continue to have my protection and my father's favor. I want you to come with me, but you won't. That's on you."

He turns to leave, but I grab his arm, fueled by more than my own anger. Fear rolls up my spine. "You don't believe me because you think you understand Serendee, but you don't. You've lived a charmed life. Your father gives you everything you want because you're goddamned royalty. Women, money, drugs, sex... there are no limits, but the rest of us... we've made our sacrifices."

"That's—"

"I'm your father's whore, Rex."

"Stop," he says. "He never—"

"Not for him, no." I look at the locked doors. "That is what these women are for. He trained me to whore myself out for the Community. For money and assets and power. I do whatever it takes to bring them in; I charm them, wine them, fuck them. Elon and Levi are tangled in similar strings. We've accepted that this is our role in Serendee, but once you walk out the door, Imogene will suffer the same fate."

In all these years, I've never been this truthful to Rex, but this isn't about me. It's about an innocent. Imogene deserves better than to be locked behind one of these doors because of his petty differences with his father.

"Don't do this to her," I say, hoping he'll do the right thing.

His jaw clenches, and his eyes dart to the ground. "I'm sorry, Silas, but the girl isn't my problem."

As he walks away, the emotion I feel isn't disappointment. It's resignation. Rex is his father's son, spoiled and entitled. Asking him to do something for someone else?

It was never going to happen.

40

Imogene

I'm packing the tent when I hear the soft clearing of a throat in the doorway.

"Clarissa," I say, surprised to see my old house mother, "what are you doing here?"

The expression on her face says it all. "I heard about your Ordering."

"Yes," I go back to sorting, "I've been rejected. Rex didn't want me after all."

She walks over and brushes the hair off my cheek and gives me a hug. "I know it doesn't seem like it, but it's not the end for you."

"It certainly feels like it."

"I don't think you know about how I ended up being a house-mother, do you?"

"No." The girl's in the domum gossiped, wondering why she didn't have a mate of her own. "Whatever the reason, you're very good at it."

"Thank you." She smiles and sits on the bed next to my bag. "I came to Serendee from the outside, recruited. I was instantly intrigued by the community and wanted to follow The Way, but Anex has to make sure we are truly loyal. Have you ever heard of collateral?"

I shake my head.

"Some people offer up money, others land or valuables. I had none of that, so I had to offer up something different." Her smile is tight. "I had to earn my place in the community and once I did, he assigned me to house mother."

"What did you have to do?" I ask, because that's the question. What does a fallen have to do to earn her way back into the fold? "I'm scared."

She places her hand over mine. "You're strong, Imogene. Beautiful. You've spent these last few weeks learning how to provide pleasure to a man. I am confident you can give Anex what he needs to lead you down the path of redemption."

As usual, she doesn't speak with transparency, no one here does. Well, no one but Elon, Silas and Levi. They've never hidden the truth from me, but the truth is clear. She gave her body to Anex. Her greatest asset.

"What if I fail again? Then what happens?"

"You won't fail. You're a fighter, Imogene. It's in your blood."

Clarissa gives me another hug and walks out of the tent. Her final words linger, tickling at my spine. I've never considered myself a fighter. Everything I've done has been compliant, focused on immersing myself in The Way, and most of all, not being like my mother.

What would she say about this? About my failed Order. About my rejection. But most of all, my punishment.

She wouldn't have stood by and waited for Anex to control her future. She would have saved herself—run. I look at the door of the tent and think about Rex's invitation. He'd offered for me to go with him, but where? How? The thought of leaving my home and everything I've ever known for a man that resents me is terrifying.

More terrifying than what awaits me tomorrow?

Rex doesn't love me. He doesn't even care for me and the accusations he's made about his mother... well, both father and son are dangerous.

The question is... which one do I pick?

41

THE SUN RISES in the east, casting the whole field in a warm pink glow. I sit on the bed in my tent. Other than the small box next to me, everything I bought is packed neatly by the door. I didn't go meet Rex. My future and my fate lie in Serendee. With Anex's command. I've seen the secular world and I don't want any part of it. Even if it means I'm Fallen.

Outside I hear the start of the day, eggs cooking in the dining tent, happy voices talking about the Solstice ceremony later in the day. I wait as I was told—when it's over, I'll settle into my new existence.

I don't know how long I sit, although it's enough time to chew my nail to the quick. Every time someone walks by the tent entrance, I look up, expecting someone to come for me. Elon? Levi? Or did they run with Rex? Will Anex send Clarissa or Margaret or will it be one of the guards dressed in black? The figures walk past, and no one enters. Eventually, I grow used to the foot traffic, which is why when the flap opens, I barely notice. It's not until he's standing right over me that I blink and take him in.

"What are you doing here?" I ask, rising to my feet. "Why?"

His jaw is made of marble—hard set and clenched. "Giving you up to my father means that I'm letting him win. I thought that by rejecting The Way, and leaving, I was protecting you. It seems my father anticipated that." He lifts his chin. "I thought that by accepting the Ordering I would be giving him control, but I realize it's the opposite. He wants me to fail—to leave you abandoned and Fallen. Vulnerable. I won't let that happen."

I look up into his stormy eyes. "So you want me to be your mate?"

"Yes." His answer is gruff. "But you must understand what I will require of you."

"Whatever you demand," I say quickly. Too quickly.

His hand slides behind my neck with a tight grip, forcing me to look up. "You will do everything I ask of you—whether it makes you uncomfortable or not. You will fulfill my every need and desire. You will keep my secrets and not betray me."

"I will do what you ask of me." I'm willing to give this man everything, even if it means violating my beliefs, but I do have one limitation. "But if you're my mate, it has to look real. I want you to come home at night. Every night."

He stares at me for a moment, but then his lips curve. "I can agree to that but understand that if I am not getting my needs met elsewhere, you will have to meet them instead."

I swallow back the rising emotions and nod. "I will."

"You will continue with your training," he continues. "The others will make sure you are prepared not just for me, but for the role of my Mate. I want you to know the truth about this community. I will not have a blind sheep standing by my side."

He wants them to continue training me? My skin burns at the memory of Silas and Levi's hands on me. Of Elon's kiss. "If that's what you want."

His fingers tighten their grip. "My brothers are all I have. I trust them with everything, including you. But they are as trapped here as much as you are. As much as I am. Together we will reveal to the rest of Serenedee that my father is a fraud and murderer. Are you capable of doing that?"

What he's asking is harder than anything else—worse than the training or agreeing to fulfilling his needs and desires. He wants me to betray my people, my community and, most of all, my leader.

I almost say no, but that vein of blood pumping through my system—my mother's blood—compels me to follow in her footsteps, to possibly find out what happened to her and to Rex's mother. Maybe I will prove him wrong and he will be satisfied. "I'm ready to be your partner, in all things."

He jerks his head toward the door. "We should go, the ceremony is starting."

"Wait." I return to the bed and pick up the box, handing it to him.

His eyebrow raises. "What is this?"

"It's your gift. For the Solstice."

"You were prepared for me to come back for you?"

"Not really." It hurts to admit that, but it's true. "I hoped."

He opens the box and pulls out the leather cord. Two beads are nestled next to one another. It's a symbol of a joined couple. He runs his fingers over the beads and then holds out the cord with one hand and then his wrist.

"Put it on," he demands.

I take the cord and wrap it around his wrist two times, then secure it with a knot. Once we leave this tent, there will be no mistaking our commitment to one another. Butterflies flutter in my belly. He holds my eye for a long moment and then pulls me to him, mouth crashing into mine. His tongue tastes sweet and his kiss is demanding—claiming. Fear skates across my skin, combined with the tickle I've come to recognize in my lower belly.

When he pulls away, I know that I have sealed my fate. There's no going back.

* * *

We're late, pushing our way through the crowd of witnesses. I hear the murmurs among the community as they take us in; Rex's fingers are wound with mine, leading us to the front of the Ordered, the cord wrapped around his wrist. I see Elon first, standing just to the side of the stage. His expression is blank, but his eyes follow us as we cut through the flock. Silas stands next to him, the hint of a smile on his mouth, as if he'd hoped we would appear. Levi just looks relieved. Like me, I know he wants to salvage this—return to normal.

Margaret is up on the stage and grins widely. She wanted this for me—for Serendee. Now that Rex has claimed me, I can join her group and do my best to serve the community.

Anex moves to the edge of the stage, his eyes sweeping over the couples, his smile warm and proud. When he reaches us, his expression falters—just for a beat—before he recovers quickly. It lasted long enough that I saw what was underneath; the look of a man that has lost something. Power, control, domination.

Me.

When he graces us with a false, warm smile, my reaction is physical, like someone dumped cold ice down my spine. I glance over my shoulder at the other Ordered, at the witnesses, at the sea of faces looking at the man commanding all of us. They are enthralled by his presence, by his words, but I know better. I know the truth and there is no turning back.

Bile rises to the back of my throat, and I force myself to look at Elon, Silas, and Levi. They are the strongest members of this community, and they too have no real power. We have nothing but one another. At that moment, everything becomes crystal clear. Rex was right. My mother was right. We should have run.

My mate's grip tightens around mine, and he holds me in place. "It's too late, Imogene," he mutters low enough that only I can hear. "Welcome to the family."

AFTERWORD

The Regressive, book 2 of The Cult of Serendee is available on Amazon.

~

Make sure you join my facebook reading group, Monarchs, for updates, sales, and exclusive content!

~

Readers,

Thank you for taking the plunge on The Order. This is a book I've been thinking about for a long time. I love cults and true crime and the opportunity to add it in with dark romance was too delicious to pass up.

I've had this book written for a while. I really struggled to find the right cover to portray what I was looking for. I want to thank Nikki Epperson for really pushing my creativity on the imagery and Cate Ashwood Designs for bringing it to life. Special thanks to Lisa and Jennifer for beta reading this. I was very unsure about it—too much of a passion project I suppose!

My plan is to write at least one more book in this series, The
Regressive. Don't be scared off my the release date, most of my solo-
work readers know I tend to release early. I am juggling my time
with this series and the Royals and that is a new challenge for me!
Thank you for being willing to take the ride!
Angel

www.ingramcontent.com/pod-product-compliance
Lightning Source LLC
Chambersburg PA
CBHW020144310726
48970CB00006B/1998